Bruce Hennigan's *The Thirteenth Demon, Altar of the Spiral Eye* is a thrill-a-second ride and an impressive debut. Intense, gripping, suspenseful, and spooky; once you open the cover, the pages will fly. Carve out some time for this one...you're gonna need it.

—Mike Dellosso
Author of *Scream* and *Darkness Follows*

In this gripping look into the supernatural, Bruce Hennigan will keep you turning pages—each one a little scarier than the last.

—Mike Yorkey
Coauthor of *Chasing Mona Lisa* and
the Every Man's Battle series

The 13th DEMON

ALTAR *of the* SPIRAL EYE

BRUCE HENNIGAN

Most Charisma House Book Group products are available at special quantity discounts for bulk purchase for sales promotions, premiums, fund-raising, and educational needs. For details, write Charisma House Book Group, 600 Rinehart Road, Lake Mary, Florida 32746, or telephone (407) 333-0600.

The Thirteenth Demon, Altar of the Spiral Eye
by Bruce Hennigan
Published by Realms
Charisma Media/Charisma House Book Group
600 Rinehart Road
Lake Mary, Florida 32746
www.charismahouse.com

All Scripture quotations are from the King James Version of the Bible.

Cover design by Justin Evans
Design Director: Bill Johnson

Visit the author's website at www.brucehennigan.com.

Library of Congress Cataloging-in-Publication Data:
Hennigan, Bruce, 1955-
The thirteenth demon, altar of the spiral eye / Bruce Hennigan.
p. cm. -- (The Jonathan Steel chronicles ; bk. 1)
ISBN 978-1-61638-280-3 (trade paper) -- ISBN
978-1-61638-578-1
(e-book) 1. Demonology--Fiction. 2. Psychological fiction. I.
Title.
II. Series.
PS3608.E56453T47 2011
813'.6--dc23
2011023450

11 12 13 14 15 — 9 8 7 6 5 4 3 2 1
Printed in the United States of America

I dedicate this book to my wife, Sherry, and my two children, Sean and Casey, for supporting me for so many years this book gestated.

But [they] were mingled among the heathen, and learned their works. And they served their idols: which were a snare unto them. Yea, they sacrificed their sons and their daughters unto devils, and shed innocent blood...

[Psalm 106:35–38]

[Prologue]

AH, THERE YOU are! I thought perhaps you had wandered off to the Chamber of Eternal Torment. Or perhaps the Well of Lost Souls. When this amusement park was at its peak, thousands flocked to experience damnation. Who would have thought that you humans would come to a park about evil? You are such strange creatures! I know this place has seen better days, but now that it has been abandoned, we relish the decaying atmosphere.

Forgive me. I am the Tomemaster, your instructor. And you, Quibble, are my apprentice. This is the recording device, the Grimvox. Guard it with your very existence, for it is an ancient device far older than this universe, and it harbors tales and secrets no human has ever heard.

Today we appear before the Council of Darkness in the ballroom of the castle. They favor meeting there on occasion. They find the putrefaction very comforting. Oh, did that lightning flash frighten you? Well, you won't do very well once we get to the Council room.

So listen very carefully. The table will be sitting in the center of the chamber. It is a pentagram, and there will be twelve covered chairs around the perimeter. Each occupant will be obscured by a shroud, so do not try to see who is speaking. They value their privacy. Once we arrive in the chamber, you will stand to the side with the Grimvox. Do not speak! Do not whimper! And whatever you do, never scream out loud!

Ah, we have arrived! Yes, it is dark in here. The twelve do not wish their faces to be seen. And there are horrors in this room you should not see. Now, allow me to speak; remain silent. Remember, it is your job to activate the Grimvox and make certain the words are being translated into our language. Begin!

"Good evening, members of the Council of Darkness..."

"Get on with it, you imbecilic cretin!"

Ah, you see that came from the chair across the table. Number six, I believe. She is very cantankerous.

"Tomemaster, is this your new apprentice?"

"Yes, number four. It is. Please try to not dismember this one. Good apprentices are hard to find. Now, I would like for the Council to entertain the story tonight of the thirteenth demon."

Ah, hear their murmuring? I knew they would be interested in this tale. And that is a good thing for you. You might not get eaten after all! Relax, my apprentice. I was joking.

"Members of the Council, tonight's tale will be related by one who witnessed the events we will hear about. Master Lucas is here, and he has a report on the latest activities of the thirteenth demon. Lucas?"

See, he comes from the shadows. So dramatic, this one. So tall and pale. What? Yes, those are tattoos moving on his bare chest. Now, pay close attention. We must get this story in great detail, my apprentice.

"Lucas, you may begin."

[Chapter 1]

Lakeside, Louisiana

ALONG THE WESTERN horizon the sun settled, bloodred—the very eye of Satan glaring down upon the man who stood in front of the horror that had once been his church. Alone on the second floor balcony, his voice echoed into the coming night.

"God, what have I done to deserve this?"

He backed up to the wrought iron railing, then gasped as he realized he was leaning against the bent, misshapen portion of the railing where it had all begun. He pushed away, bit his thumbnail, and looked around at the huge white columns and across the empty balcony. In front of him were the two intimidating wooden doors that led into the foyer of his church. Four windows were on each side, coated with caked dust. No one had been inside the church in weeks. But that did not mean it was *empty*.

He had to get to his office.

A squeaking filled the silence. The man watched in horror as the doorknob began to turn. He backed away until he felt his heels at the top of the stone stairs. Sweat poured down from his forehead, and he felt his dress shirt sticking to his ribs. The squeaking stopped. Silence descended.

"Is someone there?" he whispered. There was no answer.

He sighed and pushed his glasses back up on his nose. His heart slowed, and he wiped his coat sleeve across his forehead. The coat swallowed him. He had lost twenty pounds in the last month. "I'm not walking away this time," he said to the lifeless door. "You won't scare me away!"

The door burst open with a rush of wind, and a red mist engulfed him. He could taste the red liquid in the air; it was coppery, salty. Blood! Through the tiny red droplets on his glasses, he watched a river of it surge through the open doorway. His foot slid as he tried to stumble away, and he fell backward, bouncing off the stone banister, rolling down onto the steps. He slowed his fall halfway down the stairs and looked up at the open doors. Blood cascaded over the top step and poured down the steps, tendrils of crimson coming after him.

He slid back, tumbled once again until he came to a halt on his back on the sidewalk in front of the church. The blood came down the stairs, pooling at the base just inches from his feet. He scooted back away from the pool, watching it grow into a large circle of shimmering red.

"Do you think this is going to scare us away?"

He watched as the girl and her child appeared around the corner of the stairway. The girl's yellow hair rested on her shoulders, and she wore the same cotton dress with sunflowers as on the day she had wormed her way into his life. She couldn't have been over sixteen, but that didn't seem to matter to the toddler who held her left hand. The boy was dark-headed and somewhere between a year and two years of age. His nose was running, and he wore only a disposable diaper. The young woman picked up the child.

"No! This is not my doing. Don't you know what is going on around here?" The man pointed a bloody hand up the stairs.

"You know what I want. Time is running out," she said. The toddler smiled.

"It's in my office, and I can't get inside because of"—he gestured at the pool of blood—"this!"

"I'm not leaving, Thomas. We're in the nursery." She disappeared from sight, back toward the door under the stairs that led into the basement of the old church.

A fly buzzed by his head and landed on his glasses. He swatted at it. Another fly circled his head. He shook his bloody hair as more flies appeared and moved toward the pool of blood. One landed on the shiny, crimson surface and instantly burst into flame. More flies dove into the pool until a circle of flame hovered above the blood. It gently floated higher, growing larger with each dying fly until it was the size of a beach ball.

More flies filled the evening air, circling in dizzying arcs, until they surrounded the ball of flame. A hole opened in the front of the fly ball, and the flames showed forth from within. The man blinked as the opening turned toward him. It was a huge flaming eye! More flies arrived and flew about the flaming eye to form a spiral that pulsated and spun around it.

"We know about the girl," the raspy voice proclaimed as the eye lifted higher in the air.

At that, the man lost all reason, all civility, and scuttled backward like a crab into the road in front of the church. The hot asphalt blistered his palms. The buzzing grew louder as the voice spoke the words over and over. His heart pounded. He heard a high, keening whimper and realized it was his own voice.

Suddenly, against the insane noises, there came another roar, approaching fast, and then the sound of squealing brakes, the whoosh of hot wind, the smell of burning rubber, and the grill of a recreational vehicle as it stopped just inches from his face.

The man glanced back at the flaming eye with its pulsating spiral. It had disappeared, leaving only a pool of blood behind. The doors of the church were shut. The sudden silence was punctuated by the creaking and popping of the RV to his left. A long shadow fell over him as a figure stepped into the man's sight.

He was six feet tall with wiry muscles and dressed in a V-neck T-shirt, blue jeans, and work boots. His hair was reddish blond and short, his face tight and expressionless. His eyes were hidden behind mirrored sunglasses.

"How long has it been bleeding?" His voice was barely above a whisper.

"It just started." The man wiped blood from his face. "Are you Steel?"

"Get up." The figure disappeared into the RV.

He grabbed the grill of the RV with bloody hands and pulled himself shakily to his feet. He walked around the vehicle and entered through the open door. Inside, a table with two laptops and one large monitor sat where he would have expected the kitchen table to be. The man he presumed to be Jonathan Steel reappeared with a black backpack in one hand and a plastic container of disinfectant wipes in the other. He handed him the wipes.

"Clean up. You stink."

"Hey, I asked you a question." He pulled wipes from the container and wiped the blood from his hands. "Are you Steel?"

Steel opened a cabinet and took out a huge flashlight. "Are the lights working inside the church?"

The man wiped blood from his glasses. "I don't know. Listen, you haven't answered my question."

The mirrored sunglasses turned in his direction. "Yes. I am Jonathan Steel."

"I'm...I'm Thomas Parker. And this is my church." He tossed the bloodstained wipes into the sink.

"I know," Steel answered.

"What are you going to do?"

"We are going inside." Steel pushed past him toward the open door.

"But don't we need to sit down and talk about this?" Parker followed the man out of the RV. "Maybe over a cup of coffee? Maybe after I've had a shower?"

Steel ignored him and paused at the pool of blood. A fly landed lazily on the surface of the pool and then burst into flames. "Now there's something you don't see every day."

Parker grabbed the man's arm to turn him. He swallowed. "No one has been inside for six weeks."

Steel took off his sunglasses, and Parker was shocked by his bright, turquoise eyes. Steel glared at him. "Whose blood is this?"

Parker looked at the blood and then back into Steel's penetrating gaze. "I don't know. It just appeared."

Steel nodded and slid the sunglasses into a pocket of his T-shirt. "Then we need to find the source. Let's go."

Parker watched in horror as Steel squished through the puddle of blood and started up the stairs. He hurried after him, trying his best to avoid the rivulets of blood on the stairs. They arrived at the upper level, and Steel paused in front of the closed doors. Blood still trickled from the threshold. His head turned as he studied the walls, the windows, and finally the wrought iron railing that ran around the huge balcony. Parker followed the direction of the man's gaze and felt a chill when it stopped on the far railing. He knew that if Steel went to the edge and looked down he would see the impression where the body had landed in the soft, grassy soil. The grass still had not grown back. Steel reached for the doorknob and paused.

"Wait a minute!" Parker said. "Do I have to go with you?"

"This is *your* church." Steel frowned. "You cannot be afraid."

"I asked you to come help with the church. To clean up all of...*this*." Parker motioned to the blood on the portico. Steel just stared at him with those intense eyes. Parker wiped his forehead and sighed. "Look, you didn't see that blood gush out of that door like a living thing. You didn't see the eye of flame with the swirling spiral that came out of that puddle of blood..."

"Spiral?" Steel interrupted him. He grabbed Parker by the lapels of his suit coat and pulled him up onto his tiptoes. "Are you sure the eye was surrounded by a spiral?"

"Yes, down there." Parker slid down into his suit. "It came out of the puddle, and the flies flew around like a spiral."

For a second Steel's skin relaxed; his gaze seemed to settle on a distant memory. His hands relaxed, and Parker slid back down onto his feet. Then just as quickly as the change had come, the stony face returned. Steel's gaze returned to Parker.

"We are both going in. Now." Steel turned and pulled the doors open. They flew outward toward them, and Parker hid behind Steel's bulk to avoid the mist of blood. As they stepped inside, the temperature plummeted, filling the air with a chilling, icy vapor. Steel stepped into the church's foyer, his breath misting in front of him. Parker hurried after him. He glanced around at the chunks of ice that covered the offering table and icicles that hung from the old chandelier. Everything was frozen and smelled like freezer-burned meat. The outer doors slammed behind them, engulfing them in darkness.

"What is going on?" Parker huddled up against Steel's back.

Steel's voice seemed calm and unchanged. "Someone is trying to scare you, Reverend Parker." Light gushed from Steel's flashlight, and Parker screamed.

Huge, red spiders hung around them, suspended from the ceiling, their scrabbling arms coated with frost, their multifaceted eyes black with menace. As the light burst through the darkness, the nearest spiders retreated along their spindly webs into the dark shadows of the foyer corners.

"Where did they come from?" Parker shouted.

Steel walked toward the inner two doors that would lead into the sanctuary. "Ignore them. They don't like the light."

Steel pushed open the doors, and the cold, bitter air was replaced with a hot, fetid wind redolent with the fragrance of vegetation. Parker stumbled over something and looked down at a huge vine stretching across the center aisle. Huge roots and vines covered the pews, the aisle, the walls, and the stained-glass windows. They stretched upward to the edge of the roof. The inner doors slammed behind them, and Parker bolted forward against Steel's unmoving back.

"For a man of God, you sure are skittish," Steel growled at him over his shoulder.

"Are you kidding?" Parker stammered. "Who wouldn't be?"

"I've seen worse," Steel said.

"You've seen *worse*? How could it be worse?"

"Never ask that question."

Parker fought off his trembling. He should be the strong one. Not Steel. He tried to stand up straight and smooth out his coat. "Now that we're here, I need to find something." A huge curtain of vines was draped across a door leading out of the right side of the sanctuary. "My office is over there." He pointed.

"We'll get there." Steel passed the flashlight beam over the ceiling. Strange writings covered the old acoustic tiles. He fumbled in his backpack and retrieved a digital camera. The darkness was interrupted by flash after flash as Steel took dozens of pictures of the ceiling. Parker saw ghostly figures in the afterglow of each flash. Finally, he closed his eyes until Steel was finished.

"Pictographs of some kind. I don't recognize the language," Steel said as he slid the camera back into his backpack and pulled out a small video camera. "We'll need a linguist."

"A linguist?"

Steel motioned toward the front of the sanctuary. An altar table sat in front of the pulpit. It was covered with blood that dripped and ran in tiny threads to the floor. A huge, dead flower arrangement sat in the middle of the puddle of blood. Behind the pulpit and choir loft, something glowed with an orange light. "What is that?"

Parker pushed his glasses up on his nose. "Something is in the baptistery."

Steel hopped over the low choir rail and weaved his way through the three rows of chairs in the choir loft. He stood on a chair and glanced into the baptistery. Parker hurried after him and climbed up on a chair next to Steel. Inside the baptistery, where there once existed the warm, welcoming waters of baptism, a pool of radiant energy filled the deep chamber. Its surface moved with eddies of orange and red energy.

Steel switched on the video camera and began recording. "Baptism by fire?"

"Of course not. What is it?" Parker felt himself drawn into the mesmerizing ebb and flow of energy currents.

"An energy field. Something in this church is manipulating other dimensions of space and time," Steel said.

Parker glanced at him. "Dimensions?"

Steel turned off the video camera and looked at Parker. His face was bathed in the reddish glow of the baptistery. "We'll need a physicist."

"We need a linguist and a physicist. What about a florist for that dead flower arrangement?" Parker threw his hands in the air.

"Reverend, you have no idea what you're up against." Steel played the flashlight beam over the choir rail. "Who else is in here?"

"No one," Parker said.

"I thought I saw someone move in the choir loft."

Parker shook his head. "If you could just help me get through those vines over there, I need to get something from my office..."

"You're lying to me." Steel flicked the beam into his face.

Parker put up his hands to block the light. "I'm not lying. There is no one in here but us. No one has been in this sanctuary in weeks."

Steel pointed the light toward the vines over the door. "So, what is so important in your office?"

"Records, paperwork, uh..." Parker mumbled, stepping back involuntarily. Something squished beneath his feet, and immediately the air filled with the sound of soft chittering, the sound of a thousand tiny legs tapping and moving. Steel focused the beam of light on the floor. Spiders were all around them, scuttling along the vines converging on Parker. He backed into the altar table, and blood splashed down his legs. He bounced away and ran toward the door leading to his office. A curtain of red spiders converged on the vines and blocked his way. "Mr. Steel, do something!" he screamed.

"The light isn't stopping them," Steel said. Suddenly a gust of wind swirled to life behind Parker, swallowing him in a tornado of debris and dust. Parker felt himself lifted helplessly into the air. Wind buffeted him, spinning him upside down until he hung in the center of the vortex ten feet above the floor. Steel backed away from the funnel of air as bits of glowing energy spun from the baptistery, coalescing into a tumbling mass of gleaming metal slivers.

Parker watched the tiny metal flecks hurtle across the loft to pause just outside the vortex. Slivers of metal tumbled and spun and assembled themselves into tiny, metal spiders. The metal arachnids swirled into the vortex. Sparking and flashing in the glow of the baptistery, they ripped at his clothing, shredding his suit coat, ripping his pants, even tugging off his shoes.

Parker's open mouth finally found sound, and his scream tore through the roar of the wind. Suddenly Steel was beneath him, pulling him down. Together they fell out of the vortex of wind. Parker pushed himself off of Steel and, without pausing, ran down the aisle, flung through the inner doors, and pushed through the outer doors onto the portico. He tumbled down the stairs and came to rest in the parking lot, his eyes filled with sweat, blood, and dead leaves. Bruised and scratched, in only his underwear, he stood up and ran down the hill to the parsonage where he lived, his mind filled with unspeakable horrors.

[Chapter 2]

BLOOD FOLLOWED JONATHAN Steel. It flowed freely from the wounds he suffered in his relentless pursuit. It bathed his tortured memories. He tasted it. He smelled it. He could see it. In the musty interior of the sanctuary, Steel inhaled the metallic odor of blood and watched as the whirlwind collapsed on itself. The flashing metal spiders disappeared into puffs of dissipating energy. The baptistery darkened. All around him in the dim interior of the sanctuary, the spiders dissolved into pools of dark crimson that soaked into the floor until all of the blood disappeared.

He struggled to his feet, his back aching where he had struck the front pew. He retrieved the flashlight and picked up his backpack. One of Parker's shoes was wedged through an arm strap. He held it in his hand, studying the torn leather and frazzled shoestrings. He surveyed the sanctuary one last time. The writing had disappeared from the ceiling. All activity had stopped when Parker had run from the building. Steel had seen things like this before but never on this scale.

Maybe Thomas Parker should be frightened.

"And we were doing fine until you lied," he muttered and started toward the outer doors. The sun was below the horizon, painting the sky with streaks of orange and red when Steel walked out of the church and closed the doors behind him. He inhaled the fragrance of coming rain and mowed grass and exhaled the bitter taste of blood.

Lakeside Community Church sat on the top of a wide, low hill that sloped away in all directions. Diagonally across the street a residential neighborhood ran down the slope of the hill toward downtown. On the corner was the parsonage, the home of Reverend Thomas Parker. Across the street from the parsonage an open field led into the playground of the local elementary school. Behind the church the waters of Redcross Bayou made their way south toward the Red River, separated from the church by a huge field of sunflowers.

Steel reached into his shirt pocket and took out his sunglasses. Broken glass tinkled on the concrete. He had never lost his sunglasses before. The reverend had serious problems. Whatever Parker was involved in was complicated. Someone was liable to get hurt, maybe even killed. It had happened before. In fact, he had almost walked away from this situation until Parker had mentioned the eye.

Ah, yes, the eye.

He stilled himself, quieting his thoughts. Had he seen it himself inside the church?

Steel pulled out his digital camera, turned it on, and cycled through the pictures on the camera's color display. A cold chill ran down his spine as one image filled the tiny display. There, etched in dark red on the ceiling, was the symbol of an eye surrounded by a spiral.

From the tiny camera screen it glared at Steel. His pulse quickened and his mouth became dry. Could *he* be afraid? He took out his cell phone and dialed.

"Cephas, Steel."

"Ah, Mister Steel." An ancient voice spoke from the cell phone. "It's been weeks since you called. To what do I owe the honor of your call?"

"I may have found it."

"You've said that before." There was a note of humor in the voice.

"This time I have proof."

The sound of the old man's breathing came over the speaker. "Then you may, indeed, have reached the end of your search. Or is it just the beginning?"

"Stop being so cryptic." Steel closed his eyes in irritation. "I need some help. I need a linguist with a background in anthropology or archeology. And I need a quantum physicist. Tomorrow at the latest. Can you find me someone?"

"Who would pass up the chance to work with you?"

"Don't be sarcastic."

"I am always sarcastic. I will see what I can do. Where are you?"

"Lakeside, Louisiana. I sent you an update this morning," Steel said. "Let me know when you contact them." He snapped the phone shut and glanced across the road in front of the church to a house nestled among tall pine trees. Time to talk to the reverend and his wife.

Steel dropped the flashlight into his backpack as he stood at the open door to Parker's home. He glanced inside and saw bloody footprints leading off through a foyer and back into the depths of the house.

From around the corner, a figure in white appeared and paused to regard him. Her hair was limp and thin, her face pale with dark circles beneath her eyes. She wore a white housecoat that bulged over her pregnant abdomen.

"If you're selling something, I'm not interested." She glared at him. "If you're here to rob us, go ahead. We don't have much money, and I'm too tired to stop you."

Steel lifted Parker's shredded shoe. "I'm returning the reverend's shoe."

"Oh." She placed a hand in the small of her back and rubbed. "He's taking a shower. I wondered why he wasn't wearing his shoes."

"Does he normally run around the neighborhood in his underwear?" Steel stepped into the foyer and closed the door behind him.

"It wouldn't surprise me." She reached out and took the shoe from his hand. "Come into the kitchen while I rinse this off."

Steel followed her through a compact but dark living room and into a spacious kitchen. The woman hobbled across the tiled floor and dropped the shoe in the sink. "You can sit at the table."

"You must be Reverend Parker's wife."

"I'm not the maid." She turned her back on him and began running water in the sink. "My name is Emily."

Steel sat at the kitchen table and placed his backpack on the floor. "When are you due?"

Emily moved in slow motion as she held the shoe beneath the running water. At first he thought she hadn't heard him, but then he noticed her gaze shift to the window above the sink and focus on something far away. "Within the week, I hope. It hasn't been an easy pregnancy." She shook water from the shoe and placed it in the dish drainer beside the sink. At least she was tidy.

Parker appeared in the door to the kitchen, his face ashen, his thick, dark hair slicked back. He wore sweatpants and a T-shirt. Two scratches oozed blood from his forehead. "I'm sorry I ran. I was so scared…" His face blanched when he saw Emily at the sink. "Emily? What are you doing out of bed?"

"You went into the church, didn't you?" She turned toward him, limp hair falling across her eyes.

Parker saw the shoe in the dish drain. "Emily, he insisted."

"You promised me you wouldn't go back in. Not after what happened to Gerry."

Parker slumped in a chair at the table. "I need to get inside."

"Do you want our baby to grow up without a father?" Emily said.

"Let's not go into that again, Emily. Why don't you get us some coffee?"

Emily reached for the coffee carafe and placed it in the microwave. Probably left over from breakfast. "What have you told him, Thomas?"

Parker placed his head in his hands, massaging his temples. "Not much."

"My name is Jonathan Steel. You can stop referring to me as 'him.'"

Emily looked up from the microwave. "Very well, Mr. Steel. I'm not in a very good mood. I'm pregnant and our church is falling apart. My husband comes running in from outside in his underwear, his feet and head covered with blood after promising me he wouldn't go back into the church. What in the world would make you want to go back in there?" She glared at Parker and then glanced back at Steel. "I suppose you want coffee too?"

"I don't drink coffee. Why don't you tell me what happened. From the beginning."

"Yeah, Thomas, tell him about Ketrick."

Steel looked at Parker. "What's Ketrick?"

"Robert Ketrick is a local businessman…"

"Businessman?" Emily popped open the microwave door and pulled out the steaming carafe of coffee. "The devil himself. A tyrant. He owns Lakeside. All of it."

"He doesn't own the bank," Parker said.

"And you don't think that Benton Hobbs won't turn belly up when the right price is offered? What will happen then? The only thing Ketrick won't own is the church."

"Why would a businessman be interested in buying the church?" Steel asked.

Parker shrugged. "I haven't figured that out. Probably wants to build an apartment building that looks right down Main Street. A couple of months ago he made me an offer. Of course, I turned him down."

"You should have sold it to him." Emily retrieved two cups from the cabinet. "Then the church would still be alive. And so would Gerry."

The air grew suddenly still, and Steel drew in a deep breath. "Who is Gerry?"

"Gerald Smithson is—was—one of the deacons." Parker pushed his glasses up on his nose and his gaze shifted to the tabletop. "When I refused to sell the church, Ketrick joined the church. A week later he brought up a new offer at a business meeting."

"The business meeting from hell." Emily spilled coffee into the two cups.

"Ketrick was willing to purchase the church property and then donate twenty acres of land on the outskirts of town for a new worship center. My congregation split down the middle. After all, we would have to raise the money to build a new worship center. Gerry spoke up against Ketrick, and tempers flared."

Emily came over to the table and plopped the cup of coffee in front of Parker. "And then Ketrick killed him."

"It was ruled an accident." Parker backed away from the sloshing coffee.

"Accident?" Emily waved her coffee cup in the air. Hot liquid fell on Steel's hand. He tried not to flinch. "Thomas, that's your problem. You see good in everybody. Even a ghoul like Ketrick." She leaned across the table, locking eyes with Steel. "Broke his neck in the fall. You can still see the dent in the ground where he landed."

"Emily, it's my job to see the good in everybody. No one is beyond forgiveness. Even Robert Ketrick." Parker blew on the hot coffee, then looked up at Steel. "At Gerry's funeral at the church, his coffin flew up off its stand and dumped him on the floor. What few people came to the funeral ran out of the sanctuary and haven't been back."

"That was six weeks ago. I told Thomas not to go back in until we got some help." Emily laughed, placing a hand to her mouth. "We tried the local church association—some help they turned out to be. They had no idea how to handle the things going on up there. And all of the good members of Lakeside Community Church just disappeared into the woodwork. Like roaches."

"That's when someone sent me an e-mail suggesting you," Parker said.

"Should have just sold the church," Emily said. She turned away from her gaze out the window. "Just what are you, anyway?"

Steel reached into his shirt pocket and pulled out his card. Emily came over, took one look at it, and tossed it on the table.

"'A helper in time of crisis'? You've got to be kidding."

"Emily, please." Parker took her hand.

Emily jerked her hand away. "Thomas, this is ridiculous! We don't even know who this guy is. And how do we know he can help us?" She turned dark eyes on Steel. "Just why do you do this, Mr. Steel?"

Steel rubbed the back of his hand. He'd been waiting for the question. Everyone asked it. He closed his eyes, and the memory was there in spite of every effort to make it go away. He could still see her face, looking up at him with blood bubbled on her lips. *Stop them. Promise me you will stop them!* Don't talk, Steel had said. Help is coming. *Promise me!* she'd gasped. Steel had blinked away tears and promised.

He pushed away the feeling of loss. He had no use for that. He looked up at Emily. "I made a promise a long time ago. I always keep my promises."

Parker looked at her and said, "See, Emily."

"Whatever! I'm going back to bed." Emily picked up the empty coffee cup and shuffled over to the sink, dropping it to clatter on the porcelain. "I say let that fiend Ketrick have the church." She cast one last glare in their direction and left the room.

Parker blinked in dismay and sighed. "I'm sorry, Mr. Steel. Emily doesn't usually act this way. She's under a lot of stress. It's our first child, and her pregnancy has been difficult. And then these things start happening in the church."

"And she hates Ketrick," Steel said as he looked back at Parker. "She doesn't have much use for me, either."

Parker took a sip of his coffee. "So what do we do now?"

Steel didn't smile, his eyes riveted on Parker. "There's more here than you're telling me, Reverend. Until I know more, we can't even begin. I'll have to find out the whole story. When you decide to stop hiding things from me, we can really get started."

Parker's face paled. "I've told you everything."

"What's in your office?" Steel asked.

"Uh, some important papers that might help us," Parker said tentatively.

Steel sighed. "I've contacted an associate who will try and find me those two consultants I mentioned. Is there somewhere I can hook up my RV?"

"We have a connection behind the office annex. But it's awfully close to the church sanctuary. There's also a missionary house next door for any of your consultants."

Steel stood up and shouldered his backpack. "I need some sleep. It was a long drive from Gulf Shores. You going to show me the hookup?"

Parker shuddered. "I guess so."

After setting up the RV behind the church and detaching his SUV from the tow bar, Steel watched Parker through the windows of the RV as he walked away into the darkness to return to his house. Steel's computer monitor blinked, and the image of Cephas Lawrence graced an icon.

Steel hit the answer button, and Dr. Cephas Lawrence appeared. His wild, white hair was more unruly than ever. His drooping eyes and bushy mustache underscored a look of fatigue.

"You look terrible. Was it that hard to turn on your computer?" Steel said.

"You have missed your opportunity for celebrity, Jonathan. You should have been a stand-up comic." Cephas raised an eyebrow as big as a gray caterpillar. "I am an old man, Jonathan, and I am dealing with New York City. They want my building, a battle I may lose. For certain, there is sleep I am losing."

Steel sat down in front of the monitor. "What will you do with your collection?"

Cephas shrugged. "That is the real question. You have seen how many artifacts I have. I will need a large space if I have to move. My building is perfect. I have the upper two floors, and the rest is for my friends."

"That's your problem. The city probably wants them out."

Cephas leaned back in the image, and Steel noted his fiery red pajamas with tiny robots. "I am giving them a home. It is God's work for me."

"I like your pajamas."

"Do not deny an old man a simple vice. They are very warm."

"So, any success on my requests?"

"O ye of little faith." The man mumbled as he slurped a cup of tea. "Do you realize how difficult it is to find a physicist this time of night who is willing to drop whatever experiments he is in the middle of to run off to Louisiana to work with Jonathan Steel?"

"It's not too difficult for you, Cephas. I'm going to send you some images of an energy pool you can forward to our physicist." Steel hooked up his video camera and began downloading the footage.

Cephas placed his tiny reading glasses on his nose. "Of course, you expect me to work miracles. And I have. I am a great-uncle to a renowned physicist in Dallas, Texas, who is even now packing the bags for a trip. You'll have your physicist by noon tomorrow. Now, what about this linguist you requested?"

Steel opened a program on his computer screen and browsed through the images from his digital camera. He flagged the images of the writing on the ceiling. "Take a look at these writings. Have you ever seen this language before?"

Cephas squinted, his monitor reflecting in his glasses. "Very interesting. It looks vaguely familiar. You know, I worked with an anthropologist in Louisville, Kentucky, who might be available."

"Good, that's all I have right now, Cephas."

Cephas tilted his eyes upward in the computer monitor. "And what about the eye?"

Steel drew a deep breath. "It is there in the images from the ceiling of this church."

"Then you must be careful, my friend. I shall renew my research on this issue and be prepared if you have, in fact, found the demon with the spiral eye. Good night." Cephas tapped his keyboard, and the screen went blank.

Steel went to the bedroom in the rear of his RV and paused to glance at a photograph of an elderly man and a younger woman. Their images smiled back at him, and he frowned. "I may have found it," he whispered to the ghosts of his past.

[Chapter 3]

JOSH KNIGHT TOUCHED the lip bead. It still hurt from the recent piercing, but Ila approved, so he could stand the pain. He stood in the darkened garage of his home and ran a hand over the smooth surface of the motorcycle.

"It was your dad's, wasn't it?"

"Yeah." He looked up at Ila. She wore her black dress and long, black gloves. She had bleached her hair to a ghostly white, but it made her dark, brown eyes jump out of her pale face. "You look good."

"You didn't like my new look at first, boyfriend." She smiled and sat on the motorcycle. She reached up and ran a gloved finger across the hoops in his left eyebrow. "But then you came to your senses, didn't you, baby?"

But she didn't know the real reason he had dyed his hair pitch-black or why he had pierced his ears, eyebrows, and lip, or why he would join her clan of vampire wannabes. He could outlast whatever phase she was in. Had since they started dating at fifteen. "We're going to be late for the concert. I'll go get Mom's keys."

Ila grabbed his arm as he stepped away. "No, baby. Let's take the motorcycle."

Josh shook his head. "I can't. Mom doesn't want anyone riding it."

"I know that you take it out sometimes at midnight. Marcus told me."

"Marcus should keep his mouth shut. OK, maybe later. But not tonight." He pulled away from her and walked into the house to the dining room. His mother sat at the table with three men. Where had they come from? An ancient man with graying hair sat across from her and was tapping a yellow legal pad.

His mother ran a hand through her short strawberry blonde hair. She was nervous. "Mr. Grayson, I haven't strayed from the curriculum."

"Other dimensions, Claire?" A younger, nervous man at the other end of the table interrupted. He held up a sheaf of papers. "E-mails and letters from church members about this."

"I respect you and your positions as elders in the church, but what I am teaching in my life group is perfectly biblical. There are many scriptures that talk about the extra-dimensional capabilities of God."

"What about near-death experiences and quantum physics? We don't teach the occult," Grayson said.

"Recent research into NDEs suggests the presence of a nonlocal consciousness, and it may be tied to these extra dimensions. I think there is scientific evidence for the soul. In today's godless culture, if I could just..." Claire said.

"Our church is not your laboratory, Mrs. Knight." The third man was small and thin and wore a sour look. "Leave your physics at the university."

Josh watched his mother's face redden. She stood up and glanced at him. "Josh? How long have you been standing there?"

The three men looked at him. Grayson's mouth fell open.

"This is your…son?"

Josh swallowed and felt Ila ease up behind him. She was carrying her black parasol—not the best timing in the world. She stepped around him. "You gonna judge us just because we're different than you?"

Claire's eyes widened, and she pointed to the door to indicate Josh and Ila should leave. "I need the keys to the truck." Josh held out his hand. "We're going to a concert."

"A Christian concert, I hope." The younger man said.

"They're not Baptists," Ila said and giggled.

Claire drew a deep breath and took the truck keys from her jean pockets. "Go. Now."

Josh glanced once at the men and then back at his mother. "Mom, you knew teaching that stuff would get you in trouble with these trolls. I tried to warn you." He turned and left the kitchen.

"Wait!" Claire followed him out into the garage. "You should not call elders of the church 'trolls,' Josh."

"I can call them what they are. Stupid, arrogant—"

"Josh!" Claire raised her voice, and she seemed to stumble.

"They want to string you up, that's for sure, Mrs. K," Ila said. "I'd kick them out of the house. Mom and I left the church months ago because of people like them."

Claire seemed to regain her strength. "OK, Josh, be home by midnight. We have to go to Louisiana tomorrow."

Josh felt like he had been kicked in the gut. "What? Louisiana? Why?"

"I got a call from Uncle Cephas."

"The old dude in the ghostbuster building?"

"He is your great-great-uncle, Josh. Not some old dude." Claire rubbed her forehead.

"I have talked to him maybe once in my life, Mom. What does he have to do with going to Louisiana?" Josh asked.

"There's a phenomenon there he needs me to look into. And..."

Josh swore and lashed out at the nearby metal shelf. Paint cans showered over the garage floor, and Ila backed away. His mother paused in shock.

"Another one of your higher dimensions? I'm sick of this, Mom! Dad is gone. Stop trying to find him. I've moved on—why can't you?"

Josh turned and stormed away before she could react. He grabbed Ila by the hand and pulled her after him toward the truck.

[Chapter 4]

THE NEXT MORNING Parker pulled his car into the curb in front of a three-story plantation-style building with a picket fence. Steel sat next to him in the passenger seat.

"You haven't said a word since you told me we were going to visit Ketrick," Parker said.

"I don't have much to say." Steel massaged his tired eyes. He had not slept well the night before. His dreams were filled with the haunting image of an eye surrounded by a black spiral tattoo. "This is downtown Lakeside?"

"Well, downtown is the town. Shouldn't we have called Mr. Ketrick and made an appointment?"

Steel shook his head and stepped out of the car. "I like to surprise people. This is his office?"

"Yeah." Parker got out of his car.

"Where did he get his money?" Steel asked.

"His father was an oil tycoon. He died when Ketrick was young and left him a fortune." Parker locked his car, and they headed into the building.

Ketrick's office was on the top floor of the three-story mansion; the view allowed him to look out over the town he was rebuilding. Steel opened the door into Ketrick's reception room, and a woman sitting at a glass and chrome desk turned toward them. She wore a black leather dress that moved like a second skin as she stood up from her chair. Her hair was short, dark, and plastered to her head. When she smiled, Steel noticed her lips were covered in very dark lipstick.

"Well, looky here what the cat dragged in." Her voice dripped with southern charm. "Just what can I do for you boys?"

"We're here to see Mr. Ketrick," Steel said.

"Tell him Reverend Parker is here," Parker said.

The woman's smiled faded, and she pouted. "Well, I'll put you in Mr. Ketrick's office. Then I'll rush right on down to get him."

She ushered them through an inner doorway into a huge, stately room. She pointed to a set of plush leather chairs a person could get lost in.

"Mr. Ketrick is in a board of directors meeting, and I'm sure he just can't wait to drop what he's doing to see you. Yep, drop it like a hot potato." She studied her black lacquered nails. "Oh, where are my manners? Coffee?"

"No coffee," Steel said.

The woman lifted her eyebrows and looked in Parker's direction. "What about you, Mr. Reverend?"

"Sure." Parker shrugged.

"I'll go grind the beans." She sauntered out of the room and closed the door behind her.

Parker sunk into one of the chairs, and Steel walked around the office. He paused before his reflection in a glass case hanging on the wall. A dozen or so ancient swords and knives were displayed.

"Ketrick collects these?"

"That's what he tells me." Parker answered. "Antique swords, antique knives. I hear he has an entire room filled with ancient torture devices in his home. Sort of fits his business philosophy." The woman reappeared and set a tray with coffee and cups on the table.

"By the way, ya'll, I'm Vivian Darbonne, without the apostrophe. Mr. Ketrick's administrative assistant. I'll be in my office doing my nails if you two need anything." She smiled and left the room.

Steel raised an eyebrow. "Interesting assistant."

Parker wormed his way up out of the engulfing cushions of the chair. "Ketrick surrounds himself with beautiful women."

"And you allowed him to join your church?"

"Our doors are open to anyone."

"Maybe that's your problem." Steel walked behind a huge wooden desk in the middle of the room. Papers and photographs were scattered across the desk.

"Are you finding everything you need?" A deep, resonant voice echoed from the back of the office. Steel looked up to see Robert Ketrick enter the room. He was tall and bony with chiseled features over a skeletal face with bright green eyes and black hair pulled back in a long ponytail.

"Sorry." Steel stepped from behind the desk and cast one last glance at the papers scattered over the wooden surface. "I was just admiring these photographs. Antique weapons?"

Ketrick smiled, revealing large, white teeth. His gaze burrowed into Steel and then glanced down to the desk. "The photo on top is a reproduction of a stone knife from Central America. It is part of my collection. I keep it at home, and I'm having it appraised for insurance purposes, Mister..."

"Steel." He shook Ketrick's hand. It was dry and scaly, and his fingers were long and thin. Ketrick stared at him for some time. He hesitated and then withdrew his hand.

"Have we met?" Steel asked.

Ketrick rubbed his hand across his face. "For a moment I thought you looked very familiar. Perhaps it is your eyes." Ketrick drew himself up and clasped his hands together. "But the answer is no. I don't believe we have ever met."

Parker stood up, drew a deep breath, and glanced once at Steel before continuing. "I have asked Mr. Steel to investigate some unusual occurrences at the church, Mr. Ketrick."

Ketrick turned away from Steel and stepped behind his desk. He rearranged the papers and flicked his head, throwing the long ponytail over the back of his desk chair as he sat. "What type of occurrences?"

"Demonic," Steel said.

Ketrick's face froze, and he squinted. "Demonic? As in demon possessed? I think you're mistaken, Mr. Steel. Judging from the last business meeting I attended, I would say the church is 'deacon' possessed."

"That's not funny," Parker said. "Robert, I called you two weeks ago about this. You wouldn't talk to me."

Ketrick turned his palms up, and his long arms were splayed in a gesture of openness. "Thomas, why would you think I have any knowledge of this? Perhaps you have some hooligans on your hands involved in vandalism. Why not call Sheriff Sweeney?"

"Hooligans?" Steel said. "These *hooligans* can control extra dimensions of space and speak in an ancient tongue."

"I hear some of the new designer drugs can produce that effect." Ketrick turned to face Steel. His bright green eyes sparkled. "Tell me, Mr. Steel, are you an expert on demons?"

"I've dealt with my share of evil, Mr. Ketrick." Steel held the man's gaze. "These events are real. Reverend Parker is not making them up. And it is curious these events began shortly after you joined the church."

"Surely, you're kidding me?"

"Is this your attempt to drive us out of the church building, Robert?" Parker raised his voice.

Ketrick tore his gaze away from Steel and glared at Parker. "Why on earth would I want to drive you out of the building? I had the transaction in my hands, Parker. The vote would have gone through, and you would be looking at a new church on the edge of town out by the new four-lane highway."

"But you're a Christian, Robert. How could you bring such dissension into the church?" Parker's lips were trembling.

"Just because he's a church member doesn't mean he's a Christian," Steel said.

Ketrick shifted his gaze to Steel, and a sly grin appeared on his face. "You are correct, Mr. Steel. I am a church member. I came 'by statement,' as you called it." He looked back at Parker. "But you never bothered to check into my past, did you? You just assumed I was a Christian. You couldn't see beyond your excitement at having a rich businessman to swell the bank account of the church. Me, a Christian? I'd rather be dead."

"Ketrick, you said..."

"I never said anything, Parker." Ketrick sat forward in his chair and pointed a thin, bony finger at Parker. "I am not a Christian. Christianity is as dead as that church building of yours."

"I'm not here to debate," Parker said.

"Oh, look at your clenched fists. Are you going to hit me? Like your deacon tried to? What was his name? Gary? Jerry?" Ketrick sat back in his chair. "How many members have been showing up on Sunday?"

Parker looked helplessly at Steel. He unclenched his fists and studied his empty hands. "Nobody has been showing up."

"Precisely. Your church members ran at the first sign of trouble. They deserted you. Your church is dead. I have no interest in it anymore. I just came from a meeting with the board of directors of the bank. In a couple of days I will own the bank, and when I do, I'll foreclose on your church and your parsonage; then I can get it for a bargain." Ketrick grinned. "Mr. Steel, since you're some type of investigator, let me ask you a question. Has Parker told you about his last church?"

Parker settled back into his chair. "What could you know about that?"

Ketrick stood, seeming to grow in strength and stature, towering over his desk. The ponytail fell over his shoulder to dangle over his chest as he leaned forward to touch an intercom switch. "Ms. Darbonne, please bring Reverend Parker's file in here."

"I have a file?"

"Unlike you, I do my homework."

The door opened, and Vivian glided across the floor. She extended a pale arm toward Ketrick with a file folder in her hand. He took the file in his large hands and let one finger caress her palm.

"Thank you, Vivian."

Vivian turned toward Steel. "Something wrong with my coffee?"

"Too hot."

She laughed, and her black eyes glittered with mischief. "How droll," she said and left the room.

Ketrick settled in his chair and opened the file. "Let me see, your former church was in northeastern Texas. I understand it was a small church. An old-fashioned church. One of those churches just a couple of funerals away from closing. With lots of little blue-haired old ladies. Tell me, Reverend Parker, did it take long for them to want you to start a family?"

Parker pushed his glasses back up on his nose. "They didn't know we, uh, couldn't have children. Emily didn't want them to know."

"Too many gossips in those little churches, right?" Ketrick winked. "So, you contacted a fertility clinic in Dallas for a medical workup." Ketrick looked back at the file. "It's a shame most insurance programs don't cover infertility workups. And they're so expensive."

"Emily said God would take care of us."

"God works in mysterious ways, Mr. Steel." Ketrick looked at Steel and tapped the pages with a long finger. "I gather from the records, Mrs. Parker became the church treasurer, and soon all of the family bills stopped showing up. It doesn't take an accounting degree to fill in the rest of this ledger, does it, Mr. Steel?" Ketrick's eyes were bright with victory. "You got away with petty larceny, isn't that right, Parker?"

"I get the picture, Ketrick," Steel said.

"But it doesn't end there, does it?" Ketrick glanced down at the pages. "Let me see, the two of you underwent marital counseling..."

"I said, that's enough!" Steel did not waver when Ketrick's eyes met his.

"He didn't even tell Lakeside Community Church about his checkered past. They don't know his wife is a thief." Ketrick ran his tongue over his perfect teeth. "And now we know that the good reverend is a liar."

Parker erupted up out of the chair, knocking the small table over and spilling the coffee across the carpet. He leaned up against the front of Ketrick's desk. "How dare you call me a liar! You lied to me about your membership! My church was fine until you came along."

"Really," Ketrick whispered. He sat back in his chair and steepled his long fingers. "Perhaps Mr. Steel should have a chat with that young woman you've been seen with."

Steel stepped up behind Parker and gently pulled him away from the desk. Ketrick closed the file and smiled in satisfaction as he continued to speak. "I suppose you are just counseling her, right, Reverend?"

Parker tensed beneath Steel's grasp. Steel pushed him toward the door. Ketrick stood up and laid the file aside. "How rude of me not to ask about the other woman in your life. Thomas, how's your wife these days? Saving money for the bassinet?"

Parker tried to speak but could only stutter in anger. Steel pushed him out of the office past Vivian Darbonne's grinning face and onto the sun-filled street. Parker jerked out of Steel's grasp and unlocked the car doors. He slid into the front seat and started the engine so hard, the ignition growled at him. "He made me look like a fool."

"I think you did that on your own," Steel said.

Parker shot him a withering glance and then collapsed onto the steering wheel. "My past has nothing to do with what's going on in the church."

"Everything about you matters," Steel said. "This possession is about you. It's about your past and your present."

Parker slapped the steering wheel in anger and looked out his window at the park across the street. Trees moved in the summer breeze. Children played around a small pond, feeding a frenzied flock of ducks.

"So you found out my wife lied," Parker whispered. "Does my church really need to know that?"

"You should've told the members. One lie just produces a

string of more lies. For instance, you didn't say anything about this other woman."

"She's a church member who needed some money from the benevolence fund, that's all. I wouldn't be surprised if Ketrick started the rumor to discredit me. Just another set of lies." Parker glanced at him. "Have you ever lied, Mr. Steel?"

Steel tensed. He watched a couple stroll along a walking track that wound its way through the park. The woman paused, reaching up to straighten the man's hair. "I'm here to ask *you* questions, Reverend."

"Well, you're getting your answers and making matters worse in the meantime." Parker threw the car into gear and headed back up the hill toward the church.

[Chapter 5]

STEEL RETURNED TO the RV and decided to go for a run. Normally it would be insane to run in the high humidity and heat of mid-June in the South, but the sky was overcast with gray clouds the color of an old tin roof, and the wind was picking up as a thunderstorm moved into the area. The air was fragrant with the aroma of ozone and fresh rain.

Halfway through his run the bottom dropped out, and he was soaked by the time he returned to the front of the church. He pulled off his tank top and squeezed out the water. He noticed a car parked at the foot of the stairs. The rain had lessened and the window rolled down. The woman behind the steering wheel was probably in her sixties, with skin the color of chocolate and short, gray hair shot through with white. She wore huge dangling earrings made of carved wood. "Mr. Steel? I'm Dr. Elizabeth Washington, your expert with the gift of many tongues." She wore huge, round white sunglasses, and she tilted them up on her head as she looked him up and down. "Honey child, you're half naked and soaked."

Steel felt his face redden, and he tried to pull the wet tank top back on. It caught on his head, and he jerked it down over his chest. "Sorry."

"I'm not complaining," Dr. Washington said. "How far did you run?"

"Six miles."

"In this heat and humidity? You're out of your ever-loving mind. I power walk in the morning while it's cool. But I don't think it'll be as cool here as it is in Tennessee. I do four miles a day. Maybe you can try to keep up with me." Her amber eyes twinkled. Dr. Washington pulled her sunglasses back over her eyes and squinted at the church. "So, where's the nearest hotel?"

"You won't find one in Lakeside. That's the parsonage where Reverend Parker lives, and next to it is a 'missionary house' where you can stay."

"Will I be sharing the house with missionaries?" She glanced back at him and pulled her sunglasses down so he could see her eyes. "Or with you?"

Steel swallowed and closed his open mouth. "Neither. I'm staying in my RV."

"You brought your own hotel?" She sighed and glanced up at the church.

"It's easier that way. I have computer equipment."

"And the writing is in there?" Washington nodded and glanced up the stone steps to the church sanctuary.

"Yes. We can take a look at it once you're settled in. And I'm dried off."

"Where's your RV?"

"In back." Steel gestured over his shoulder.

"Hop in and I'll give you a ride." Dr. Washington motioned to the car.

"I'm soaking wet."

"It's a rental. I'm sure this heat will dry it out in no time."

Dr. Washington smiled. "Besides, I'm just picking at you. I'm old enough to be your grandmother. Cephas put me up to it."

"That old coot," Steel said as he climbed into the front seat.

"He said you were a bit of a porcupine. Funny, I don't see any quills." Dr. Washington started the car and pulled around the back of the south wing of the church to the office annex. "After Dr. Lawrence told me about the writing in the church, I couldn't resist the chance to work with you." She grinned as she glanced over at him.

Steel opened his mouth to respond and couldn't think of a thing to say. Somehow he had lost control of this conversation. He glanced over the back of the front seat into the rear of the car. A briefcase and duffel bag sat on the fabric. Lying across them was a long, dark wooden stick with the head of a lion carved at one end. She brought the car to a halt in front of his RV and glanced at him.

"I'll just get the key for you." He slid out of the car and stumbled over a root. He would have a few words with Cephas over this.

Dr. Washington got out of the car and stretched. Steel retrieved the key from the RV and paused as the sound of gears grinding echoed from around the corner of the annex. An ancient pickup truck with a small camper shell on the back rounded the far end of the annex and pulled into the shade of the oak tree. The passenger door opened, and a teenage boy hopped out. His hair was unwashed, greasy, and jet-black with dye. He wore a black T-shirt and black jeans. A gold bead gleamed from the skin just below his lower lip. His ears were pierced with half a dozen small hoops that flashed in the sunlight. Metal bars and beads pierced both eyebrows.

"The least you could have done is let me keep my phone." He slammed the door and threw one caustic look in Steel's direction. "Dude, what are you looking at? Where can I get lost in this redneck town?" He glanced around and finally stormed off across the churchyard toward the distant school playground.

The silence was deafening after Josh slammed the door. Claire Knight leaned against the steering wheel and massaged her tired eyes. When she opened her eyes, she felt calmer and looked out through the windshield. The two figures, a man and a woman, blurred suddenly as her vision clouded and her calm disintegrated into frustration. She opened the truck door and fought to clear her failing vision as her hands tingled. Now was not the time for this!

Claire felt a hand on her arm and looked up into the eyes of a short, trim African American woman. "Hi, I'm Dr. Elizabeth Washington, but you can call me Liz. Honey, are you all right?"

Claire smiled as her vision cleared. "I'm fine. Just a little frustrated by my son. He doesn't want to be here. And since my husband passed away years ago, I've been raising him alone."

"Baby, I understand. I raised five of them. All tall and handsome and full of vim and vigor. How do you think I got this white hair? You'll survive. Just love him." Her smile was infectious.

Claire felt herself relaxing, and the tingling in her hands began to fade. She straightened her shirt and pulled up her jeans. She pulled a crumpled tissue from her pocket and dabbed her eyes. "Thank you."

"Why don't we go meet Mr. Steel? I think you'll like him. Whoo, is he handsome!"

Claire's eyes widened and she laughed. "OK."

"Honey, there may be snow on the roof, but there's still a fire in the fireplace."

Claire turned and caught her first clear sight of Jonathan Steel. He was tall, a bit over six feet, and a wet tank top clung to his chest. He was muscular but not bulky. Short, wiry reddish blond hair hugged his head. He had a lean face and high cheekbones with a straight nose. His eyes were deep pools of turquoise that seemed to be filled with surprise. Or was it irritation? She swallowed and walked across the wet grass to meet him. And then, like pieces of a puzzle tumbling into place, she remembered where she had met him.

How many years ago had it been? Her husband, Arthur, had taken her to a reception in hopes she would help him impress Lieutenant Miller. Miller had project money, and Arthur was hoping he would be chosen to head up the man's gene mapping project. Arthur had been uncomfortable in his tuxedo, and she had tried to straighten his unruly hair.

After they arrived, as Arthur set out to impress Miller and his benefactor, she had stepped back and crunched someone's foot under her heel. She turned and saw a tall, severe figure of the man behind her, the gun he had tucked into a shoulder holster, and his bright, turquoise eyes. His gaze filled with fury as he glanced at her, and then he was gone. Had he been some kind of security? Or was he somehow connected with Miller? She hoped not. The affair with Miller had not turned out well.

Steel tensed at the sight of the woman from the truck. She brought her teenage son? He didn't need a mother and her teenage son walking into a dangerous situation. Alarm bells sounded in his mind. Cephas had some strange sense of humor.

The new arrival's eyes were red and puffy. She was tall and

willowy with short red hair and an oval face. She dabbed at her jade-colored eyes with a tissue.

"Mr. Steel? I'm Dr. Claire Knight. Your friend Dr. Lawrence was supposed to send you an e-mail." She held out a hand and Steel shook it. Her skin was warm and moist.

"He did. But he didn't tell me you would be bringing your son along." Steel felt a tremor of anger in his voice.

"I really don't have anyone to leave Josh with. He's not too happy about leaving his friends."

Steel gazed off toward the playground. Josh was sitting in a swing dragging his feet through mud. Josh glanced back toward them and lifted his hand in an obscene gesture. "Seems like a nice kid."

"His father died a few years ago, and Josh has been a holy terror since. I had to bring him with me. I can't trust him to be alone." She turned her gaze back to him. "I don't think he'll be any trouble. I'll tell him to stay out of the way."

"I'm just concerned about safety." Steel's voice softened.

"Safety?" Claire glanced down the hill at her son. "Josh needs some time to decompress. I know you don't approve of him, but if you want my help, he's part of the package." She looked back at him with defiance in her gaze. Steel felt an annoying tremble when he looked into those jade-green eyes.

"Let's drop it for now. Why don't the two of you go on over to the missionary house while I shower and change clothes? I'll come over in a while and bring you up to date on what we're dealing with."

"Fine." Her face relaxed, and she shaded her eyes against the sunlight. "Would you mind bringing Josh when you come?"

Steel opened his mouth and then closed it in frustration. "I'll be glad to drag him along."

Josh watched the adults look his way and spat in the grass. Louisiana of all places! Redneck city! He'd decided to forgo showering for a couple of days just to show her. And in this stifling humidity it wouldn't take long to work up a good stink.

A shadow fell over him, and he looked up into the face of a teenage girl. She had bright, yellow hair and dark eyes and wore a dress covered with sunflowers.

"I'm Summer. Who are you?" She sat in the swing next to him.

"Josh. I'm not from around here."

"I'm not either. But that doesn't matter. Want to go inside?"

Josh touched his lip bead with his tongue. "Inside? Where?"

She pointed to a small building at the edge of the playground. It had a dirty window, and on the outside, two huge pipes poked out of the ground. Some kind of well pump house? "Over there."

Josh's eyebrows furrowed. "What is in there?"

Summer smiled, and he felt his heart skip a beat. "So, you want to have some fun?"

Josh swallowed as the implications of her invitation ran over him like a cold chill. He studied her figure and her demure smile. For a moment he thought about Ila. But the opportunity to irritate his mother was irresistible. "Sure."

"Hey, annoying kid."

Josh stood up and looked up the hill. The man from the RV was calling to him.

"Yeah, what do you want?"

"Your mother wants me to drag you over to the house. Get up here or I will." He turned and walked back toward the RV.

Josh gritted his teeth. He turned to talk to Summer, but

she was gone. "Hey, where'd you go?" A pile of dead weeds lay beneath the swing, but the girl was nowhere in sight. "Did you let that big jerk scare you off? Well, that's another reason to annoy him. Yep, he goes on the hit list." He started up the hill with a silly grin on his face.

After his shower Steel pulled on a pair of cargo shorts and a T-shirt and walked out of his tiny bathroom. The boy sat at the computer consoles. "Bro, you've got some heavy equipment here."

"Bro?" Steel said.

"Bro! Dude! Man! Get it?" Josh said.

"OK, *Bro*, who said you could touch my computer?"

Josh looked up, and his lip bead glittered in the light from the computer monitor. His hair glistened with sweat and grease, and he exuded a foul odor. "What, I need permission? I'm here, so I just assumed I could."

"Never assume anything around me. You don't touch my equipment unless you ask first. Understand?" Careful, he's just a kid, Steel told himself.

Josh's face reddened, and he tossed the mouse he was holding down on the table. "Fine! I wouldn't want to break your little toys, *Bro*."

Red fire engulfed Steel's mind, and he reached over and grabbed Josh's shirt at the chest. He picked him up until the boy's feet barely touched the floor. He drew his face close, his nose almost touching Josh's. "We need to come to an understanding. Get rid of the attitude. I didn't ask for you to be here. As far as I'm concerned you're just excess baggage. So stay out of trouble and stay out of my way. This situation might be dangerous."

"No problemo," Josh squeaked. "So, are you the danger? Because, man, you need some serious therapy."

Steel closed his eyes and drew a deep breath. He slowly lowered Josh to the floor and stepped back. "Let's start over. I'm Jonathan Steel."

"Joshua Knight."

"So, you know something about computers?" Steel said awkwardly.

"Yeah." Josh picked at his lip bead.

"Like what?"

Josh pointed to one of the computers. He rattled off the hardware and operating system specifics as if he were a seasoned programmer. He made suggestions on how to improve the computer's efficiency.

"Not bad. Where'd you learn all of that?"

"I've got a photographic memory. And the highest IQ in my grade." He paused, and his finger twirled the lip bead. "But dude, just try and convince my mom."

Steel nodded. He only had a brief memory of his mother. "Sorry about your father."

"Yeah, no more than I am." Josh stood up. "So, we going over to this other house, or do I sleep on the floor?"

"It can be arranged." Steel growled and led him out the door of the RV.

[Chapter 6]

CLAIRE STUMBLED THROUGH the dark interior of the missionary house until she found a light switch. Pale light illuminated the walls, and she located the thermostat. The hot, musty air was stifling. The central air conditioning unit thrummed on as she turned the thermostat down. She was about to take her bags down the hall to one of the bedrooms when the front door opened and Steel stepped in off of the front porch. His face bore the same stern expression of disapproval as before. Josh pushed in behind him and surveyed the dwelling.

"Where's Opie?" He pulled off his black T-shirt and exposed a white tank top. He tossed the shirt on a nearby chair and collapsed on the couch. "Dude! Sure is hot in here."

Claire sniffed. She placed her hands on her hips and glared at her son. "Josh, you stink."

"I know." He wore a smug look. "If you had told me about this little field trip earlier, I would have had time to shower."

"I told you last night." She felt uneasy and glanced at Steel. "Josh, there is a bathroom down the hall with a fully functional shower. Hit it."

Josh ignored her and raised his arms and crossed his hands behind his head. "I would rather compete with the mildew."

"If you're smart," Steel said, "you'll do as your mother said and go take a shower." There was an unmistakable quality of authority in his voice, Claire noticed. Like when she saw him in the ballroom. She hoped he didn't have a gun.

Josh glared at Steel and then shrugged. "Whatever, bro." He got up and went back toward the bathroom. Claire tensed as Josh passed her, expecting the usual outburst. Instead she heard the sound of a shower running. She exhaled and leaned against the wall. Advantage Steel. She glanced up at him.

"I guess that's what I've needed at home since my husband died. A security guard. Or were you special forces?" She said.

Steel's head snapped in her direction with alarming suddenness. He stepped closer, and his eyes were wide with shock. "What did you call me?"

Claire tried to step away, but he grabbed her arms. She swallowed. "OK, so maybe you were just security for the reception."

"What reception?" he said through clenched teeth.

"With my husband. It was a little over five years ago. You were there. I stepped on your foot..."

"You know me?" His face changed, almost softened and he pulled her down beside him on the couch. "Do you know me? Answer the question."

Claire grimaced. "You're hurting me."

His face relaxed just a bit, and he released her. "Sorry. This is important, Dr. Knight. Do you know me?"

"I only met you once. I can understand if you don't remember me. I stepped on your foot at the reception, and you walked away. That was all. I remember you because of your eyes. I'm sorry. I was at a reception with my husband. Lots of military types and philanthropists. I didn't know anyone there, I swear.

He was trying to get money for his research, and I ran into you. That was all. You had an earpiece and a gun."

"A gun?" Steel leaned back on the couch. "A gun?" Steel's mind reeled with the information. One tiny piece of a larger puzzle just fell into place, and he was back in time, back to the gun club.

It was November, five months since he woke up on the beach. He stood on the deck of the Pierces' beach house. He should have been proud of the work he had done as their handyman, but a tight, worrisome paranoia kept surfacing. The man with the spiral tattoo might be out there. He might be watching right now. He stood there beneath a clearing night sky and felt the cool air. Like an alarm bell, his anxiety increased day by day. He needed to find something to bring him peace, reassurance. He needed a weapon.

The next day he found a local gun club. It was located out in the deep pinewoods of southern Alabama. He walked into the metal building that served as an office, and a young man with no hair and a huge goatee waited on him from behind a counter.

"What's up?" he asked.

"Do you have a pistol range?"

The man frowned and opened a notebook in front of him. "I don't recognize you. Only club members are welcome. What's your name?"

"Jonathan Steel."

The man studied the book, and a surprised look came onto his face. "Oh, here you are. Looks like you haven't been here in quite some time. OK, did you bring your own gun, or do you want to borrow the usual?"

"When was the last time I was here?"

"Oh, looks like two years ago. See?" The man turned the notebook around, and Steel studied the page. The date was almost two years previous with a time stamp of 10:17 a.m. His signature was scrawled by the date and time, J. Steel.

"Do you have any records on me?"

"Naw." The man frowned. "That hurricane last year pretty much wiped out the office. It was a little travel trailer right outside. All that was left was the logbooks. Which reminds me. I'll let you shoot today, but you're going to have to fill out a new application and pay the club fee."

"Do you remember when I was here last?"

"I've only been here little over a year."

"Are there any other members around that might have been here?"

"No." The man averted his eyes and suddenly seemed nervous. "You didn't hear?"

"Hear what?"

"Well, my older brother was one of the founding members." The man gazed off into space. "Six of them. About seven years ago, they founded it. And then, over a year ago, I guess it's

been, they all went deep-sea fishing to celebrate the club's anniversary. Never came back. Just disappeared off the face of the earth." The man had traveled far away now in his memory, and his eyes became unfocused. His voice grew softer. "There was a storm that day. Coast Guard says the ship probably sank in the storm." He shook his head and returned his attention to Steel. "I took over the club. Most of us are new."

Steel's mind raced with the implications of this information. "I'll need to borrow a pistol. I'll pay for the ammunition."

"Sure." The man slid the notebook under the counter. "You can have a box on the house since you are a former member. But after you're done, I need you to register for a new membership. Got it?"

Steel nodded, and the man reached under the counter. "How about a Glock 9mm? Seventeen OK? What you used last time."

Steel watched him lay the gun on the counter. It was silent, still and dark. It was more than just a gun. It was a link to his distant past. He reached for it and hesitated. What would happen if he picked it up? Would his past come rushing back to meet him? What if he was a trained murderer?

He touched the gun. His fingers caressed the cold, oiled metal, and nothing happened. He picked up the pistol and measured its weight. It felt natural in his hand, almost an extension of his arm. The man behind the counter placed a small box of ammunition on the counter, and Steel found himself opening and inspecting the gun as if he had done it a thousand times.

"Yes, this will be fine. Where's the range?"

The man pointed across the room past a soda machine to a back door. "Through there. Targets are by the back door if you want to use the zip line. Tactical targets are out to the left. Ear protection is on each table. There's no one here right now, so you can make yourself at home."

Steel picked up the box of ammunition and walked through the back door. He picked up a couple of large targets of a man and went to one of the tables. The target fit on a pull line, and he worked the cord, sending the target out to fifty feet. He placed the ear pads over his ears and loaded up the magazine with bullets.

Steel raised the gun, and it felt right; it felt good in his hand. He braced himself and studied the target. He closed his eyes. "Don't think," he whispered. "Just react."

He opened his eyes and began squeezing off shot after shot. When the last gunshot echo died, he lay down the gun. He had placed half the shots in the heart and half between the target's eyes. And he hadn't even thought about it. His heart wasn't even racing. He stepped to the next table and sent a target out to 150 feet. He loaded up the gun and repeated the process.

When the smoke cleared, he had placed the shots in the exact same deadly cluster. He looked at the gun in his hand and dropped it on the table in front of him as if it were a deadly snake. He pulled off the ear pads and let them hit the dirt. Suddenly he had a memory.

A man, standing next to him, wearing a wide-brimmed Panama style hat and sunglasses with a white Meerschaum pipe clenched in his teeth. "Why do I have to do this?" he'd asked him.

"Boy," his father had said, "you have no idea what is out there waiting for you. You've got to learn to defend yourself," the man had continued as he took the pipe from his lips.

"I'm past all of that. I'm back to normal. I'm old enough to take care of myself. You've made me take martial arts, taught me how to fly an airplane, go mountain climbing. My whole life you've pushed me, but this time I'm saying no. I don't want to learn how to shoot a gun."

The man had taken off his sunglasses, revealing bright greenish-blue eyes. "You don't have a choice. If you don't learn how to shoot, I'll shoot you myself. Right now." A pistol had appeared in the man's hand as quickly as a breath, his sunglasses tossed into the grass.

In a blur, he had snatched the gun from his father's hand even as the sound of the gunshot had reached his ears. The bullet had whizzed past his right ear, and he had turned, twisting his father's arm to make him drop the gun and then fluidly tossing him over his hunched shoulder. His father had landed with a thud in the grass. He had found the gun suddenly in his hand, pointed at his father's prostrate form. He had blinked for the first time and looked at the thing in his hand. His father had slowly stood up, and his eyes had glittered with excitement.

"Just as I thought. You don't need lessons."

Steel glanced once again at the gun and shook his head of the memory. He never wanted to touch a gun again.

Steel shook his head, and his eyes came into focus. Claire was still sitting across from him on the couch. Liz came in and squeezed between them, with a pitcher of ice water and several glasses on a tray. She placed the tray on the coffee table. "Something cool to drink, Mr. Steel. You need to tell us the tale of our church."

Steel grabbed a glass and guzzled the water in one continuous swallow. He sighed and sat forward. "Thomas Parker is the pastor of Lakeside Community Church. He contacted me two days ago about a problem with his sanctuary. It seems to have become possessed."

"I haven't seen any real demonic possession in years." Liz's eyes gleamed with excitement. "Of course, my interest is purely academic. I wouldn't want anyone to get hurt."

"Someone already has." Steel filled them in. Claire pulled a notebook out of her satchel and slid her red reading glasses over her nose.

Josh appeared from the hallway. His hair was clean, and he had scrubbed his face. He wore a black T-shirt and gym shorts. Josh disappeared into the kitchen. As his story came to an end, Steel leaned back on the couch.

"I really need to see more of these writings, Mr. Steel. You only sent me a sampling, and I couldn't tell enough about them to draw any real conclusions except to confirm they're ancient."

"This pool of energy you saw, Mr. Steel, did it radiate heat?" Claire checked her notes.

"The air felt warm to the touch, but I didn't dare put my hand in the field."

"Definitely. You wouldn't find a phenomenon like that on Earth under natural conditions." A quaver filled her voice as excitement built. "I think you may be right that we are dealing with a possible extra-dimensional phenomenon. This would be an amazing scientific discovery."

"Hey, I've got a phenomenon for you. It's called hunger." Josh came into the room and leaned against the wall. "Is there anything to eat in this house? Or do I need to resort to cannibalism?"

Claire gazed at him over her reading glasses. "Is that all you think about?"

"That. And girls. Mom, it's almost five o'clock. That burger I ate in Canton is long gone."

Steel reached into his backpack and produced a cell phone. "Here." He tossed the phone to Josh. "There's a pizza place out on the highway. Order enough for us all, and I'll buy."

"Dude, anything I want?" Josh asked. "I don't need you picking me up by my shirt again."

Claire glanced at Steel. "What?"

"Sure," Steel said. "But you have to eat everything. Or I'll feed it to you myself."

Josh rolled his eyes. "Bro, you are so in need of tranks!" He turned and walked into the kitchen. He began opening and shutting drawers with great energy until he found a phonebook.

"You grabbed him by the shirt?" Claire slid her glasses back into her satchel and stood up.

"We had a discussion in my RV about boundaries," Steel said.

"Boundaries?" Claire glanced at Josh. "Well, I'm sorry if he violated your boundaries."

"No problem. For a teenager he's acting pretty normal."

Liz stood up and retrieved an equipment pack. "Well, I for one want a look at the church while we're waiting for the pizza." She pulled out an enormous digital camera. "I need to image the entire ceiling in ultraviolet, infrared, and regular light." Liz reached to the corner of the room and retrieved her stick leaning against the wall.

"You told me you power walked every day. I didn't know you needed a cane," Steel said.

"Four miles a day. My hips are still as good as when I ran track in college. As for this stick, I don't use it for walking." She lifted it and slammed the end against the floor. "I use it for poking. Things that bite can hide in cracks and crevices among the ruins I like to explore. I'd rather a snake strike this stick than me. As I said, herpetology is an interest of mine."

"Herpes who?" Josh asked from the kitchen.

"Snakes, son."

Liz walked across to Steel and held the top end up to his face. The head of a lion stared back at him. "An African chief gave this to me. I never go on site without it."

Claire reached out her finger and touched the woodcarving. "It's beautiful. I'm afraid my equipment isn't as artistic. I'll get my dull, boring instrument package." She paused as she crossed in front of the window and stopped. She looked up the hill at the church. A white van with a satellite antenna sat at the foot of the stairs. "I think we have some visitors, Mr. Steel. Looks like the media have caught wind of the goings on in the church."

Steel glanced out the window and stiffened. "Why is *he*

here?" He threw open the door and rushed out. Claire glanced once at Liz, and they followed after him.

Josh closed the phone book and clicked off the cell phone. He had ordered five pizzas, and he would make sure he ate every single bite in front of the high and mighty Jonathan Steel.

"All right, bro, I ordered the pizzas..." he said as he walked into the living room. The front door stood open. The adults had left. Josh hurried out onto the front porch. Steel led the way up the hill toward the church. Josh ran after them.

[Chapter 7]

IT WAS THERE deep inside of him, always waiting...always hungry...always nervously caged. But Steel kept it under tight control—most of the time. When it escaped, the fury and anger took him like a perfect storm. At first it simmered, gathering heat and steam, and then it boiled over into an explosive fury. Steel walked up to a man in a long, black trench coat talking to Thomas Parker, tapped the man on the back, ignored the news crew standing at the foot of the stairs, and punched the man dead in the nose.

The man tumbled back, his perfectly combed black hair suddenly awry, his tie stained with dripping blood, his sunglasses hanging at an impossible angle.

"Mr. Steel!" Claire rushed up and pulled Steel back.

"Leave me alone, Dr. Knight." Steel spoke through clenched teeth, jerking his arm out of her grasp. "I'm just getting rid of the vermin."

The man stood up slowly, pulling a handkerchief from the inside of his coat to dab at the blood running from his nose. "I could have you arrested for striking a federal officer, Steel."

"I've heard that one before. Why are you here?" Steel growled.

"Anywhere you crop up, Steel, I'll follow. You know that."

Parker stepped between them. "FBI Agent Ross is here at the request of Sheriff Sweeney and Deputy O'Reilly." He pointed to a pot-bellied middle-aged man leaning against the squad car. Sheriff Sweeney tipped his broad-billed hat and spat tobacco juice on the ground. A tall, thin man in a similar uniform got out of the car, his eyes shifty and pale. Deputy O'Reilly fingered his gun and grinned.

"Afternoon to you, Mr. Steel," Sheriff Sweeney drawled. "Agent Ross, are you going to file charges?"

"I hope so, Sheriff." Deputy O'Reilly's jaw worked at a piece of gum, his eyes filled with anticipation. "I ain't arrested nobody in months." Sweeney laid a restraining hand on his deputy.

Ross took off his sunglasses and glanced briefly at Josh and Claire. His eyes were deep pools of brown. "No, I won't be filing charges. It's not the first time he's hit me."

"Nor will it be the last." Steel stepped back, feeling the fury die down back to a low simmer. "What do you want, Ross? And who brought in these news clowns?" Steel pointed to the reporter. Her mouth was open in shock, and the cameraman was pointing a huge shoulder-mounted camera in their direction.

"Anonymous tip." The cameraman said.

Ross reached out and shoved the front of the camera down. "Cool it, Spielberg." Ross glanced at Steel. "Nothing to see here." Ross's nose had stopped bleeding, and he put his sunglasses back on, stuffing the bloody handkerchief into his pocket. How could the man stand to wear the trench coat in the summer heat? "Now, Sheriff Sweeney and I want to ask you and Reverend Parker about a certain pool of blood that was seen here at the foot of the stairs earlier today."

"We went inside the sanctuary and couldn't find a source."

Steel motioned to the stairs. "The rain must have washed it away."

The news cameraman followed Ross with the camera as he walked over to the steps and studied them one by one until his eyes came to rest on the closed doors at the top of the stairs. "Then you wouldn't mind if we went in?"

Parker hurried over and stood between Ross and the first step. "I don't think it's safe."

Ross took off his sunglasses and raised an eyebrow. "A church isn't safe? Have you been handling snakes and drinking strychnine?"

"Well, not snakes..." Parker's voice trailed off.

"Let them inside," Steel said.

"What?"

"You've nothing to hide. Let them have a look."

Parker hesitated, running his hand through his hair and tugging at his sagging jeans. "Go on in. But I warned you."

Ross led the way up the stairs with Parker following, the news crew circling them like vultures. Steel started up the steps and Josh joined him.

"Bro, that was a pretty good punch back there."

Steel glanced at the kid. "Yeah."

"Dude, would you ever punch me like that?"

"No. Ross and I have a history." Steel reached the top of the stairs and turned to study Josh. "You, on the other hand, are just a teenager."

Josh fingered his gold bead. "You know, bro, for someone who likes to help people, you sure are violent."

Steel had no comeback. Josh was right. He turned his back on the boy and watched as Ross flung open the doors. Parker put his arms up in a defensive posture, but the air was still and warm. No wind. No mist. No blood. Ross stepped into the foyer and reached over and flicked on a light switch. The church looked normal—abandoned, but normal.

Josh sighed. "OK, I'm still bored."

Parker looked back at Steel as Claire and Liz joined him. "What's going on?"

Ross looked around the foyer, the news camera gyrating wildly expecting to catch demons in action. "So far, I don't feel threatened, Reverend Parker. I don't even see any blood. But these offering plates are a bit intimidating."

Ross pushed open the inner doors and walked down the aisle. The pews gleamed in the overhead lights. The carpet bore the normal stains of decades of use. The ceiling was white and empty of writing. Parker pushed past him and ran up to the podium. The altar table was clear of blood and flowers. Parker climbed up into the choir loft and looked over the baptistery edge. He whispered to Steel, "There's nothing in here but a dead roach. No energy field. I don't understand."

The reporter stepped into Steel's line of sight, her hands on her hips. "Like, where's the demons?"

"In Reverend Parker's mind." Ross shook his head, slipping his sunglasses back over his eyes. "Looks like we've been hoodwinked."

Steel walked down to the front pew and silently shook his head. Parker held up his hands. "I'm not convinced this is over."

"Yeah, the fat lady didn't sing," Josh said.

"Son, be quiet," Claire said.

Josh turned his back on the adults and walked up into the choir loft and peered over the edge of the baptistery. He didn't see any demons. Big deal! But at least he would be going home sooner than he expected. He would get away from this backwater town.

Then he saw something move in the shadows of the baptistery—it was Summer. She motioned to him.

Josh had wondered where she had gone. "Hey, where did you go earlier?"

She smiled from the shadows. "Doesn't matter. Meet me at the shack. OK?"

Josh nodded. "I'll bring pizza."

Claire blinked as they exited the darkened church interior. Disappointment lay like a hard lump in her chest. She had really wanted to find the energy field and study it. Had it all been a hoax? She glanced at Steel. Although he had intimidated her at first, he seemed an honest man, perhaps a little too honest. Tact was not one of his attributes. If he said he'd seen the energy field, then it must have existed.

Reverend Parker turned off the light switch and closed the door to his newly cleaned church. "I don't know how you did it. But I hope they are gone."

Steel's eyes were riveted on Ross as he mumbled something to the sheriff and they both climbed in their vehicles and drove off. Steel turned back to Parker. "Don't get your hopes up just yet. I've never seen things clear up so quickly. It doesn't seem right."

Parker smiled and turned to Liz.

"Dr. Liz Washington, anthropologist and linguist," she said. Parker shook her hand. "If you don't mind, I'd like to take a look at your church archives. No need in wasting a visit. Church history fascinates me. Maybe later?"

Parker nodded. "Of course. And you are?" He glanced at Claire.

"Dr. Claire Knight." She took his hand in hers.

"Sorry you didn't get to see any extra dimensions. Now, if you'll excuse me, I need to go check my office." He motioned down the steps.

A blue and red car pulled up to the door of the missionary house. Claire tapped Steel on the shoulder. "The pizzas have arrived."

Steel nodded absently, his thoughts obviously still far away in the church. Claire kept gazing at those eyes, and suddenly she stumbled, reaching out to catch Steel's arm. His hands clamped on her upper arm, stabilizing her unsteady gait. She blushed and tried to regain her composure. "Do you mind letting me hold onto you until we get to the house? I'm really tired, Mr. Steel."

"Sure." Steel's voice became hoarse. His face relaxed. He looked away. "You can call me Jonathan."

Parker watched them descend the old stone steps and then turned back to the double doors. He jerked them open and stepped inside. No spiders! He opened the inner doors and stepped into his empty sanctuary. No vines!

Parker ran down the aisle and through the door toward his office. He reached for the handle, and it wouldn't open. Of course, he had left it locked. He fumbled in his pocket and took out his key ring. His hands shook as he found the key and unlocked his door.

The inside was hot and the air was stale. He flipped on the light and glanced around the room. No blood! He sat at his desk and turned to face the back wall, pulling open a cabinet face to expose his safe.

Parker wiped sweat from his forehead and blinked when his glasses started fogging up. He took them off and laid them behind him on the desk as he twirled the old-fashioned combination dial.

"Boo boo da!"

Parker jumped, fell out of his chair, and landed on the floor behind the desk. He peeked up over the desk, and the child was sitting on the blotter with his glasses in his hands. "Blvvddddd!" The child stuck out his tongue and coated the lenses with spit. Parker jerked them out the baby's hands.

Summer stood behind the baby. "That wasn't very nice. Now, what are you looking for?"

"Summer, I'm getting something out of my safe. I'm glad to see you're OK. I was so worried about you." He slowly regained his seat and rubbed the sore spot on his bottom.

"If you're looking for the recordings, I have them." She smiled.

Parker swallowed and turned to the safe. He spun the dial once more and opened the door. Inside, a large, ancient book bound in leather was on top of his other precious memories. He turned back to Summer.

"What is this?"

"I have a friend to meet, Reverend. I have the recordings. But I put an old bookmark in that book. Read the passages on those pages, and if you can find the object it's talking about by midnight Friday and give it to me, I'll disappear, and so will your precious recordings." She picked up the child. "Just remember, I'm in the nursery, and I won't go out in public with the baby if you give me what I want." She looked at the baby. "Say good-bye to Daddy."

[Chapter 8]

PARKER STUMBLED BACK to his house. "The church clears up, and then this? God, what more am I supposed to handle?" He collapsed at the kitchen table and opened the book. Parker felt a hand on his shoulder and stiffened. "Emily?"

"Who else would it be?" Emily sat at the kitchen table next to him. "So, is it true?"

"The church is back to normal," Parker said.

"I still think you should let it go. Give it to Ketrick." Emily ran a hand through her short, dark hair and sighed. "We'll just have to move on and start over."

"I'm tired of running from the past, Emily. When we came here, I had a vision for this church."

"Until Ketrick showed up. Honey, the people just turned and ran away from the first big challenge. They won't support a contemporary service. They want to squat in that old building until it falls apart. In the meantime, what do we do for money? We do have bills to pay, particularly when this baby is born."

Parker nodded and pointed to the book. "I may have found a solution."

Emily leaned forward. "What is this?"

"I found this in my office after the sanctuary went back to normal. It's an old book, and most of it is handwritten, probably a journal. The author is Sidney Blakemore, one of the founders of the church." Parker opened the leather-bound book. "Look at this."

Emily reached over and turned the book toward her. "It's a chest."

Parker pointed to the hand-drawn illustration. "Covered in gold, from what I can decipher from this bad handwriting. But listen to this, 'Whilst investigating the mystery of the altar of the spiral eye, I became acquainted with an ancient Indian legend of a chest containing two gold crosses encrusted with precious stones. It is rumored the chest is buried beneath the altar of the spiral eye.'"

"Where is this altar?" Emily drew closer to him.

"Somewhere under the church according to these writings. If we can find this, Emily, these crosses would be worth a fortune. This may be what Ketrick is looking for. This may be why he wants the church."

"Oh, I doubt that," Emily said.

"Why?"

Emily shrugged. "Oh, I don't know," she said. "Ketrick seems more of a power person. He wants the property for something else, I'm betting—probably a shopping mall."

Parker nodded. "Maybe you're right. But if this book is true, then we have to find this altar."

"What is the spiral eye?" Emily relaxed into his side again.

"I have no idea."

Steel paid the pizza man, and Claire carried the five extra large pizzas inside. Liz hugged four two-liter soft drink bottles to her chest.

"Honey, you've got one hungry child!"

Claire nodded, slowly placing the pizzas on the kitchen table. She felt more stable now that her balance had returned. "Josh could eat all of them." She looked behind her at the room. "Where is he?"

Steel looked around the living room, and his gaze settled on Claire. "I can't have Josh running off and getting into places where he may be in danger."

"But the church looked fine."

"Don't bet on it." He crossed to the window and glanced up at the church. "Claire, is Josh a Christian?"

Claire joined him at the window. "Yes, why?" She felt a tug at her arm, and Liz handed her a plate with one piece of pizza. Liz mouthed the word "eat" and pointed to the pizza.

Steel glanced back at her. "I need to make sure, Claire. If not, the enemy could use one of us against the other."

"He was baptized when he was ten." She glanced out the window and watched Josh run down the hill toward the house. "Why? Is he in danger?"

"Maybe I'm overreacting. I hope none of us are in danger anymore. But I don't think he should be going back into the church without us." He looked at her, and his eyes filled with anger.

Before she could reply, Josh burst through the door. She stepped back out of his way. Her eyes never left Steel's troubled face. Josh hurried to the table and opened a pizza box and placed Steel's cell phone next to them. He took several slices of each of the pizzas and deftly exchanged them so that he had one extra large pizza. He grabbed a two-liter bottle of soda and headed back toward the front door. Claire stopped him with a hand held out to bar his exit.

"Josh, please don't go back into the church without one of us with you." She made him look her in the eye.

"No problemo, Mom. I'm heading over to the playground." He hurried out the door and disappeared up the hill. Claire watched him go. What danger had she brought her son into?

"I had no choice but bring him," Claire said. "Uncle Cephas told me this would be a chance of a lifetime, to see evil incarnate and to possibly prove there is access to other dimensions of space through a supernatural realm scientists don't want to acknowledge." Claire felt her knees weaken. "Look, you can't intimidate me, so forget it."

"I'm not trying to intimidate you." Steel's face reddened.

"Then what do you call this?"

"This is who I am. This is how I act. I'm not a diplomat. I get things done."

"Uncle Cephas said you were a bit of a porcupine," Claire said. More like a rabid wolverine, she thought. Silence filled the air, and she swallowed. "Now, tell me about that FBI agent you hit."

Steel looked at her and nodded. "There's nothing there. He's on a wild goose chase, believing me to be a threat of some kind. But all he does is stir up trouble in my wake."

Steel turned his back on her and sat at the table to eat his pizza. Claire opened her mouth to press on, and Liz put a hand on her shoulder. She shook her head.

It had been five weeks since waking up on the beach when Steel first met Special Agent Franklin Ross. He ignored the pain in his side and managed to finish the twentieth bench press before allowing the rod to settle back onto its resting place. He heard a voice say, "Should you be working that hard after what you've been through?" and he looked up into the face of Special Agent Franklin Ross. Ross wore his sunglasses even though they were inside the rehabilitation wing of the hospital and far from the bright August sunlight outside. He took off his sunglasses and stared at Steel.

"After the guy with the spiral eye tattoo attacked me, I guess I've gotten paranoid," Steel said.

"Got a minute?"

Steel sat up and reached for his towel and wiped the sweat from his forehead. "I have plenty of time. What can I do for you?"

Ross glanced around at the workout room and motioned to a conference room in the corner. "How's the ribs?"

"Healing slowly." Steel followed him into the room.

Agent Ross wore the same long, black trench coat, white shirt and red tie. He sat down and motioned to a chair across the table. Steel settled into the chair.

Ross pulled a small notebook out of his shirt pocket and flipped it open. He studied his notes and rubbed his chin. He looked back up at Steel, his dark eyes devoid of any emotion.

"Your psychiatrist, Dr. Pierce, told me about the incident in group therapy last week."

"It's OK." They'd put Braxton, the man who attacked him, in a padded cell. He wouldn't hurt anyone again—although Steel could see that strange spiral tattoo in his dreams.

"Well, I did some checking on Braxton," Ross said. "It seems Mr. Braxton is not exactly your model citizen. He was the suspect in several crimes, but there has never been enough evidence to indict him." Ross stood up and tapped the notebook against the palm of his left hand as he paced across the room. He stopped in the far corner and slowly turned. "I also did some checking on you. If your name is Jonathan Steel. And if the month and day on that frequent dining card really is your birthday. So, I took the liberty of running your fingerprints." Ross stepped closer to the table. "Your DNA." He sat down again and squinted at Steel. "And even tried facial recognition. You're a ghost."

Steel swallowed and looked away. "What are you saying? I'm some kind of mercenary?"

"Or a criminal. Those abilities you showed when you took out Braxton prove you've had some kind of special training."

"Anyone can train in martial arts, Special Agent," Steel said.

"There is a shadowy connection between Braxton and some possible homicides." Ross tapped his notebook and glared at him. "I can't prove anything. He was just in the same place and at the same time of some strange murders in the past

five years. And there is evidence he had an accomplice." Ross smiled. "Maybe it was you."

Steel felt his heart race, and his spit dried up. The warm flow of anger washed over him, and before he knew it, he was across the table. He grabbed Ross by the neck, and they tumbled into the wall. Ross shoved at him with his hands, but the red haze had taken Steel and he knew nothing but rage. He lashed out and caught Ross in the face. Blood splattered on the wall.

"Don't even put me in the same category as Braxton! Understand? He's evil." Steel was shouting. He barely remembered security pulling him off of Ross. He barely remembered Ross standing across the table, blood streaming across his shirt. Finally the wave settled, and the blood drained from his face and back into the harsh, tight ball of fury that lived in his gut.

Dr. Pierce appeared at his side, her dark hair pulled back into a ball. She glared at Ross. "What did you do to him, Ross?"

Ross wiped blood from his lip. "What did I do to him? He attacked me!"

"You provoked a patient on my ward to violence. Get out!"

"I could file charges!"

"This is a psychiatric ward."

Ross reached into his jacket and pulled out a folded manila envelope. "Fine! Here are your new papers, Steel. You get to pay taxes again. And I get to keep an eye on you." He slammed the envelope on the table and stormed out.

Dr. Pierce turned on him. "What do you think you're doing?"

Steel felt his heart break. The last thing he wanted to do was to disappoint Dr. Pierce. "I'm sorry."

Dr. Pierce shook her head. "Take him back to his room and get him a sedative. And while you're at it, get me one too."

It was months before Steel saw Special Agent Ross a second time. He was soaked in sweat from his workout in the open garage under the Pierces' house when he got a call from April. "Jonathan?"

"Hello, Dr. Pierce."

"Stop that. I hope I didn't disturb you?"

Steel dropped the barbell into the sand and shook his head. "No, April. I was just under the house working on something, but it can wait. It's good to hear from you."

"It's good to hear your voice too. How are you doing?"

Steel looked out at the beach and the rising sun peeping out over the ocean. "I'm doing well. I get stronger each day. And I'm making progress on the house."

"Well, that's why I'm calling. Dad and I thought we'd come out for the weekend."

Steel felt his pulse quicken. "Great! I mean that would be good. Do I need to go find a hotel room?"

"Of course not, silly. Dad said you had settled into the downstairs bedroom. That's the guest room, and we have rooms upstairs. It's you we'd be imposing on."

"No, you're not imposing on me," Steel said. "Your father can check on the progress on the house. I have some questions for him, so it would be a good idea. When are you coming?"

"We should be there around six." April said.

"Tonight? I guess I'd better take a shower. I mean, clean up." Steel rolled his eyes.

"By all means," April said. "We'll see you at six, and don't eat dinner. Dad is cooking steaks." The line went dead.

Steel held out the phone and looked at it. He looked up at the ocean. For the first time in this life he could remember, he felt happiness. He hurried up the stairs into the house. He had a lot to do.

By five that evening Steel had cleaned up the house and straightened up the downstairs. It was amazing how much of a pig he had become. He realized that in the past few weeks he had stopped caring about everyday things. He couldn't afford to let that slide again. April was coming to see him!

He drove to the nearby outlet mall in Foley and bought all new clothes. Other than the scrubs he had worn in the hospital, he had only bought some shorts and tank tops. Now, he wore a nice pair of khaki slacks and a red polo shirt. He looked at himself in the mirror of his bathroom. His hair had grown out since the surgery, and it was almost shoulder length, the reddish tint burned out by exposure to the sun. His turquoise eyes were clear and rested. The wounds had healed on his face, and he felt strong and healthy. He smiled at the face in the mirror and gazed into his own eyes. The smile slowly faded, and he sighed.

"Who are you?" he asked himself.

The doorbell rang.

Steel rushed out of the corner bedroom and across the den through the kitchen. They were early. He tried to calm his racing heart and stopped to catch his breath. He reached out and opened the back door, making sure he had a huge smile on his face.

Special Agent Franklin Ross stood on the doorstep. He pulled off his sunglasses. "Hello, Mr. Steel. Mind if I come in?"

Steel stepped back in shock at the sight of the FBI agent. Behind him, two local policemen stood on the porch overlooking the driveway.

"What is this about?" Steel managed.

Ross stepped into the foyer and motioned to the two policemen. "You two can wait in the car. I've got this under control." As he shut the door behind him, Ross studied the huge den of the condominium. "You've moved up in the world, Steel."

"It's not mine. I'm working for Dr. Pierce. What do you want?"

"I need to ask you a few questions." Ross stepped past him and sank into the sofa.

"What kind of questions?"

"Where were you this morning at about eleven o'clock?"

Steel blinked and tried to calm his racing thoughts. "I was over in Foley buying some new clothes. Why?" Ross reached into his pocket and pulled out a packet of cigarettes. "No smoking in the house, Special Agent."

"I won't light it. I was doing so well until you came along. I had quit the smoking. Given up the booze. My ulcer had healed. But then you had to pop up." He stuck the cigarette in his mouth.

"You said you found out nothing about me. Why would you be stressed out over me?"

Ross inhaled the unlit cigarette and sighed. "Call it intuition. I know you are going to bring a heap of trouble into someone's life. In this case, the Pierces. I tried to ignore it, but my gut is always right. And then, this morning I get a call from the local police about a murder. Turns out the dead man was holding a piece of paper in his hand with your name on it."

"My name?"

Ross reached into his coat and took out a plastic evidence bag. Inside was a charred piece of paper. He stood up and held it in front of Steel. "Recognize your handwriting?"

Steel felt a cold chill come over him. It was a page from the gun club log book with his signature. "What happened?"

"Seems there was a fire at this gun club. The whole thing burned to the ground. We thought the proprietor died from the fire until I found this." He pulled out a picture. It was a close-up of the man Steel had met at the gun club. The skin on his scalp was cracked and bleeding, but behind the right ear was an unmistakable bullet hole.

"Nine mil, Steel. Says here on the page from the log sheet that you used that kind of pistol at the club. Did you turn it back in?"

Steel kept staring at the picture as his mind raced. The man was dead. He had been murdered just days after Steel had showed up and started asking questions. Coincidence? "I left the gun at the club."

Ross dropped the picture and the evidence bag on the coffee table next to him. Steel felt the anger stoke within. "I wasn't even in the area. Here," He took out his wallet and pulled out the receipt from the outlet mall. He glanced at it and then held it up for Ross to see. "There. A time stamp. I paid for these pants I'm wearing at eleven seventeen a.m. The clerk's name was Sam. He asked me if I was interested in offshore fishing, his second job. Give him a call and see if he doesn't remember me."

Ross took the cigarette out of his mouth and studied the receipt. He seemed to wilt. "Mind if I have that?"

"No." Steel pulled it away and tucked it back into his wallet. "When you get a warrant. Then you can search the house for a gun. I don't have one. The guy was probably robbed and killed, and it has nothing to do with me."

"Then why did he have this page in his hands?"

Before Steel could find an answer, the back door burst open, and April Pierce stood there, her father right behind her. She was wearing shorts and a bright, yellow blouse, her dark hair pulled back into a ponytail.

"Jonathan, are you OK? There are policemen outside." She stopped when she saw Ross standing by the coffee table.

"He's fine, Dr. Pierce."

Richard, an older stocky man with thick, white hair, came around Jonathan and noticed the picture on the table. "Who is this?"

"Someone who was murdered this morning," Steel said, his eyes riveted on April. She came over to him and reached out and touched his arm. Electricity ran across his skin.

"Murdered? Why is the FBI talking to you?" She looked over at Ross.

"Jonathan may be tied to the murder," Ross said.

Richard held the picture in front of him. "This is Cooter Boudreaux. He runs the gun club."

"Cooter?" Ross frowned. "His real name is Eugene. I don't know which is better."

Richard looked up at Ross and then over at Steel. "And why do you suspect Jonathan had anything to do with this?"

"He paid a visit to Cooter's gun club earlier this week," Ross said.

"I was trying to trigger memories." Steel felt his face grow warm. "I wanted to see if I knew how to handle a gun."

"Did you?" Ross asked.

Steel looked up at Ross. "Yes."

"Those were your targets still hanging on the zip line, weren't they? A perfect grouping in the head and heart. Seems you're quite the marksman."

"That doesn't mean I killed him." Steel was breathing fast now. "You've seen the receipt. You know I wasn't out there today."

Richard spoke up. "I know Cooter very well. I treated him last year for drug addiction. I had heard he was using again. I'm sure this murder is nothing more than a drug deal gone bad. If you want to pursue this any further in my home, you'll have to show me a warrant. You can leave now."

Ross grabbed the picture and the evidence bag and picked up the cigarette he had dropped in the struggle. "Let me get one thing straight with all of you. We have no idea what Mr. Steel has done in the past. He shows every sign of having the skills to pull off just about any crime. For all we know, he may be a thief or a serial killer or a career criminal. I'd think twice about letting him spend another night in your home, Dr. Pierce. And if I find any evidence linking him to this murder, I will be back with a warrant."

Ross put his sunglasses back on and walked out the door. He paused and glanced at Steel. "Oh, by the way, Steel, ask Dr. Pierce about your tattooed friend." He closed the door.

Steel looked over at April. "What is he talking about?"

April frowned. "I didn't want to tell you over the phone. Braxton escaped from his cell a couple of weeks ago."

Steel felt his heart race and backed away. "I have to leave. I'm putting you in danger . . . "

April grabbed both of his hands in hers. "Jonathan, look at me. Look at me!"

Steel was breathing hard. He managed to focus on her face. "Jonathan, I know in my heart you are not a criminal."

Steel looked down at her hands and fought for control. "I hope you're right."

[Chapter 9]

"THIS PLACE STINKS like a sewer!" Josh looked around at the inside of the shack. It was some kind of pumping station for a huge culvert that dumped water into Redcross Bayou.

"It hasn't affected your appetite," Summer said. She sat on the huge metal pipe that occupied the center of the room. Josh had placed the pizza box on the wheel that opened and closed the pipe.

"Don't you want something to eat?" he asked Summer.

"I'm not hungry for that. Hurry up and finish. I want to show you something." She hopped down from the pipe and opened the door. A hot, humid wind blew into the tiny shack, carrying with it the fragrance of daffodils. "I like the name Summer," she said. "You know, the summer solstice is coming. The longest day of the year."

"Where are we going?"

Summer reached out and took his hand. "I'll take you there." She led him out of the shack. A long industrial-strength chain-link fence ran across the back of the playground and up the hill into a huge field of sunflowers behind the church. She opened a gate, and they stepped out onto the bare bluff overlooking the bayou. A huge clump of vines hung down from the levee just at the foot of the shack, and the girl reached over, brushing it away like a curtain. An old stone culvert at least six feet in diameter below them emptied turbid water into the bayou twenty feet below.

"We're going in there?" Josh asked, but the girl did not answer him. She let go of his hand and stepped down a dirt path to the lip of the culvert. He followed her through the veil of vines and into the mouth of the culvert. Cool, musty air bathed his face, and in the far distance, at the edge of the light, he saw her beckon to him.

Darkness swallowed him about twenty feet into the culvert, and he almost turned back. But far ahead, he saw a glimmer of light. As he drew nearer, the light grew stronger until he stood at the foot of an old metal ladder in the wall of the culvert leading up to an open trap door. Pale, green light shimmered from above, and he hurried up the rusted rungs of the old ladder.

Josh emerged in a tunnel with walls of ancient stone and mortar. The tunnel stretched away from him toward a huge metal cylinder at the far end. The green light came from the other side of the cylinder. He walked around the hulking metal shape and felt heat radiating from the surface. On the far side was a small chamber. In the center of the room sat a raised stone platform about the size of a kitchen table. It was made of oddly shaped stones fitted together so precisely the seams were almost invisible. The light came from the opening in the cylinder, and its top funneled into the ceiling. Black, twisted gas lines hung from the old wooden rafters above him. The front of the cylinder bore a huge open door. Deep within its recesses a green fire burned.

"It used to be a furnace for the church." A voice echoed

eerily in the chamber, and Josh whirled. A woman stood across the room, and her dark, beetle eyes glittered in the pale light. "Now it's used as an incinerator to burn up all the trash."

"Who are you?"

"Vivian Darbonne." She stepped toward him, and her movements were as graceful as a stalking panther. "Without the apostrophe."

"Where's Summer?"

"Summer? That sweet little ole girl called herself Summer? How precious." She glanced toward the incinerator. "Unfortunately, she is our prisoner, Josh. When Mr. Ketrick found out you were the new kid in town, he asked Summer to bring you here." She stepped closer and looked at him closely from head to toe. "Nice piercings. Yes, you will do nicely."

"Uh, they were for my girlfriend, Ila. What do you mean, Summer is your prisoner?" Josh glanced around. There didn't seem to be any escape from the room except for the tunnel behind the incinerator.

"Let's just say she took something from Mr. Ketrick that is very important. And until we find it, she stays here in the church." Vivian moved closer to him. "You might could help her, sugar."

Josh shook his head in confusion. "This isn't making any sense. Help her how?"

Vivian was so close now, Josh smelled pepper on her breath and saw the pores in her skin. She leaned in to him and inhaled. "Oh my, the fragrance of raw youth. Sorta like a wet puppy dog with raging hormones. Delicious! Now, here's where you come in, Josh. You can help Summer by allowing me to complete this here transformation you started for your old girlfriend."

Josh's heart pounded, and he felt dizzy. "I don't know. I think I'd better go."

"Whatever for, sugar?" Vivian frowned. "Tell me, where would you go, Josh? Back to your mother, who cares nothing about you? You know she's going to leave you, just like your father did."

"That's crazy."

Vivian studied him and then suddenly laughed. "You know she'll fall in love again. She's so lonely. Just like you. You know it in your heart, Josh. And where does that leave little ole Josh? Off to some boarding school? Maybe a reform school? Anywhere just so long as you'd be out of her hair. Isn't that what you've been thinking?"

Josh's head began to pound, and he felt a pain behind his right eye. Suddenly Vivian ran a finger along the angle of his jaw. "You don't need them, sugar. We can give you all the power and strength you could ever imagine. And then you can save Summer. She's in there, waiting. Don't worry. She won't burn up. Neither will you."

Josh glanced at the door leading into the incinerator. He took a step forward, reaching out to touch the warm metal. "My mother has been distant the past few months, as if she is hiding something."

"Another man, perhaps?" Vivian said.

"No, this is wrong. I'll go to the police." Josh stepped away from the incinerator.

Vivian swore loudly and stalked across the room. Spittle spewed from her lips like venom. "Josh, the police have already been here! The FBI was here just an hour ago. They won't find Summer. So, you listen up, and you listen good. I'm giving you until midnight Friday to make up your mind." She came up to him and pressed her face close to his. She had lost her friendly accent. "But you must decide by Friday. Understand? And to make sure you don't go telling Mr. Steel about this, I'll make sure you forget what we just talked about until the time is right and you want more than anything to turn your back on them. When the time comes for you to make the choice, you will remember this place. You will remember Summer! Now, get out of here!"

Pitch-black thicker than tar fell on Josh. He screamed and stumbled back against the stone wall. "Hey! Where are you?"

Silence greeted him, and something spindly and fibrous moved across his face. He swatted at it and slid along the rough wall. Old bricks met his touch. "Summer!" he shouted.

The darkness was thick enough to cut with a knife. An insect ran up his arm, and he slung it away. More insects fell into his hair, and he jerked his head to dislodge them. He swallowed and fought down panic. Did he hear their tiny legs swishing? Were these the spiders Steel had talked about? He hurried along the stone wall, and his hand passed over a rough brick edge into an opening. He turned into it and felt a step against his feet. He reached out. It was a stone stairway leading up! The chittering, scraping sounds came nearer.

Josh scrabbled up the stone stairway, and it turned away from him in a corkscrew. He fell once and scraped his knee on the rough edges. More insects on his neck! He brushed them away and bolted upward. Suddenly his head banged against a metal surface. He swore and reached up to touch a rusty metal panel. He pushed against it, and it swung upward and outward. He climbed up out of the stone stairway and slammed the trapdoor on the things that were coming up the stairway beneath him. He heard them bang and pop against the underside of the metal door like an obscene rain.

Josh found himself beneath the wooden altar table in the church sanctuary. Welcome light streamed through the stained-glass windows, and he climbed out from under the table and stood up.

Something grabbed him from behind and pulled him back onto the altar table. He looked up at the silhouette of a figure standing over him. Did she have blonde hair?

"Summer?" he asked.

"Not even close," the thing rasped and jumped up onto the table with him. Her legs grew large and rubbery, shooting in all directions like twisted tendrils of root that wrapped themselves around his legs, his arms, binding him to the table. Josh struggled against them as the thing's arms transformed into vines and her hair sprouted into a million writhing rootlets. He opened his mouth to scream, and the face exploded into a mass of squirming twigs closing off his last breaths.

"Now, you just go and forget that little ole conversation, you hear?" The voice rasped in his ear, and he was out.

"Oh, no!" Liz stood up from the table, and her hands went to her mouth.

"What is it?" Steel asked.

Liz pointed toward the open window of the dining room. "The lights. In the church."

Steel glanced at the window, and he heard Claire gasp behind him. Outside the sun had set, and the sky was an unsettled dark blue on the cusp of twilight and night. The stained-glass windows of the church flickered and glowed with arcane light. "I told you it wasn't over. Get your things."

"What about Josh?" Claire asked.

Steel turned around and noticed his cell phone. "He left my phone here. Does he have one?"

"I made him leave it at home. Is he in danger?"

Steel studied the concern in her face. "I'm sure he is with his friend eating pizza. He'll be safer with her. Get your instrument pack."

Steel led them across the yard to the front of the parsonage. He banged on the door, and it swung open. Parker stood in the doorway, and in the background he saw Emily holding a book. She shut it quickly and pushed it aside.

"Things have heated up again in the church. We're going in."

Parker gasped and leaned around Steel to look at the church. "No! That can't be! I thought it was over."

"I'm sorry. The enemy must not have wanted any outside attention, so things went back to normal with the news crew and Ross. Now it's returned to the way it was. We need to go in tonight and take some measurements and make a record of the writing."

Parker nodded and turned back to Emily. "Emily, I have to go back into the church. It isn't over."

Emily tensed, and her face was hidden in shadows. "No, Thomas, it isn't over. Not yet."

Steel cast one last lingering look at her and the book lying on the couch. Parker slid his feet into loafers, and Steel pulled him out into the dark night.

[Chapter 10]

A COARSE WIND TUMBLED down Main Street, driving trash and dirt up the hill to blast against the team as they mounted the stairs to the church. The debris coalesced into a dozen tiny dust devils that died by hurling themselves against the old stairway. Steel paused at the top of the stairs and wiped grit from his face. He turned to survey the members of his team.

"We're going in for one reason: reconnaissance. We're not here to fight any battles. Be aware that inanimate objects may have the appearance of life. Don't touch anything. Don't move quickly. Don't react to any voices. Remember, what you see and hear is an illusion. Are we ready?"

Liz nodded as she shouldered her digital imaging equipment and gripped her lion stick. Claire made one last check of her sensor probe and the LCD readout panel attached to her backpack. Parker swallowed, his eyes fixed on the door. Steel turned and opened the doors.

A cold gust of wind hurtled out around them and carried a fine mist of condensed water vapor. The sound of a thousand howling voices filled the night. Claire studied her readout, holding the handheld LCD up to her eyes. "Temperature is thirty-five degrees Fahrenheit."

Steel turned on his flashlight and stepped over the threshold. The wind lessened inside the foyer, and things moved in the shadows. Snakes had replaced the spiders. Dozens of writhing, hissing poisonous snakes squirmed from a tunnel of rootlike fibers encircling the foyer. The snakes hissed and struck at Steel, but they seemed fixed by their tails, unable to reach far enough to do any harm.

"What happened to the spiders?" Parker avoided the snapping snakes.

"I guess they weren't frightening enough," Steel said.

"Amazing!" Claire waved her sensor probe toward the snakes. A cottonmouth struck the probe with a metallic click. Claire pulled back. "How can snakes survive in an atmosphere where the temperature is almost freezing?"

Liz held up her video camera to get a picture of the snakes. "Most of these species are indigenous to this area. I recognize copperheads, rattlesnakes, and water moccasins. But a few of these species are foreign to this area. They may come from the rain forests." She poked the lion stick at the snakes, and their fangs clicked on the hard wood.

Steel turned to the inner doors leading into the sanctuary. "Let's move on." He pushed open the doors, and a gust of hot, humid air poured from the chamber. He stepped inside and played his flashlight across the interior. "Well, this may explain your snakes."

Claire pushed past him and stopped in the aisle with her sensor probe weaving back and forth. "Ninety-six degrees Fahrenheit and ninety-eight percent humidity. Hotter than outside."

Steel walked down the aisle and stepped over huge vines.

The interior of the sanctuary was completely covered with more vines and leaves than before. Pews were intertwined with huge leaves and flowers. The walls were covered, and the vines extended onto the ceiling and covered the outer third of its perimeter. His gaze was drawn to the ceiling, and he saw the spiral eye surrounded by other graphics. The demon of the spiral eye was here.

"Oh, my." Liz stood in the center of the sanctuary with her eyes turned upward. She was studying the band of drawings that spiraled outward from the center of the ceiling toward the periphery and ended just at the edges of the vines. "Look at this. Glyphs and drawings. Your pictures did not do this justice." She directed her video camera at the ceiling. After several passes to document it, she exchanged the video camera for a digital camera.

Claire paused before the altar table and glanced at a huge pile of vines and leaves. Then she noticed the glow from the baptistery. She hurried up the stairs to the rear of the choir loft. Stepping up onto a chair, she glanced over the edge of the baptistery. Steel appeared at her side.

"It's beautiful, isn't it?" Claire breathed deeply. The air smelled of ozone and sulfur.

"What is it?"

Claire reached out with the probe and waved it over the energy cloud. "I detect neutrinos, weak gamma rays, heat, light in all the visible spectrums. And at the center of the cloud is a nidus that appears to be a singularity. But—that's impossible!"

"A singularity?"

"A microscopic black hole. If we were exposed to it, we would be dead. But there appears to be some type of containment field. Which is also physically impossible." She had donned her red reading glasses, and the green lights of her instrument display played across her face. Claire looked up at Steel, and her eyes were bright with excitement. "Jonathan, this is an extra-dimensional phenomenon. If I were to breech an energy field containing a singularity, it could be disastrous."

"How disastrous?"

"Global destruction." Claire exhaled her breath.

"There's something alive down here," Parker screamed.

Steel turned his attention away from the baptistery. Parker stood next to the altar table, and his hands were covered with blood. Blood gushed from beneath the tangle of vines and poured onto the floor. The vines moved, emitting a low moan. Steel jumped down from the choir loft and ran to the table. He brushed aside the leaves. A hand protruded from the vines. He pulled more vines away, scattering blood-soaked leaves in all directions.

"Help me." He glanced over his shoulder at Parker. But Parker backed away and fell over a root. Fumbling to his feet, he stumbled down the aisle toward the door, through the corridor of snakes, and out into the night air.

Claire appeared at Steel's side, and together they began tearing away the vines. Liz dropped her camera on the front pew and joined in, sloshing through the blood, pulling aside vines and roots covered with the sticky goo. A face appeared in the vines, a gold bead gleaming from the lower lip.

"Josh!" Claire screamed, and she tore frantically at the vines. Josh's eyes opened, and he struggled to sit up. Steel bodily lifted him from the mass of fibers and stepped back.

"Dude, what's up?"

Claire grabbed him and pulled him to her in a hug. He protested, freeing himself from her embrace. "What am I doing here?" He looked around at the interior. "This is the church, isn't it? Or did Reverend Parker turn this into a rain forest?"

Steel jerked Josh away from Claire to face him. "I told you not to come in here! I warned you it was dangerous."

Josh glared at him. Above his indifferent gaze his hair was filled with dried leaves and dust. "Look, all I did was meet my friend for pizza. And then..." A puzzled look came over his face. "I don't remember how I got here."

Claire brushed the dead leaves from his clothes. "All that matters is that you're all right. When I saw that blood gushing from under the vines, I thought you were dead."

"What blood?" Josh glanced around him. The blood had disappeared. There was no trace of it. Steel looked around in amazement. Liz dusted her hands off and picked up her lion stick.

"I don't like this place. Let's get the rest of our measurements and pictures and get out of here." Liz retrieved her digital camera and backpack and walked toward the baptistery.

"I agree. If the two of you have seen enough, I suggest we retreat and evaluate what we have," Steel said. "We're pressing our luck as it is."

Liz stepped up into the choir loft with her camera aimed at the wall over the baptistery. "Just let me get one more..."

The air was suddenly filled with an insistent clacking coming up out of the baptistery. Two huge claws appeared first, followed by the dark, ugly eyes of a monstrous scorpion. The thing was as large as a truck, and it scurried over the front edge of the baptistery. Liz gasped in shock as the huge scorpion scuttled over the chairs in the choir loft, hurling them aside with its huge pedipalpi. It headed straight for her, and from its rear, the long, glistening stinger arched upward and plunged down toward her.

Liz fell back and swung her lion stick at the descending stinger. The glistening tip clattered against the stick. Liz rolled away as the stinger thudded into the wooden pew beside her. Splintered wood showered her. Steel pushed Claire and Josh down the aisle and ran to help Liz. Liz stumbled to her feet and swung her lion stick and caught the scorpion between its huge, beaded eyes. The thing pulled back in pain and rubbed its huge pedipalpi over its eyes. The stinger came at her again, and Steel grabbed the lion stick. He swung it with all his might and knocked the scorpion's tail away. He shoved Liz down the aisle.

"Get out of here, now!"

Josh paused halfway down the aisle. "Dude! That is awesome!"

Steel grabbed Josh and pulled him down the aisle as the stinger imbedded itself in the carpet beside them. They ran down the aisle as the scorpion settled over the podium. Its tail retracted and came to rest above its swaying front appendages. Steel slammed the inner doors behind him and, ignoring the writhing snakes in the foyer, hurried out onto the balcony. He shut the sanctuary doors on the evil that lay within and tried to recover his breath.

"Just an illusion, huh?" Liz remarked, straightening her hair and wiping sweat from her face. "Honey, next time we go up against Satan, remind me of that little tidbit of wisdom." She lifted her lion stick and studied the long gash in the wood. "No snake or insect has ever been able to scratch this wood. I think I need to go lie down." She headed off down the steps.

[Chapter 11]

PARKER FELL THROUGH his open doorway and slammed the front door behind him. He leaned against the solid wood and fought for control of his erratic breathing. Twice now he had run away from the horrors within the sanctuary. He had tried to stay. But the blood gushing from underneath the pile of vines had been too much. He shoved his hand against his mouth and bit down to keep from screaming. The horrors he had seen replayed themselves in his mind. Gerry tumbling to his death. Blood gushing from the altar table. How much more could he take?

As Parker made his way to the kitchen, he watched a spider scramble across the floor and he slid to a stop. He slammed his foot down on the thing and felt it squish beneath his shoe. He stepped back, tripped over something on the floor, and fell against the edge of his couch.

As he lay in the darkness, pain exploding through his shoulder, tears sprang to his eyes. He sobbed quietly until the moisture ran back into his ears. He was a fallen man, a broken man, a total failure. How could God ever use such a coward?

Another spider jumped up onto his hand, and he hurled it away, rolling away from his painful shoulder onto his right side. He bumped into Emily. She lay next to him on the floor with her legs outstretched into the walkway and her white shirt dotted with spiders.

Parker jerked up and started brushing the spiders away. "Emily!" He screamed.

He knocked a huge spider off of her face, and her eyes fluttered and she licked dry lips. "I'm so tired, Thomas. I tried to get some water, and I fainted. I think it's time."

Parker shook off the feeling of dread and jumped to his feet. He hurried into the bedroom and grabbed Emily's hospital bag. He hurried back to the front door and threw it open onto the night. Steel and the team were walking back toward the missionary house.

"Jonathan! Help! Emily has passed out, and we're going to the hospital." Steel glanced at him and began running down the hill. Parker hurried toward the kitchen and deftly stepped over Emily's legs. More spiders crunched under his feet.

Parker fumbled with the key holder hanging by the back door and finally found the car keys. Bursting through the back door, he slid into his car, tossed the bag into the back seat, and backed it out of the garage. He gunned the engine to bring it down the driveway and into the turnaround by the front porch. Steel arrived, breathless and sweaty. He leaned in through Parker's open driver side window.

"What's wrong?"

"Emily passed out. And she may be in labor. We've got to get to the hospital."

Steel peered over the front seat toward the back. "Where is she?"

Parker looked behind him. "Oh no! I left her on the floor."

Steel pushed against the door as Parker tried to open it. "I'll get her. Just wait here." Steel disappeared through the front door of the house and emerged with Emily in his arms. Parker got out and opened the back door, and Steel laid her on the back seat. Steel pushed him toward the passenger side.

"I'm driving. You're navigating."

Parker didn't argue as Steel slammed the car in gear and left hot rubber on the driveway. Parker craned his neck over the back of the seat and mumbled directions for Steel to get to the hospital as he tried to check on Emily. Passing streetlights flashed on her pale face, and she writhed on the seat. No spiders. Thank God!

"Dr. Brown, why did you do this?" She mumbled.

"I have my cell phone if you want to call Dr. Brown," Steel said.

"I don't know a Dr. Brown. Emily's doctor is Dr. Miller."

Steel glanced at him. "Then who is Dr. Brown?"

Parker looked once more at his wife's troubled features. "I don't know."

The emergency room at Women's Center in Shreveport bulged at the seams. Patients and their families milled in the waiting room like fire ants. Steel lifted Emily into a wheelchair, and Parker shoved his way through the chaos toward the check-in desk. The triage nurse took one look at Emily's pregnant form and motioned to the elevator.

"Take her on up to the labor and delivery unit on three."

A nurse was waiting when the elevators opened on the third floor, and she tried to take Emily from Parker. "You can wait over there in the waiting room; I'll let you know something once we get her evaluated."

Parker tightened his grip on the handles of the wheelchair.

"I left her once tonight. I'm not leaving her again. And she was covered with spiders."

"Spiders? You might want to call an exterminator. We'll check her for bites." The nurse smiled and gently pried his hands from the handles. "I'll come get you in about ten minutes and you can stay with her. Right now, it looks like she needs immediate attention." The nurse turned her eyes on Steel. "Why don't you take your friend to the waiting room?"

Steel nodded and took Parker's arm, leading him into the waiting room. Steel sunk into a chair, but Parker couldn't keep still. He paced the waiting room as he saw Emily's body sprawled on the living room floor.

"Why did you run out on us at the church?" Steel asked.

Parker stopped in mid pace and whirled. "How dare you? My wife is in serious condition in there. I found her on the floor. She was almost unconscious. She fainted, and I wasn't there for her, Jonathan. No, I was up at the church chasing snakes. What would have happened if I hadn't run away?"

Steel stood up and crossed to him and placed a hand on his sore shoulder. "I'm sorry. Sometimes I'm a little too direct."

"Yeah, tact isn't one of your gifts." Parker shrugged off Steel's hand and winced at the spike of pain from where he'd struck the floor.

Steel looked away and cleared his throat. "Look, I'm not your enemy. I'm here to help you. Does this have anything to do with the woman Ketrick mentioned?"

"What?" Parker stiffened and looked off into the distance. "I already told you. Someone in the church was asking me for money from the benevolence fund. That's money only for extreme emergencies, and then she started a vicious rumor about me."

"Blackmail?"

"Sort of. But as God is my witness, there's nothing going on there."

"So, you and Emily aren't having any marital problems?" Steel asked.

"How can you ask me that at a time like this?"

"The sooner you tell me the truth, the sooner everything will get back to normal," Steel said.

"Get back to normal? What is normal, huh?"

Parker leaned against the wall and pounded his forehead into the hard surface. He felt a hand on his shoulder. The grip was firm and pulled him roughly around. Through tears, he looked into those intense eyes of Jonathan Steel.

"If you come clean with me, if you tell me what is going on in that church, I can help you. I made a promise and I always keep my promises, but you have to help me. If you do, Thomas, I will see that you will preach this Sunday to your congregation. I promise you we will get everything back to normal. Trust me," Steel said.

The door opened to the waiting room, and a nurse dressed in scrubs looked in. "Mr. Parker, your wife is not in labor. She's very dehydrated and malnourished. No spider bites. I've called Dr. Miller, and we're going to give her some fluids overnight. You can stay in the room with her."

"What about the baby?" Parker asked.

"The baby is fine. Good heartbeat. No problems. If your wife is feeling better in the morning, she can go home." She paused. "She kept asking for Dr. Brown. We don't have a Dr. Brown on our staff. Has she seen anyone else besides Dr. Miller?"

"No. We don't know a Dr. Brown."

The nurse paused to think and reached into her pocket. "We found this in her bag. I was going to call Dr. Brown, but I'll let you inform him."

She handed Parker a folded index card. Along the top was the hastily scrawled name, Dr. Daniel Brown. "I've never heard of him."

The nurse smiled and crossed her arms. "Maybe he's the doctor of one of your wife's friends. We ladies are always trading notes. You can come see your wife anytime you want." The nurse turned and walked away. Parker looked longingly after her and turned back to Steel.

Steel took the card from his hand. "Go be with your wife, Thomas. She needs you. I'll find Dr. Brown and let him know what's going on."

"Are you sure?"

"Yes. I'm here to help. Now go."

Parker released his fears and worries into the hands of Jonathan Steel. He nodded and walked down the cold, sterile hallway to be with his wife.

[Chapter 12]

Claire looked up from her laptop as the door to the missionary house opened. Steel stepped in with a troubled look on his face.

"What's going on with Emily?" she asked.

Steel glanced at her and blinked. "Emily? Oh, she's fine. Just dehydrated. Thomas is staying at the hospital with her tonight." Steel shook his head. "Things are getting out of control. I've never seen anything like we saw tonight in the church."

Liz appeared from the kitchen with a cup of hot tea in her hand. "I'm still trembling. Honey, there isn't a scorpion on the face of this planet that could be that large."

"How's Josh?" Steel said as he paced around the living room.

"He's fine. Too fine, if you ask me. I would be in a coma if I'd been through what he went through," Claire said.

"Every teenager is invincible," Steel said. "Where is he?"

"Taking a shower. Two in one day. You're good," Claire said.

"I want to talk to him when he gets out of the shower and see if he remembers how he ended up in the church."

"OK," Claire said. "You were right about us being in danger. I should have listened more closely to you."

"Yes, you should have. Look, we've been through a lot

tonight." Steel looked away. "We need some rest. Why don't we go over your readings in the morning?"

Claire sighed. She was hoping he would talk about it tonight while it was still fresh on her mind. But he was obviously focused on something else. "Are you telling us everything?"

Steel paused in his pacing. "I'm not sure. I'm going to my RV and try to get some rest. When Josh gets done, send him over." Without another word he left.

Claire looked up at Liz and drew a deep breath. "Does he honestly think any of us are going to be able to sleep tonight?"

Liz raised an eyebrow. "Only if I could keep one eye open."

Steel studied the index card as he stepped into his RV. Between what had happened to Josh and Emily, matters were getting increasingly complex and out of hand. He switched on his computer and accessed the Internet. In moments he had an office address for Dr. Daniel Brown matching a phone number on the card. Steel found an online map website and learned that the office was on the edge of town.

He studied the name on the card and unfolded it. On the inside, one word was scrawled. *Mif??pri??tone.* Steel squinted in thought. He'd never heard of the word. And the question marks were obvious attempts to figure out some missing letters. He heard a sound and turned to see Josh step inside.

"Hey, bro." His hair was a mess. The rat's nest look seemed to be the latest fashion trend. He wore a pair of gym shorts and a psychedelic T-shirt with a huge smiley face poking its tongue out in a raspberry. At least he didn't stink. His eyes strayed around the room and came back to rest on Steel. "You told me to come talk to you before I went to bed."

Steel rubbed his tired eyes. "Oh, yeah. Sit down."

Josh sat on the couch and fingered his lip bead. His eyes darted around the interior of the RV.

"You can't remember what happened to you this afternoon?"

Josh shook his head and squirmed on the sofa. "I went to meet my friend at the playground. I offered her pizza and then…" Josh's forehead furrowed in thought. "And the next thing I knew, I woke up in the church underneath all those vines."

"I asked you not to go in the church without us."

"Dude, who made you my boss?" Josh stared at him, and his face grew red. "You're not my father."

Steel drew a deep breath and blew it out. "Josh, you and your mother may be in danger."

"Mom told me the scorpion was just an illusion. She said you told everyone nothing could hurt you in there. So, what's the big deal?"

"I was wrong. Look, we don't know why the enemy is in this church, and anything could happen in that sanctuary."

"What is this 'enemy' business?" Josh crossed his arms and looked at the computer screens. "Bro, you make it sound like we're in some kind of video game."

"I refuse to even call Satan by his name. He is the enemy. He is the father of lies. He will do anything to destroy us." Steel waited until Josh's gaze came back to meet his. "In fact, Satan is the only enemy we really have to worry about. He is the father of all evil. And he will harm you without remorse or guilt or second thought. I know. I've come up against his demons in the past. They play for keeps." Steel shuddered at the thought, recalling the image of the spiral tattoo around a man's eye. "Josh, I asked your mother to come and help me out. She agreed to be a part of the team. Since I put the team together, that makes me the leader. If you want to remain safe, you must do what I tell you. In other words, I am the boss."

"Just don't get any ideas about taking my father's place."

Steel leaned back in his chair, surprised at the suggestion. And then he realized he had forgotten to ask Claire more about the reception. Could there be a connection between Josh's father and his past? "Tell me about your father."

"What's there to tell, bro? He was never at home. Always traveling to promote his work with his precious genetic research."

Steel nodded. He had only one memory of his father, and it dealt with the man trying to shoot him. "I understand. I don't think my father was very good at his job, either."

"Dude, I'll make you a deal. You tell me about your father, and I'll tell you about mine."

"What is this, true confession time?" Steel frowned.

"We're a team, right? Didn't you just say that? I mean, bro, how long has it been since you've worked with somebody? Or are you so good at what you do you don't need nobody?" Josh said. "I mean, you are a jerk, and it'd be nice to know why."

"And you're not exactly Winnie the Pooh," Steel said.

Josh raised an eyebrow and touched the lip bead. "Did you just call me Winnie the Pooh?"

"Sorry."

"Dude, do we have a deal, or do I leave?"

"Why are you pushing me on this?" Steel asked.

Josh blinked as if trying to recall something. "I woke up under those vines and was almost snagged by a giant scorpion. This is your show, bro. Not mine. I want to know why this is happening, and it has something to do with you, doesn't it?"

Steel nodded. "Fine. I'll tell you."

Thunder drove him up out of unconsciousness. The man's eyes flew open, and his body jerked up from the sand. He squinted into the gloom around him as rain streamed down from his hair into his eyes. He stumbled to his feet and studied the sand around him. Houses and condominiums stretched down the empty beach. The ocean surf pounded him from behind, and he tumbled forward onto the beach. He struggled to his feet again and glanced down at himself. He was naked, and his skin was covered with coarse white sand. Blood oozed from a dozen cuts on his abdomen and legs. He lifted his hands to study them. His left index and middle finger were bent at an odd angle, and as the numbness faded, he felt the pain of the broken bones. Blood dripped into his eyes and blinded him with a crimson wave. He felt a deep cut about three inches long just above the hairline. He tasted blood and saltwater. Dizziness swept over him, and he wobbled forward away from the surf.

Just ahead through the rain, a stairway stretched up to the outdoor deck of a beach house. He clawed his way up the stairs, and his blood ran down the steps with the rain. He lurched across the open deck to a back porch. His pressed his face against the metal mesh and managed to pull open the door and fall inward out of the rain. A woman sat at a patio table eating tacos. He reached out his good hand toward her and managed to say, "Help me." He was unconscious before his head hit the floor.

Red and blue lights swirled above him, and the raindrops seemed to slow, almost stop in the reflection. He saw black raincoats with yellow writing and felt the cold plastic of an oxygen mask. More pain as the needles came. He heard the roar of the ambulance, the staccato sound of the gurney ticking down the hospital aisle. Pulsing hard and strong, the pain blossomed in his chest. He found himself gasping for air now as the pulsing weakened and he receded down the long hallway of darkness.

The man blinked as he awoke to a sudden orchestra of pain. He saw a hospital room drenched in white light. Sitting halfway up in the bed, he tried to move, but he found his wrists and ankles tied with cloth restraints.

"You're awake, Mr. Steel." He heard a gentle voice from the corner of the room. He saw someone outlined by pearly light. She came toward him. Her hair was dark and shoulder length, and her face was that of an angel. "Just calm down. You're having another nightmare."

"Am I dead?" he whispered.

"Far from it. Your name is Mr. Steel, isn't it?" Her voice was filled with hope.

Steel searched his mind again. It was empty. Void. No memories. "I don't know."

"I was afraid of that." The woman cradled her chin in her hand. "You've been in and out of consciousness, and it seems you have amnesia."

Steel blinked and felt the pain of the stitches in his scalp. "How do you know my name is Steel?"

She reached for something on a nearby table and showed it to him. It was a small, laminated frequent diner's card from a sandwich shop. Scrawled in the name slot was J. Steel. Steel studied the card but did not recognize it. "You found this on me?"

"We didn't exactly find it on you. There was nothing on you."

"So, you're telling me I have eight sandwiches to go," Steel said.

She laughed. "Humor. That's a start. You had a backpack with empty soft drink bottles inside to keep you afloat. We found it on Orange Beach. This card was the only other thing in the backpack. So, we assumed you're Mr. J. Steel."

J. Steel. The name meant nothing to him. "Uh, Miss . . ." Steel sat up painfully, and the restraints pulled on his arms.

"Pierce. Doctor April Pierce." She held out a hand in greeting and then pulled it back in puzzlement. "I'm sorry for the restraints. You're very strong. You broke one of the orderly's arms. Here, let me cut you loose."

Dr. Pierce pulled a pair of angled scissors from the pocket of her white coat and snipped the restraints from his feet and hands. "You were a mess when they found you. Two broken ribs. Two broken fingers. A subcapsular hematoma on your spleen, which didn't require surgery. Numerous abrasions and cuts. You've been here for ten days, bouncing from lucidity to insanity a dozen times." She paused as she snipped the last restraint. "I don't think you're dangerous anymore."

"I hope I'm not dangerous, but then we don't know, do we?" he said. "What kind of doctor are you?"

"Surgery resident." She pushed the dark hair back out of her face. "But not for long. I'm switching to psychiatry next week. After two years of surgery residency and no sleep, I've decided on another field of medicine." Dr. Pierce stopped and left her hand on his arm. "I should've listened to my father. He's a psychiatrist. Anyway, I've taken a special interest in you. The other residents don't mind me backing out on some of the surgical cases. They need all the practice they can get. So they let me work with you since you're now more of a psych case."

Steel kept silent as he searched his thoughts. "You say I was found on a beach?"

Dr. Pierce nodded. "Yes, during a really bad storm."

Steel recalled rain falling and darkness and sand in his cuts. Then there were the medics and the ambulance. Yes, he recalled some of that. He closed his eyes and tried to sort through the chaotic images of hospital and personnel. He found some blurred images of Dr. Pierce along with other health personnel standing by his bed. His hand lashing out caught an orderly in the stomach, and the man lurched across the room and fell over a chair. He remembered that clearly along with something else. Rage. Anger. Fury so white hot it had boiled to the surface when the man had tried to restrain him. He recalled another image of a man in a shirt, tie, and a long black coat with his eyes hidden behind sunglasses.

"Who's the guy in the suit?" He looked at Pierce.

"Oh, him?" Dr. Pierce straightened with surprise. "He's an FBI agent. He was here to try and identify you. Special Agent Franklin Ross."

"Has he found anything?"

"I'm afraid not, Jonathan . . . "

"Jonathan?"

"We picked a first name for you. I suggested Jonathan. I wanted you to feel unique. I hope you like it. He was a friend to David in the Bible. You remember King David? The guy who wrote the Psalms? One of my favorite books in the Bible."

"I'm glad your favorite wasn't Deuteronomy," Steel said. He stopped and drew in a breath. "Where did that come from?"

"See, you're remembering something already." Dr. Pierce pulled up a chair and sat in front of him, and the fragrance of cotton blossoms wafted over him. "You're already beginning to recall some basic, ingrained information. Much of your memory is encoded and unconscious. For instance, your memory of books, historical facts, etc. Let's try stimulating your memory."

Dr. Pierce opened the top of his tray table and revealed a mirror. Steel leaned forward and looked at himself. His hair was reddish blond, short, and shaved away at the hairline above his right eye. A row of black stitches ran across the top of his forehead. But the most startling feature about his face was his turquoise eyes. He stared into the depths of those arresting eyes and felt nothing.

"Sorry, I've never seen this man before."

"Let's try something else." Dr. Pierce smiled and pushed the table away. "What's your favorite fruit?"

Steel sighed. "I don't know."

"Your favorite color?"

"Nothing." Steel shook his head.

"Flower?" Dr. Pierce smiled.

"Cotton blossom?" He said. Dr. Pierce raised an eyebrow and touched the bare flesh at the base of her neck. She cleared her throat.

"That would be the fragrance of my hand lotion. Probably not a memory. Movie?"

"Jaws," Steel said. He frowned. "It's a about a shark, that's all I remember."

"Good!" Dr. Pierce slid her chair closer to the bed. "Let me ask you something else. We did a CAT scan looking for brain trauma. We couldn't find anything acute. But there was this tiny metallic object close to the base of your brain. Have you ever had any kind of brain surgery?"

Steel felt a wave of nausea sweep over him, and his mind clouded. Surgery? Metallic object in his brain? Just at the fringes of his memory, a few flickers of light gathered, red and glaring. A spiral swirled around something. An eye? Why would an . . . He couldn't remember what he was thinking . . . Where was it? Sweat poured down his face, and he felt on the verge of vomiting. "My head is starting to kill me. And I don't feel very well."

"Then let's not push for any more information today. You've made a good start, and I don't want you to get frustrated." Dr. Pierce stood up and pressed a button on the IV stand. "How about some pain medicine?"

Something warm coursed through his veins, and the flaring, red light vanished in a wave of comfort and peace. He slumped back into the bed and smiled. "I feel like I'm on a long vacation." His tongue felt thick. "As hard as it may be, I need to be patient, don't I?"

"Yes, Jonathan Steel."

Steel smiled. He liked the name. And he liked Dr. Pierce. In fact, she was the most beautiful woman he'd ever seen. Which, considering his amnesia, wasn't saying much. The warm wave passed over him again and washed away the pain in his head. It carried him downward to a dark bed of slumber where memories and worries were no more.

Jonathan Steel limped into the meeting room and headed for the empty chair opposite the door so he could keep an eye on anyone coming in. It had been one week since he woke up. His

strength was quickly returning, and he had been transferred to the psychiatric ward. Five other patients drifted in. Mr. Sanora, an elderly man suffering from obsessive-compulsive disorder, was wearing spotless pajamas with sharp creases. Chuck came in next, chewing on his nails, his eyes focused on the floor. He was a teenager with a serious neurosis. Mr. McCoy, the manic-depressive, came next. He carried a box of doughnuts in his right hand and a bag of cookies in the other. Suicidal Mr. Watson peeked around the corner and hurried to one of the free chairs. And last came Rocky Braxton. Braxton was short and extremely thin with a shock of black hair that stood on end and a tattoo around his right eye, a dark spiral that wound its way from just under his lower eyelid out toward his cheek, back up under his eyebrow, down the line of his nose and ended just above his eyebrow. Every time Steel saw it, something itched in the back of his mind. But when he tried to pin it down, the thought skittered away like an insect. Braxton walked hesitantly into the room and hugged himself. He leaned down and whispered to Mr. Watson.

"Please, kind sir, may I have my chair? Please?"

Watson rolled his eyes and then slid out of the chair across the circle to the only other empty one. Braxton stepped up into the chair and settled down on crossed legs. He stared at Steel.

"I don't like my feet to get dirty. Do you?" he asked politely.

Steel averted his eyes and felt something burn in the pit of his stomach. His heart raced, and he touched his cheek. It was hot.

"Good morning, group. I hope you've had a good day so far." Dr. April Pierce entered the room.

Braxton raised his hand. "I'm doing very well after my morning constitutional. Happiness is a clean colon." Braxton glanced around at the other group members and nodded. "Don't you all agree?"

"Thank you, Rocky." April pulled up a chair to the head of the group. "Before we begin, I want to introduce you to my father, Dr. Richard Pierce."

Dr. Pierce stepped into the room. He was tall and stocky with thick gray hair. He smiled. "Good morning. I will be the attending physician for your psychiatry resident, Dr. April Pierce."

Braxton waved. "Good to meet you, Papa."

Richard's face showed no reaction. "I am in private practice, but I oversee three group sessions a week. Now, I understand you've met once this week already with Dr. Pierce, correct?"

Mr. Sanora raised his hand. "Dr. Pierce, the elder, I'd like to inform you we met day before yesterday from ten oh four a.m. to eleven eleven a.m. I sat in this spot, although the chairs have been moved around."

Dr. Pierce opened a black notepad and smiled. "That is good, Mr. Sanora?"

"Amil Sanora. I've been retired from the postal service for two years."

"I'm still working for the post office." Mr. McCoy bit into one of his doughnuts. "I am also an operative for the NSA and the CIA, and I am aware that your doctor-patient confidentiality prevents you from discussing that fact with anyone outside this room. Otherwise, to reveal my secret identity might cost you your life."

Braxton hugged his legs to his chest and laughed. "No, no, no!" He wiggled his hand. "I believe that would be a Hippo violation."

"It's HIPPA," Chuck said. "Not hippo."

Braxton grew very still and slowly turned his face toward the teenager. "You don't like me, do you?"

Dr. Pierce cleared his throat. "Mr. Braxton, correct? Let's move on, shall we? Now, Dr. Pierce has asked me to sit in on today's group session. I was hoping that today we could discuss some of your childhood experiences." He looked up at Braxton, and his gaze traveled around the room to Steel.

"Mr. Steel, how about you? Would you care to share any childhood memories?"

"I'm sorry, Dr. Pierce," Steel's eyes strayed to April. "I can't remember any of my childhood."

"Jonathan, you didn't even try," April said.

"I've been trying for over a week."

"Maybe the spymaster over here can look into it for you," Braxton said as he pointed to Mr. McCoy.

"Mr. Braxton," Richard said. "Let Mr. Steel talk."

Braxton glanced down at his fingers intertwined across his folded legs. "What if he doesn't want to remember?"

"I'd like to make a suggestion," April said. "Jonathan, a week ago you recalled the name of a book in the Bible. Perhaps you have a religious background. Do you believe in God?"

Steel opened his mouth to speak and paused as his mind raced. Did he believe in God? He saw motes of dust swirling in a ray of sunshine. He felt the thump of his heart and the slow rhythm of his breathing, of his life. He settled into his chair. And then he glanced at Braxton and it faded, replaced with a burning anxiety, an unsettled feeling. Irritation, that was the best way to describe it. "I think I do, Dr. Pierce."

"Why are you looking at me?" Braxton said quietly. "Am I God?"

Steel blinked and felt his face heat up with anger. "If you are God, then I don't believe in you."

Braxton hugged his skinny legs against his chest. "I never said I was. I asked you if you thought I was God. This is about what you think, Mr. Steel, not feel. But if you want me to be your God, then just look right here into my eye." His voice was so quiet and seductive, and he pointed with a thin finger at the spiral around his right eye. It seemed to move and pulse, and Steel fell . . .

Steel opened his eyes, and he knelt in a pool of blood from his swollen, bloody nose. He had been in some kind of fight. He wore tattered jeans and a tank top. He was sixteen years old. His head pounded, and his body racked with spasms of pain. He glanced up, and a man stood in front of him. He was short and balding. But his eyes held a love as deep as the sea.

"Hey, man, we've come to get you. You need to come on home." Steel looked at the man. His name was Kevin. "You know we all love you. It's time to walk away from all of this. Would you like for me to help you?"

Down the alley in which he stood a shadowy figure glanced over his shoulder as he disappeared around a corner. He felt a pang of fear and hatred and turned his gaze back to Kevin. He held hope in his hands. "I don't want to go on like this. Will you help me?"

"I promise," Kevin said.

Steel felt the memory slip away, and he found himself in the group session again. He glanced around at the expectant faces. April had gotten up and was standing in front of him. "Jonathan, did you remember something?"

"I was a teenager in an alley. Kevin prayed with me. Whoever he is," Steel said. "I was transformed into something

new. Something forgiven. But I can't remember what I was like before that."

Dr. Richard Pierce nodded. "Without the framework of your past, you will have difficulty determining who you became. But you've taken a big first step, Jonathan. You've remembered a life-changing occurrence that is so profound even amnesia can't erase it."

Steel smiled. "April, I remembered!"

Braxton's tattooed face rose like a dark sunrise over April's shoulder. "Are you starting to remember, Johnny boy?" he said in a trembling voice as he gently pushed April aside. "I helped you, didn't I? I gave you back those memories, don't you see? That means I am God, man of steel." A lopsided smile creased his thin face, and the spiral tattoo seemed to move with a life of its own. Braxton climbed up into Steel's lap, folding his legs like an insect under him, and draped his hands over Steel's shoulders with his face hovering just inches from Steel's eyes.

"What are you doing?" Steel asked.

"Mr. Braxton, return to your seat," April said.

Braxton smiled and touched the tip of his tongue to his lip. His voice lowered to a whisper. "We tried to take your memories. All of them, don't you know, Johnny boy? But I guess we couldn't take the one memory that He controls. That means you are still one of them, don't you see? We thought when you gave up the past you would be with us. But you're not, are you?"

Steel glanced over Braxton's shoulder, and April tugged at Braxton's shoulder. "Please return to your seat, or I will call the orderlies."

Braxton brushed her hand away. His tattooed eye eclipsed everything, huge, bloodshot, mesmerizing. His voice reached a new level of intensity. "In fact, you are a traitor to your god!"

April pulled at his arm again, and Braxton lashed out, shoving her across the room into her father. His legs snapped around Steel's waist, and he grabbed Steel by the throat. "It's time for you to die!" he screamed in an unearthly voice. Steel stumbled up and found his arms pinned to his side by Braxton's legs, and they fell back over the folding chair onto the floor. He struggled against the man's inhuman strength and felt his mind fading as blood flow to his brain lessened.

Braxton pressed his spiraled eye into Steel's face. "Beware the spiral eye. Remember? I'm your worst nightmare. You should be dead, but no, you survived somehow, and I'm going to finish the job." Steel felt his mind slip away into white light.

Steel was back in that place where his memory was lost like a dying man wandering through the desert. He looked up, and Braxton was gone. In his place stood a man in his mid-forties. Heavily muscled and bare-chested, he wore combat fatigue pants and boots. His face was hard, filled with flat planes and intensely burning blue eyes. He wore a white, wide-brimmed

hat that he suddenly tore from his head and tossed away. Gray spikes shot through his short, red hair.

"Did you hear me, boy? I don't care about your fanatical friends. You're going to learn to be tough if you're going to be my son. You understand? If I hit you, you're going to hit me back. You got that? Come on, you want a piece of the Captain? Come on!"

The man leaped into the air and twirled, his leg snapping out like a lever to catch him in the face, but Steel fought back...

Steel felt heat erupt within him, and the suppressed fury and anger boiled up with incredible strength. He flipped upward with incredible strength until he was standing, but Braxton clung to his neck and waist. He head-butted Braxton, and the man's skull sounded like a cracking coconut. The muscles in Steel's arms bulged, and Braxton's legs flew away from his side. He slapped away Braxton's hands, and the man stumbled back on wobbly legs. Steel twirled and, like in his flashback, lashed out with his right foot and caught Braxton in the chest. Blood showered in the air from the man's mouth as he hurtled across the room to crash into Mr. McCoy. Steel crouched in a defensive posture, and reality returned. April lay on the floor, and Dr. Richard Pierce was on the phone calling for more security. Braxton's unconscious form lay draped over a chair. Slowly the red haze of anger dissipated. Steel drew a

deep, troubled breath. Perhaps it would be best to leave his past buried.

Steel stood up and pulled a bottled water out of his small refrigerator. Josh reached for it, and Steel paused.

"What, you don't have enough bottled water? It's not like I'm asking for a beer."

"I don't contribute to the delinquency of a minor. What are you? Fourteen?" Steel said.

"Dude, I'm sixteen. Wait! Was that an attempt at humor? Are you trying to be funny?"

"I don't do humor."

"I bet you don't."

Steel tossed him the bottle of water and got another one out of the refrigerator.

"So, what happened with the chick? Did you fall in love with her?"

Steel sipped water and looked across the room at a picture on the far wall. It showed April and her father. They were smiling. "She sent me packing. Couldn't get involved emotionally with her patients. I ended up working for her father at his beach house until I could get my feet on the ground. So, you see my only memories of my father aren't the best. He seems to be a violent man who would just as soon beat me up as give me a hug. Now, your turn. Your father. Everything."

"Dude, like I said, he traveled a lot." Josh shrugged. "I think he and mother got crosswise right before he died." Josh drank some water and grew still.

"How did he die?"

Josh frowned. "He loved to hang glide. I was too young to go with him. We went up Sandia Peak. That was when we lived in Albuquerque. The cable car—made Mom nervous 'cause I was hanging out the windows." He laughed. "That was her favorite place on the planet up there on Sandia Peak, and then he had to go and ruin it by dying on us."

Josh picked at his lip bead. Suddenly he seemed small and defenseless. "See, I ran down this path to the cliff edge when he was supposed to go." Josh sat forward and threw his hands up in the air. "Mom freaked. She thought I would fall down the cliff, and she ran after me and almost fell herself. And so there we were all clutched up and Mom gasping from breath, and Dad's hang glider shot out over us." Josh looked up and pointed. "It was all purple and gold and black, and he screamed 'Wooooo Hoooooo' and waved at us." He sat back and took a swallow of water. "Dude, I swear he headed right into the sunset. It was almost poetic. But he never landed. Mom drove to the landing sight. No Dad. They looked for him for a week. No Dad. They think he might have had a heart attack or a stroke and the wind just carried way out into the desert. I was eleven years old. Bro, I was eleven."

"If you could have him back, would you?" Steel sat slowly in his chair.

Josh wiped at his eyes and chugged the water. "Yeah. I guess. I didn't like him that much when he was with us. But I miss him."

"Then you're different from me. I don't miss my dad."

Josh put his empty bottle on the table and picked up the index card. "Who's this Dr. Brown dude, more potential scorpion food?"

"No. He's a physician."

Josh grinned and amusement danced in his eyes. "Are you pregnant?"

"No. Why would you ask such a stupid question?"

Josh pointed to the card. "It's not a stupid question. Man, you gotta chill. Fill in the blanks."

"The blanks?"

Josh crossed his arms and wore a smug look. "Well, the big dude wants my help after all. Imagine that?"

Steel stood slowly and towered over Josh. "I never said you didn't have anything to contribute."

"Well, you have two choices. Beat the stuffing out of me like you did that FBI guy. Or give me the respect I deserve. Make me a member of the team. No restrictions, no hiding behind my mother's apron. And no more lectures." He stood up and glared into Steel's eyes. "I know computers. I can help. Besides, I'm bored. I got no Ila. I got no cell phone or video games. Bro, I thought we were going home until Scorpio showed up in the church. Looks like we're here for the duration. So, I want to help out. I want to be on the team."

"Where was this amazing intellect of yours this afternoon?"

"Dude, hormones will do that to you."

"OK." Steel sighed. "But you'll do everything I tell you, just like any team member. Understand?"

"No problems, bro." Josh grinned and tapped the index card. "Mifepristone. Also known as RU-486. That's why I asked you if you were pregnant. It's 'the morning-after' pill."

Steel's hair stood on end, and he picked up the card. He glared at the words as if the action would reveal any further information. "Are you sure?"

"Google it if you don't believe me." He tapped his head. "Remember, I have photographic memory."

Steel slumped into his chair. "Thanks, Josh. You can go now."

"Oh, I can go now? You mean, I'm dismissed? No 'thank you, Josh'? No, 'good work, Josh'? No 'way to go team member'?"

Steel bolted to his feet. He reached out and clamped his right hand over Josh's mouth and squeezed. "That's enough with the smart mouth, Josh. Now, listen carefully," he managed through clenched teeth as he pressed his face close to Josh's. "Thank you."

"Dude, for someone who wants to help people, you sure are violent," Josh blurted out.

Steel slowly released the young man. "You said that already."

"It's a good line. I think I'll keep it. So, what's next with this Dr. Brown?" Josh rubbed his mouth.

"I go pay him a visit in the morning."

"When do we leave?" Josh asked.

Steel glanced up at Josh. "We?"

"I'm part of the team. Give me something to do. I'll give you a different perspective." Josh balled up his fist and held it out to Steel. "What, no fist bump? OK, so you're not that cool. It's OK. I can teach you. You're what, forty?"

"I don't know." Steel looked at Josh's hand like it was a tumor. "You can put your hand down now."

"OK, so you don't remember. But you're not as ancient as Uncle Cephas." Josh dropped his fist. "Dude, look at it this way. I'll be with you, so I'll stay out of trouble."

Steel sighed. "Fine. Be ready at eight in the morning. Now, go to bed, Josh."

Josh smiled and opened the door. "Whatever you say, bro. You're the boss. By the way, nice bonding time."

"I don't do bonding."

"Dude, you are way too harsh." Josh slammed the door as he left.

Steel felt a headache coming on and tossed the card on the table. Taking Josh along with him might be a big mistake. On the other hand, he did have a very different perspective on things. He glanced down at the card. Why would Emily be consulting a doctor about the morning-after pill? And wasn't she too far along even if she were considering such a thing? Besides, Emily and Parker had been trying to have a baby for years. He leaned forward and studied the map on the computer screen, punching a button to print out a hard copy. He would soon find out.

[Chapter 13]

JOSH HAD ON the same T-shirt the next morning, and his eyes were puffy and swollen. He sat quietly in the passenger seat of Jonathan's SUV.

"Long night?" Steel asked.

"Whatever. Let's go."

Steel drew a deep breath and opened his mouth. He looked at Josh.

"Go ahead. Say it! Cuss at me!"

"I don't curse. Waste of words." Steel started his SUV. "But you may make a liar out of me. I might have to start cursing at Cephas Lawrence."

"How do you know the old man?" Josh yawned.

"He's sort of like my mentor."

"Your Yoda? Cool. He's kinda creepy to me. He came to one of my birthdays before Dad died. Dude, he kept inhaling the helium from the balloons and talking like a chipmunk."

Steel tried to hide a smile. "I'll have to remember that one."

"See, when you get to know the Josh man, you get to like the Josh man."

"Don't push it. So, if you're tired, you can stay if you want," Steel said.

Josh glanced in his direction. "Oh, no, dude. I'm a part of the team. You're not going to get me to back down. Let's go."

Steel pulled out of the driveway of the missionary house. Fifteen minutes later he pulled up in front of a dilapidated one-floor house. It was in obvious disrepair. A sign hung at an angle from the front porch. "Daniel Brown, Health Food Consultant."

Josh rolled down the window and studied the weed-choked front yard. "Bro, I'm not into early Howard Hughes. I'll just wait for you to come out."

Steel pointed across the young man's chest. "I don't think anyone is going in. See those yellow tapes."

Josh looked at the front porch. "Police tapes?"

"This isn't an office anymore. It's a crime scene. We need to go pay a visit to the sheriff."

Deputy O'Reilly stood up from behind his desk when they stepped into the sheriff's office. He was nervous and fidgety, and Steel noted he was playing with a bullet.

"What can I do for you boys?"

"I need to speak to the sheriff," Steel said.

O'Reilly wiggled his eyebrows and pushed a wad of tobacco across his mouth with his tongue. "Sheriff's awfully busy."

A door opened at the back of the office. Sheriff Sweeney stepped into view. "Buford, what are you doing?"

O'Reilly put his hands on his belt. "Keeping these varmints from wasting your time, Sheriff."

The man rolled his eyes and sighed. "What can I do for you, Mr. Steel? Looks like you got an unusual partner there."

Steel nodded toward O'Reilly. "So do you."

O'Reilly glared at him and Sweeney smiled. "Come on in."

Steel led Josh into the man's office. It was simple with an old metal and Formica desk. A mounted deer head stared down at them. Sweeney motioned to two chairs in front of his desk and then squeezed himself behind the desk. He was a bit on the obese side with thinning gray hair and a red face. "My wife won't let me keep my deer head in the den."

"Nice," Josh managed. Steel shot him a dirty look. Josh shrugged.

"Now, Special Agent Ross said some mighty ugly things about you, so before we go any further, I need to know if you're a private investigator," Sweeney said.

Steel took out his wallet and showed him his license. "Mrs. Parker is in the hospital, and last night she asked me to find a Doctor Daniel Brown for her. I went out to his office and noticed there was yellow police tape across the windows and doors."

Sweeney leaned back in his chair. "I'm afraid so. A lady across the highway from his house called us a few days ago. Said a black SUV pulled up in front of Brown's house, and someone dragged him out and shoved him in the car."

"Someone kidnapped him?" Josh asked.

"Wouldn't surprise me." Sweeney shrugged. "The man's a dope head. Used to be an ear, nose, and throat doctor in Monroe. Got drunk one day and tried to do surgery. Injected too much cocaine solution, and his patient had a seizure and died. He lost his license and ended up in jail for murder."

Steel pocketed his wallet. "I take it he's out of jail and practicing again."

"Not practicing medicine." Sweeney leaned forward over his desk. "Calls himself a health nut practitioner. I can't stop him from selling herbs and remedies. But as far as I know, he wouldn't be having a thing to do with Emily Parker."

"Any idea who took him?"

"Probably a drug deal gone bad. We'll probably never find his body." Sweeney glanced over at a stack of folders. He seemed about to say something. Steel nodded toward the folders.

"You've got something else on him?"

Sweeney cut his eyes toward Steel. "Could be."

"I could really use the help, Sheriff. If it affects the church, it affects the community."

"Tell me about it. I'm chairman of the deacon board. Gerry Smithson was a good friend." Sweeney nodded. "I think there may be a connection with a local businessman."

"Ketrick?"

Sweeney smiled. "I heard you met him yesterday."

"What is he into? Drugs?"

"I'm not sure. He's having a big brunch out at his house today. Bunch of bigwig businessmen from down south Louisiana way. Something is going on. I can't prove he had anything to do with Brown's disappearance. But…" Sweeney paused, deep in thought. He nodded slowly. "In spite of Special Agent Ross, I'm going to trust you." Sweeney continued. "I found a savings account book in Brown's junk." He reached for one of the folders and pulled it toward him. A bank account passbook slid out. He opened it and pushed it across the desk toward Steel. "Someone paid Dr. Brown three successive payments of ten thousand dollars over the past six months."

Steel glanced at the passbook. The entries were written in very bad handwriting. And at the end of each entry was one name. *Vivian.* Steel felt his blood run cold. Sweeney pulled the passbook away. "I'll make you a copy, Steel. You say where you got it, and I'll claim you stole it."

"Before you do that"—Steel pulled the piece of paper out of his pocket—"I have a list of the members of your church.

Thomas Parker gave them to me. I was going to try and speak to them, but I'm running out of time. What happened that they deserted their pastor?"

Sweeney leaned back in his chair. "Rumors are more powerful than bald-faced lies. Some say he was seeing a young woman on the side. Others say he wanted to start a contemporary service."

"That's as bad as adultery?" Josh laughed. "Man, we have three contemporary services at our church. I play the bass guitar on Saturday night."

"Young man, in this small town those two things are equally bad. Not to mention this whole thing with Ketrick wanting to move the church. Some of the congregation worship that building like it's an idol."

Steel laid the sheet of paper in front of Sweeney. "I had a talk with Parker last night in the waiting room at the hospital. He thought his wife was in mortal danger and not a single church member was there for him. I don't know what is going on with your people, but I know Parker. He is a struggling man wanting to do God's will for his church. I believe that, and I know he has made some mistakes. But he doesn't deserve to be treated like this. He and his wife are supposed to have a family that sticks with them through good and bad. Make it right. Be there for them. They need your prayers and your support. I promised Parker I would help him get his church back. I always keep my promises, no matter how uncomfortable they make me. Will you do it? By this Sunday?"

Sweeney nodded and picked up the sheet. "I'll do it." He slid out from behind his desk and went into the outer office. Steel glanced over his shoulder as Sweeney left the office. He reached for the folder.

"What are you doing?" Josh asked.

"Taking a quick peek." Steel opened the folder. A picture slid out. The man in the picture was short and squat with an obvious physical deformity. His face was round with bulging eyes and thick lips. He looked like a toad. Steel took one look at the face and remembered.

The man in the Panama hat leaned over him. His face lit up in red fire as he inhaled the smoke from his Meerschaum pipe. "Did you break him, Toady?"

The other man leaned over him. His face was thick and froglike with bulging eyes. Tears were streaming down his cheeks. "He was my friend, Captain! I tried my best to break him. Why did you make me torture him?"

The Captain motioned to a man nearby in black sweats. The room seemed to move. They were on the bridge of some kind of boat. "Take Toady and throw him overboard."

"No!" Toady screamed. "I can't swim!"

The Captain glanced back at him. "Then shut up, or I'll send you back to prison where I should have left you to rot. If he can't be broken, then I have no other choice but throw him overboard instead of you."

The Captain leaned closer, and he smelled the sickly sweet odor of the tobacco. "Sorry, son. It has to be done. Beware the demon of the spiral eye."

Steel blinked and looked around at the office of Sheriff Sweeney. Josh reached out and nudged the picture back into the folder and closed it just as Sweeney came back in the office.

Steel's face was coated with sweat as Sweeney handed him the copy of the passbook. "Here you go, Steel. Good luck. If you find Dr. Brown, you let me know right away."

Steel blinked and calmed his heavy breathing. "I won't stop until I've found him," he said hoarsely. He had more reason than ever for finding Dr. Daniel Brown. Toady, as the Captain had called him. With Dr. Brown missing, his one link with the "toad" was Ketrick. It was time for brunch.

[Chapter 14]

CROSS LAKE SPREAD out over hundreds of acres of land, supplying water to the Shreveport area. In spite of that, the lake was a huge recreational body of water. A dozen sailboats dotted the dark water. Fishing boats plied the waters. Beneath the hot morning sun, the lake was cool and inviting.

Lakeside sat near its northwestern shore, and in recent years new homes had sprung up along the northern shore, some of them owned by successful businessmen. Ketrick lived in a secure area named Pineshore Hills. Homes with square footage in excess of ten thousand dotted the rolling hills overlooking the lake. Steel had taken Josh back to the missionary house and asked him to accompany Liz to the local library for research on the snakes they had seen in the foyer. That way Steel was free to confront Ketrick about his connection with the mysterious Dr. Brown.

An ornate security building sat at the entrance to Pineshore Hills. An armed uniformed man paced outside the building and cast a suspicious eye on Steel's four-wheel drive. Steel drove past the security post and parked at a bait shop across the street next to a bayou that emptied into the lake. He went inside the store, a brick-and-glass structure filled with all types of fishing paraphernalia. The odor of fish and fried chicken was overpowering. A wrinkled prune of a woman sat behind the counter smoking an unfiltered cigarette. She was watching a wrestling match on a small television/DVR combo. When he stopped at the counter, she reached over and pressed the pause button. She turned rheumy eyes on him and sneezed.

"Excuse me, ma'am," Steel leaned back away from her as she sputtered and coughed. "I'm trying to deliver a package to Mr. Ketrick's home. Have you heard of him?"

The woman wiped her mouth with a stained tissue. "Yep." She leaned toward him and pointed out the window. "See that there castle-looking outfit with the black roof across the street and down the bayou? That's his house, all right. Anything else?"

"No, thank you," Steel replied. The woman turned back to her television, her cigarette, and her wrestling match. Steel walked out of the smoke-filled store and looked up the slope of trees across the street to the huge house the woman had pointed to. Behind the bait shop, the small bayou ran under a bridge nearby and emptied into the lake somewhere on the other side of the hill.

Steel walked down to the bayou and followed it through the dense brush. Once, he scared an alligator out of the bushes into the water. He stopped and breathed a small prayer for safety. It wouldn't do to come all the way to Louisiana to fight demons and get eaten by an alligator. To his right, he noticed a high stone fence and made his way up through the dense brush. He climbed up to the top of the fence and glanced over the top.

Ketrick's house was indeed a castle. It was square and ugly and made of huge brick stones with cone-topped towers at the corners. The backyard was immense. Lush landscaping surrounded a large swimming pool.

Steel slid over the wall and made his way behind a long row of bushes running along the fence. When he came to the end of the bushes, he studied the pool. At least a dozen servants were busily bustling around the group of people who sat in lounge chairs around the pool. Ketrick was the only one wearing an expensive suit, which he wore over a silk shirt and a string tie. He tossed his head, and the long ponytail danced in the morning air.

The rest of Ketrick's guests wore swimsuits and cool clothing. Ketrick, tall and bony, probably didn't swim. He would sink like a rock. He held a glass of champagne in his hand and bit into a croissant. Ah, the brunch of the rich and famous.

Three people sat beneath an umbrella attended to by two young women in skimpy bikinis. The oldest man was smoking a huge cigar and laughing out loud. Steel recognized him from a recent newspaper article he had run across when researching Louisiana. He was the supposed boss of a huge, organized crime syndicate out of New Orleans. In his most recent appearances in court, he was supposedly suffering from Alzheimer's disease and incapable of testifying, much less going to jail. From the way he leered at the young women, his brain functioned just fine.

The other man turned and exposed perfectly combed hair and a matching shirt and shorts. Gold rings adorned his hands, and he could have been mistaken for a Hollywood star. But Steel knew he had a checkered past. The man had recently run for US Congress and had lost. But he had kept his seat in the Louisiana legislature, much to the chagrin of Louisiana voters. The perfectly smiling features hid the fact the man had been a leader in the Klan.

Steel drew a deep breath as the third person stood up and turned around. He recognized the woman's short, black hair pulled back behind her ears. She wore a full-length light cotton drape dappled in black and white and a one-piece black swimsuit. Large, black sunglasses hid Vivian Darbonne's eyes as her gaze traveled slowly around the backyard, taking in every detail.

The woman sauntered away from the table and paused in the middle of the pool deck, as if searching for something. She turned toward the bush, and a chill ran down Steel's spine as she stopped. A delicate hand went to the sunglasses, and she revealed deep, dark eyes that bored into his. She smiled, licked her bright red lips, and made a gun out of her right hand. She pointed it at the bushes and mouthed the word "bang." She put the sunglasses on and turned back to the pool.

Vivian walked languidly across the pool deck with the black and white drape rippling in the breeze. Steel was certain she would stop and tell Ketrick there was an intruder at his party, but she passed him by. She paused just under the back patio awning and turned to face Steel. She stretched out her hand and beckoned him with one finger, then vanished into the house.

Steel eased to his feet and worked his way down the hedge to a side door leading into the house. Cool air wafted out into the hot morning humidity through the open door. He glanced toward Ketrick's party, and no one looked his way. Quickly he walked across the perfectly manicured grass and slipped into the cool interior of a kitchen. He moved deeper through the kitchen and into an enormous den.

A man sat in a recliner reading a magazine. His hands were bone white, long and spidery. He lowered the paper and studied Steel with red eyes. His pale skull was hairless. He wore a long, black coat and a black silk shirt open at the neck. Steel saw tattoos on the man's chest.

"Good morning, Mr. Steel."

Steel felt an uneasy disquiet settle over him. The mere sight of the man was disturbing. "Do I know you?"

"We've never been formally introduced." The man stood up and towered over six feet in height. "My name is Lucas. I am an associate of Mr. Ketrick."

Steel reached out his hand, and the man looked at it with disdain. "If you'll forgive me, I have problems with my immune system. I never shake hands. Don't consider it an act of incivility."

Steel lowered his hand. "I understand. Are you a business associate?"

Lucas smiled and exposed impossibly white, straight teeth. He seemed to have too many of them. He motioned to the wall behind Steel. "I am a broker. I collect items of antiquity for my client. As you can see, Mr. Ketrick is very interested in these objects."

Steel turned around. Ancient stone carvings and hideous masks covered the walls. The eyes of demons followed him across the room. He examined the glass cabinets filled with antique knives and swords. Between two cabinets, a three-foot stone circle hung on the wall. The mutilated body of a woman filled the circle. The sight of the carving made Steel's hair stand on end. It emanated evil. Steel looked away from the carving as his mind filled with nameless dread. Something about this carving was so evil it reached across the ages. He turned and found the room empty. Lucas was gone.

A shadow shimmered at the far corner of the house closest to the lake. He moved into a short hallway that opened into a huge library that was open up to the second floor level. Bookshelves covered all of the walls except for the glass French doors that provided a view of the lake. A huge oak desk sat in the center. The leather chair behind the desk swiveled, revealing Vivian Darbonne. She removed her sunglasses and smiled.

"I'm so glad you got to meet Mr. Lucas. Oh, but you poor baby. You must be so upset Robert didn't send you an invitation to the brunch." She purred. "And I could have fixed you a nice cup of coffee. Not too hot."

Steel surveyed the contents of the room. "I tried to call him at his office, but the secretary said he wasn't in today. I decided to take a walk down by the bayou." He turned toward her. "When an alligator chased me, I had to jump over the fence."

Vivian stood up and smiled. "Predators can be so sneaky," she drawled. "Mr. Ketrick won't be happy you're here, sugar. Maybe I can smooth things over with him." She walked around the desk and leaned into him. Her lips were shining and her eyes were filled with wildness. "Maybe if I whisper just right in his ear, he won't be too unhappy. So, honey, you just go right ahead and have a seat, and I'll go inform him he has a visitor." She placed a lacquered fingernail on his chest and pushed him backward. He stumbled over an ottoman and collapsed into a chair. "Now, that's more like it, sugar."

"Tell me about the checks to Dr. Daniel Brown," Steel said.

Vivian paused with her back to him. Her wrap stirred in the faint breeze from an air conditioning vent. She slowly turned, and the sultry demeanor was gone and her southern drawl vanished. "I knew you'd be good at this. Don't put your sights on me. I'm just a pawn in this game. Keep your focus on Ketrick. He's the one you need to worry about." She moved out of the room, and her wrap danced in the air. Steel wiped the sweat from his brow.

He stood up and walked over to the desk. He spied a drawing of a riverboat casino on a Louisiana river at the bottom of a tall bluff. In Louisiana, casinos could only conduct their business on riverboats. Beside it was another drawing of a lavish hotel sitting at the top of a hill overlooking the river. The entrance was grand and fashioned after a pyramid, similar to the ones built by the Mayan empire. From the top of the pyramid entrance a huge medallion gleamed in the sun, emblazoned with the dismembered torso of an ancient goddess—the same carving that hung on the wall in the den. Ketrick seemed to have an obsession with it.

For a moment Steel considered the significance of the two men he had seen by the pool. Organized crime and the riverboat casinos sometimes went hand in hand. There was a hefty casino industry in Shreveport, and it was possible that organized crime was moving into the area. But if the two men by the pool were involved with Ketrick, then it was a good bet Ketrick was probably involved in gambling traffic in New Orleans. The good citizens of his perfect "Main Street" town would frown on his unsavory associates.

Steel turned. Framed photographs of politicians and movie stars hung along the wall. Each picture carried an autograph in the lower right hand corner. He paused before one picture of a handsome man with silvery hair shaking hands with Ketrick. The testimonial read, "Keep up the good work! Wulf." Beneath the name Wulf a tiny number 12, barely legible, was enclosed in quotation marks.

Steel spied another photograph and picked up the picture frame. It was an old 35 mm snapshot showing a young black-haired teenager standing next to a tall man in a black overcoat. Behind the two, Steel could see the stone disk that inspired the reproduction hanging in the den. This must have been a younger Robert Ketrick. Even in the fading photograph, he could see the man next to Ketrick had reddish eyes. Lucas had been there with Ketrick? And Ketrick couldn't have been more than fifteen or sixteen. And yet Lucas looked the same in the picture as the man he had met in the next room. He had not aged a day.

Steel placed the picture frame back on the shelf and was about to sit in a chair when another picture caught his attention. As he walked toward it, ice ran in his veins. It was a photograph of Ketrick in a sailing jacket and shorts sitting on the edge of a sailboat. He was arm in arm with Rocky Braxton. The man was younger and had short, black hair, but the spiral tattoo around his right eye was unmistakable. In the lower corner was scrawled a testimonial, "To my weird Uncle Bobby. Love, Rocky."

"Find something interesting?"

He whirled. The young girl before him was short and lithe with long, yellow hair. Her face was perfectly oval, and her eyes were black. She wore a knee-length cotton dress covered with sunflowers.

"Who are you?"

"Josh's new friend. I'm Summer. He's a cute kid. I like him." She giggled and touched a fingernail to her lips and smiled.

Steel drew a deep breath. "Why are you here?"

"Bobby's my uncle." She smiled, and for a second Steel smelled the fragrance of dried rose petals and old dust. She turned, and standing behind the desk was Robert Ketrick. He motioned to a seat in front of his desk.

"I didn't know you wanted to attend today's brunch, Mr. Steel. Please, have a seat. Summer, why don't you go get Mr. Steel some pate?"

Summer nodded and cast one last look at Steel. "I love liver." She left the room.

Steel grabbed the picture of Braxton and shoved it at Ketrick. "Explain this."

Ketrick leaned forward, and the ponytail fell forward across the right side of his well-tailored suit coat. His string tie dangled forward, and Steel was shocked to see a scorpion in a Lucite block as the tie clasp.

Ketrick frowned, and his eyes filled with sadness. "Oh, my poor nephew Rocky. So mixed-up. So sad. I tried my best to mentor him. That was my sailboat harbored in Panama City Beach. A couple of years ago I took him under my wing for a summer. I'm afraid he repaid my kindness with treachery. Something drove him over the edge of sanity into madness. Poor Rocky."

Steel stared at the picture. "Poor Rocky?"

"His undoing was an ancient knife used long ago in arcane rituals. He stole it, and if I'm not mistaken, he used it to kill someone. He died in the attack. What a pity." Ketrick's eyes danced with mischief as leaned back in his chair. "Did you know my poor nephew?"

Steel slammed the picture down on the desk, and the glass shattered. "You know I did, Ketrick! He killed…" Steel paused gasping for air as the smell of thunder and blood flooded over him. "…someone I cared deeply about."

Ketrick pursed his lips and his gaunt features filled with sadness. "My condolences, Mr. Steel. I will soon call the police, and they will arrest you for trespassing. So, I suggest you leave, now. Perhaps we can address your questions some other time. Say, next Monday?" Ketrick stood and crossed to the French doors and opened one of them. "If you follow the path down to where the bayou meets the lake, you can walk back through the snake-infested brush to your car."

"How did you know I came that way?"

Ketrick pointed to the ceiling over the door leading into the study. A tiny red light gleamed. "I have security cameras everywhere, Mr. Steel. And I record everything that transpires. I knew you were coming long before the reptile in the bushes spooked you. Good day."

Steel walked across the room toward the French doors as his thoughts raced. Lucas, Summer, and Vivian belonged to Ketrick. What was he up to? Ask questions, he thought. Probe! Don't just walk away! Turn over another rock. "Who is Lucas?"

Ketrick raised an eyebrow and smiled. He motioned over his shoulder, and Lucas seemed to appear literally out of the shadows of the hallway. "An old associate of mine."

Steel licked his lips and stalled for time. He had to get more answers, but the memories of the knife and the blood were overcoming his senses. "He finds you these artifacts? Like that one?" Steel pointed to another reproduction of the stone circle.

Ketrick placed a hand on his face, deep in thought. "Lucas, should we tell him?"

Lucas's red eyes gleamed with an unearthly sheen. "I told you he would be the one."

"The one?" Steel asked.

Ketrick nodded. "Yes, would you like to see the past? I can do this for you. With Lucas's help. I can give you a memory of mine. But you will not like it."

Steel shook his head as Lucas stepped closer. "Give me a memory?"

"You've lost all of yours, poor boy." Ketrick shook his head. "Lucas."

Lucas paused and reached toward Steel, and then a pained expression came over his face. "I cannot touch him."

Ketrick nodded. "Of course. I forgot. You can do this through me."

Steel fell backward into a deeply cushioned chair. "What are you doing?"

Ketrick stepped closer and smiled. "I knew your parents. I was an exchange student in Mexico. Only fifteen. So young then. But far from innocent. Your mother helped me find the artifact." He gestured toward the stone circle. "Would you like to see her? See her as she was young?"

Steel shook his head. "That is not possible. It's evil. It's of Satan."

"Yes, most temptations are, Mr. Steel. But think on this." He leaned down, and his bright green eyes gleamed. "I can give you back a precious memory of the day you were born. Just take my hand."

Lucas reached out a bony hand and placed it on Ketrick's shoulder. Ketrick extended a hand toward Steel. The fingers curled and twitched with nervous energy. Every fiber within Steel told him to stop, to turn and run away. But he had to know! He shoved his hand forward and grabbed Ketrick and was somewhere else.

[Chapter 15]

For weeks Bobby had felt a sensation tighten and grow within his gut as if something was coming, something meant just for him. Week after week digging through ancient manuscripts under the careful eye of his teacher, Christine, had paid off. He had sensed, no, he had known the thing he sought was under the ground, buried, waiting just for him. And now workers digging ditches for new electric cable in the heart of Mexico City had found that something. Something ancient. Something evil.

In the downtown area the excavation site marred the concrete and steel, an open wound into the earth. He pushed his way past the curious onlookers and flashed his museum ID to gain access to the site. A group of men from the archeology office stood on the edge of the pit, and their excited voices babbled on about the find. Bobby ignored them and slid down a ladder into the cool, dark past.

Sunlight slanted into the depths of the pit, and the smell of old, sodden earth filled his nostrils. Something about this pit excited him, sparked within him a new anticipation of power, of destiny. He pushed his way between two men and stared down at a huge, round, flat rock covered with the figure of a woman carved into ancient stone.

The horrific scene thrilled him. The image of the severed head, the torn arms, the separated legs, and the torso of a woman covered a stone disk almost eleven feet in diameter. The woman wore a serpent belt adorned with a human skull. He couldn't pull his eyes away from the wounds carved into the stone until he felt a hand on his shoulder.

"What are you doing here, Bobby?"

Bobby pushed his dark hair back out of his eyes and stared into the face of the Captain. He was a bit shorter than Bobby, and his gaze did not waver beneath his wide-brimmed Panama hat. He puffed on a peculiar Meerschaum pipe. He was the curator of the local museum where Bobby had come for the summer.

"I wanted to see the find." Bobby motioned toward the stone disk.

"And he brought me." Christine appeared behind the Captain. Her face was flushed with the exertion of chasing Bobby, and her reddish blonde hair was plastered to her scalp. She massaged her pregnant abdomen.

The Captain pulled his pipe from his mouth. "I told you to stay at the hacienda. We're leaving in the morning, and I don't want anything to happen to our baby."

She ignored him and peeked over his shoulder at the stone disk. "But I had to see it! Now I can finish my thesis."

The Captain put a hand on her shoulder and pushed her back toward the ladder. "Well, now you've seen it, and you're going back."

The woman carried a macramé purse slung on her shoulder, and she reached inside and removed a camera. "At least let Bobby take some pictures for me." She handed the camera to Bobby. "For the paper, Bobby. Will you please?"

Bobby glanced at the camera. He had no interest in taking pictures. All he wanted was to touch the stone disk. He took the camera and gave her his best smile.

"I'd be happy to. You go on with the Captain."

The Captain put his pipe back in his mouth and clenched down on it with ferocity. His eyes raked across Bobby one last time as he directed his wife back toward the ladder. Bobby tucked the camera in his pocket and turned back to study the stone disk.

"I'm glad you managed to pull that one off. The good Captain would have had you back at the museum without ever touching this precious stone," someone whispered in his ear.

Bobby glanced up. A man towered over him. His pale, white skull was bare. His face was youthful, but his red eyes bore the weight of years. He wore a long, black coat over a black shirt open at the throat. The edge of a tattoo could be seen just at the edge of the shirt. A scar the shape of a star marred the pale flesh of his left cheek. "What do you see?"

Bobby studied the bright, fiery eyes. "I'm not sure. But it's wonderful."

The man's red tongue darted over his teeth. "Would you like to know more about it?"

Bobby nodded as his mind filled with excitement and anticipation. He felt as if he were on the verge of a monumental development, as if his entire life had led to this moment. The man pointed to the image of the mutilated woman.

"This woman's mother became pregnant. The new child within her mother was a boy, an heir to great power. This woman could not abide such a threat to her power from her unborn brother. She was jealous and plotted to have her mother killed so the child would never be born. But someone told the unborn child."

Bobby felt something stir within him, an excitement unlike anything he had ever felt. His hands trembled in anticipation. His heart raced. "He wasn't happy his sister wanted him to die, was he?"

The tattooed man frowned. "No, he was not happy. In fact, so powerful was this new ruler that he sprang forth from his mother's womb fully grown. His rage knew no limits. He took a large, golden knife, and he hacked his sister to pieces and threw all but her head down the mountainside."

Bobby's eyes glittered with excitement as he watched the man's scar glow with the crimson flush of blood. "What was the man's name?"

The tattooed man smiled, and his face glowed with triumph. "He was not a man. He was a god. And his name is one you'll grow to love and revere. Would you like to know more?"

"Yes!"

"What is your name?"

"Robert. Although most people call me Bobby." He frowned.

"You shouldn't let people talk down to you, Robert."

"Bobby, come with me. Now." Bobby glanced up at the Captain standing on the edge of the pit.

"I'll be right there." Bobby shouted up to the man. He pulled the camera from his pocket and began to snap pictures of the disk until the Captain walked away from the pit. Bobby held out the camera to a passing archeology office worker. "Can you take our picture? Por favor?"

The worker took the camera and nodded. The tattooed man put an arm around Bobby's shoulders, and the man's flesh was as cold as ice.

"I'd better get back to the museum. The Captain will be waiting for me." Bobby looked into the eyes of the tattooed man.

"Of course. Would you mind if I came by later to talk?" he asked.

"No."

The tattooed man placed his hands behind his back and turned away. Bobby cast one last longing look at the disk. He leaned forward and let his hand stray across the rough stone. It felt like electricity danced up his arm, and he gasped and drew in a deep breath. For a second he saw the woman's body, saw the blood, smelled the ancient odor of fear and evil. He smiled and scrambled up the ladder from the pit.

Night had fallen, and the courtyard was lit with many torches by the time he arrived at the museum hacienda. Servants were bustling around the courtyard and up and down the stairs to the second floor entrance of the house. Bobby hurried into the main courtyard. The air was hot and muggy and smelled of antiseptics and sweat. A scream echoed down from the second floor. Bobby stopped a short woman hurrying by with a pan of water.

"Maria, what is happening?"

Maria's eyes were wide with fear. "It is the mistress of the house. She is having the baby."

Bobby watched her hurry away and looked up at the balcony. The Captain stood there, minus his hat. His shirt was soaked with sweat. "Bobby! Good, you're back. Watch for Dr. Santiago. I was hoping we could get back to the States, but Christine is in labor."

Another scream cut through the air, and Bobby flinched. He thought about the stone disk. He pictured the pregnant mother giving birth to a full-grown man capable of hacking his sister to death. Why did he think such things at a time like this? He liked Christine. She had been kind to him over the last few months when most of the adults at the museum ignored him. She had seen his potential and had asked him to help find the disk of Coatlicue, the mother of the woman on the stone. Where had that mother's compassion gone? How could a mother sit by and watch as her daughter is killed?

"Am I interrupting something?"

Bobby turned, and the tattooed man stood in the open archway leading into the courtyard. "No. My teacher is having her baby. She may be in trouble."

Bobby watched the man's face flush with crimson. For a second a smile played across his lips. Bobby studied the man's red eyes and felt a shiver course over him. For a second, he felt a sense of dread at the man's presence.

"Bobby, who is this gentleman?" The Captain was suddenly behind him. Bobby whirled. The Captain held a bloody blanket to his chest. The head of a baby lolled against his bloody chest.

"Is that your baby?" Bobby asked.

The Captain looked down at the child and blinked. "Yes. His name is John."

Bobby leaned forward and watched the newborn child squirm in his father's grasp. For a fleeting second the baby's eyes flew open, and the startling color of turquoise gleamed in the torchlight. The Captain looked over Bobby's shoulder.

"I asked you who that man was. He's not Doctor Santiago."

"Just someone I met at the dig."

The tattooed man smiled and exposed his white teeth and red gums. "My name is Lucas."

The Captain was silent for a moment, and his greenish-blue eyes stayed riveted on the tattooed man. "I don't want you to have anything to do with him, Bobby."

Bobby nodded. "Of course, Captain. I'll show him out." Above them, another scream pierced the night. The Captain grabbed Bobby's arm and turned him back. He thrust the baby into his arms.

"Here. Hold him until Consuela comes for him. My wife needs me." The Captain hurried away and disappeared up the stairs.

"What a beautiful child." Lucas smiled.

"I think you need to go," Bobby said. He glanced at the squirming baby in his arms.

"I will go. In a moment. But first, I must tell you more about the child you hold in your hands." Lucas leaned forward, and a finger strayed toward the baby. He paused

just before touching the baby's forehead. "Your destiny and his are connected. But it would seem that destiny may have given you an unprecedented opportunity." Lucas walked across the courtyard to the fountain. "Come. Follow me."

Bobby glanced at the baby and hurried after the man. "What are you talking about?"

Lucas sat on the edge of the fountain. "Pick the baby up by the leg."

Bobby frowned. "Why?"

"Trust me."

Bobby blinked as something swelled within him, a heat that burned its way to his fingertips. He reached down and took the baby's right leg in his hand and gently lifted the baby into the air. The baby's blanket fluttered to the ground.

"Good. Now lift him up in the air." Lucas's voice grew hoarse.

Bobby lifted the naked baby up until his face was level with his, his arms and left leg dangling. The baby ceased his squirming, and for a second, his eyes flickered open as if to study Bobby.

"Now, drop him in the water."

Bobby looked at him. "In the fountain?"

"Yes. One quick release, and your future will be secure. Just like you dropped the scorpion."

Bobby blinked. That morning he had dropped a scorpion on Consuela, the girl he hated so much. He could still remember her screams. "How did you know?"

The tattooed man stood up and drew very close, and his eyes gleamed in the scant light. "I know everything about you, Robert. It is a matter of record, that your mother committed suicide. But the truth is, you were playing with the gun and it accidentally went off and she died. You wanted the gun to kill your father. He's the one who deserved to die, right?"

Bobby began to tremble, and his grip weakened on the baby's leg. "No one knows that."

"I told you I have had an eye on you for some time. And now, if you listen carefully to my advice, I will complete your training."

Bobby felt the heat intensify and felt his mind blur. An inexorable force seized his mind, and he lifted the baby higher as he reached over the edge of the fountain.

"Good. Now, just relax your grip. One simple movement, and your adversary is gone. And all you have to do is blame it on Consuela."

"Son of the devil! What are you doing?" Bobby whirled, and Consuela appeared out of the darkness. Huge, red welts covered her face from the scorpion stings. She snared the baby from Bobby's grasp and pulled him to her chest.

The Captain appeared on the upper level. "What is happening?"

Consuela retrieved the blanket and wrapped it around the baby. "Bobby was going to drown the baby."

The Captain glared down at Bobby. "Is this true?"

"I don't know, sir. I just lost my mind, I guess." Bobby fumbled for words. He watched the man's face redden with anger.

The Captain glanced at Lucas. "Take your friend and get off my property. Now."

"But sir . . . "

"Now. Pack up your things, and have your friend drop you off at the airport. You can catch the first flight out in the morning. I don't want you around my son another moment." He motioned to Consuela, and she hurried up the stairs.

"You have failed your first test, Bobby," Lucas whispered.

Bobby flinched when he heard the name. He studied the man's features hidden in shadows. "What have you done to me?"

"I have done nothing. You have done this to yourself. Every choice you have ever made has led to this moment. Come. I'll take you to the airport. When you get home, you can begin the completion of this plan. Soon you will be eighteen, and you can finish the business you started with your father. And then, you will inherit his company and his riches."

Bobby looked at the hacienda he had once called home. Down that hallway was the woman who had been the closest thing he had to a mother. "What about the baby?"

Lucas shrugged. "He will try and stop you some day. And when that day comes, you must kill him."

Steel jerked his hand out of Ketrick's grasp and struggled for breath. Ketrick's face reddened, and he whirled on Lucas.

"Why did you show him that last part?" Spit flew from Ketrick's lips.

"It is necessary," Lucas said.

Steel was reeling from the memory. The image of the mother he could not remember. He glared at Ketrick. "You knew my mother? You know who I am!"

"Yes. I'm quite familiar with you, Mr. Steel." Ketrick rubbed his hands together and then wiped spit from his lips. "They named you John, if you're interested. It may have been short for Jonathan. I don't remember. Fascinating how everything comes full circle, isn't it? I was there on the day you were born, and now, I'm here on the day you will be arrested for trespassing. You know, you won't be much good to Reverend Parker if you're in jail. So, I suggest you put your curiosity aside and forget about the past. You wouldn't like it, even if I told you. Now if you will be so good as to leave."

Steel stood up shakily and glanced once at Lucas. His bemused smile was chilling.

Steel stumbled backward through the French doors and left blood on the handle. He glanced down, and only then did he notice the blood running down his fingers from the cut in his palm. Ketrick stopped at the open door and noticed the blood. He reached down with a long, bony finger and dabbed at a spot of blood on the door handle. He raised his finger delicately to his flaring nostrils and sniffed the spot of blood. Smiling, he placed his finger in his mouth and savored the moment as his eyes closed in concentration. He opened his dangerous eyes. "You have good blood, Mr. Steel. Very good blood. Take care of it. It tastes almost as good as the blood that was left on the knife Rocky used."

Steel blanched, and he squeezed his hand in a fist. His heart pounded with horror. When he had seen the picture of the knife on the desk in Ketrick's downtown office, he had thought it looked familiar. Now it all came back to him. The gold, curved blade covered with her blood. The mosaic tile of the handle shaped like the backswept wings of a hummingbird. He glared at Ketrick as his mind reeled. He was unable to find words.

Ketrick grinned, and the red blood outlined his chiseled white teeth. Ketrick pursed his lips and steepled his bony hands together. "The police returned the knife to me once the inquiry into poor Rocky's death was over with. But don't worry. I cleaned all of her blood off the knife before I displayed it. I wouldn't want to dishonor the dead. See you later, alligator."

Ketrick quietly closed the door, and Steel lost control, running dizzily across the yard to fall in the bayou. He swam away from the castle and away from the hideous beast who lived there, toward the brush, toward the less frightening prospect of hungry alligators, rushing onto the shore, tearing through the bushes and shrubs, briars and vines ripping at his flesh until lungs almost bursting, he collapsed against his car, fumbled in his pockets, and in a blind panic drove away from this most private hell.

[Chapter 16]

STEEL'S CELL PHONE warbled and pulled him out of his stupor. He blinked and glanced around. Water surrounded him, and he realized he was on the long bridge over Cross Lake. He did not remember the drive from the bait shop. Pulling across the grassy medium at the end of the bridge to the opposite side of the highway, he headed back across the bridge toward Lakeside. He answered the cell phone, and blood ran down his arm.

"Hello, my friend. How is the search going?" Cephas's voice was very calm.

"Ketrick was there when I was born," Steel said hoarsely. "He knew my mother and father, Cephas."

Cephas was silent for a moment and then said, "Jonathan, this is getting very confusing."

"Cephas, he had the knife! He admitted to knowing Braxton. He called him his nephew. He knew about the murders."

Steel listened to Cephas breathing on the other end of the phone. "Jonathan, this has just gotten very dangerous for you. There are supernatural forces at work here that have conspired to bring you and this Ketrick together. I fear for your safety.

Walk away from the church. Walk away from the job. If you do not, you may die."

Steel glanced around at the passing countryside, so placid and still in the summer day. It all seemed so normal. "Cephas, you know I can't walk away from this. I have to know about my past. If Ketrick is telling the truth, he can tell me who I am."

"But do you want to learn such a thing from this fiend?" Cephas asked. "At what cost?"

"I don't have much choice. Lucas told him Ketrick's destiny was to kill me."

"Lucas?"

"Some kind of bizarre creature, Cephas," Steel said.

"He may be the repository of the demons. A placeholder, if you will. Who knows, Jonathan?" Cephas said.

"He was there in Mexico with Ketrick the day I was born. He gave me his memories."

"Ah, that is interesting," Cephas said. "Remember that Satan is the father of lies. Why would you believe this man?"

Steel blinked and tried to clear his thoughts. "Ketrick was angry about something Lucas revealed. I think what I saw was the truth."

"Jonathan"—Cephas's voice took on a guarded tone—"do not become a vigilante. Let the legal system handle Ketrick. Do not take matters into your own hands. If it is true that Ketrick and Braxton knew each other, then Ketrick is most likely in league with the demon of the spiral eye. This demon was drawn to this area by forces beyond our comprehension. There must be some plan, Jonathan. And I fear your pastor friend is somehow involved."

Steel felt his heart rate slow. "Cephas, I came here to take out that demon. Nothing is going to stand in my way."

"Very well, Jonathan. I'll look for what I can find on Mr. Ketrick and Lucas. If I find something, I'll call you immediately. So go with God, my friend. Remember to whom you owe your allegiance as you face these forces of darkness. Do not let the enemy deceive you, for he will do everything to stop you."

"I will, Cephas." Steel ended the phone call as he passed through Lakeside and drove to the church. He pulled up in front of the missionary house. Liz Washington was talking with Josh. The young man nodded in Steel's direction and headed into the house. Steel climbed out of the car, and Liz intercepted him.

"Jonathan, come with me. I've made a startling discovery." Liz's amber eyes glowed with excitement, and she took his good hand in hers and pulled him down the street. Before he could protest, she started up the hill toward the church.

Steel's scratches and cuts stung from his sweat as Liz led him around the church and into the field behind. Shoulder-high sunflowers towered around them. Liz pushed the tall flowers aside with her lion stick and motioned excitedly toward the back of the property. Steel saw a chain-link fence running along the bluff overlooking the bayou. Liz squeezed through a gap in the wire and held it open with her lion stick as Steel followed. The bayou churned twenty feet below him, feeding water to the south where it emptied into the Red River.

"What do you see, Jonathan?" Liz asked in her best professorial tones. She rested her hand on her lion stick and smiled at him.

"Redcross Bayou. A bluff. A levee." He shrugged. "What am I missing?"

"Turn around."

Steel turned and looked back toward the church. The hill was highest at the bluff, and from their vantage point he could see over the office annex and right down Main Street. The land surrounding Lakeside undulated in greens and browns. Trees swayed in the breeze. In the far distance he could even see Cross Lake gleaming in the sunlight just as the Founding Fathers had promised. It was a breathtaking view for a land as flat and featureless as Louisiana. "If Ketrick wants to build condos here, the tenants will have a nice view."

Liz pointed the stick toward Main Street. "That's the point. Now, you tell me. Why would you have such an elevated view in a land that is so flat? Think, Jonathan."

Steel wiped his bloody hand across his brow. "I'm sorry, Liz. I'm so tired I can't play professor and student."

Liz nodded, and her features softened. "Have you ever heard of Cahokia?"

Something tickled in the back of his mind. "Cahokia? Not really."

Liz grabbed his arm in excitement. "It was one of the best-known mound civilizations in North America. Around A.D. 900 the citizens of Cahokia built a flat-topped, four-sided pyramid on the Illinois side of the Mississippi River. They built one of the first cities known in America. Their culture thrived on agriculture and river trade, Jonathan. Right here in northeastern Louisiana is another mound site, Poverty Point. The inhabitants were called the mound builders. They were natives who built their pyramids out of soil."

"So, the church is built on an old mound?"

"Yes! An undiscovered mound of this size is a rare find, Jonathan. Imagine, a thousand years ago a culture flourished right here on Redcross Bayou. Look over here." She led him along the bluff to where the sheer wall took on a more gradual slope down to the water. Liz leaned out over the precipice and with her lion stick pushed at weeds and vines coursing down to the churning waters. She was oblivious to the danger. Her face was alive with excitement and discovery. With the stick, she lifted a huge expanse of vines and uncovered an undulating horizontal series of ridges in the bluff wall.

"See, stairs cut into the bluff wall and reinforced with limestone. They had a harbor down on the bayou and carried on trade. An entire civilization of farmers lived around this huge mound." Liz stood up, and sweat glistened on her brown skin. "I checked toward the south, and there is a drainage culvert cut through the mound to carry rainwater into the bayou. I bet the engineering firm found artifacts from the mound builders and never reported it. Typical behavior. If they'd reported it, the state would've halted the project. No work, no money. Some ditch digger probably sold the artifacts online."

Steel listened to Liz drone on as a thought tickled at the back of his mind. Suddenly he started back toward the church. Liz followed until Steel stopped in the middle of the sunflower field and looked all around him. His mind went back to the picture of the pyramid in Ketrick's office, the proposed riverboat casino and hotel. It all fell into place.

"What is it, Jonathan?" Liz asked.

"I know what Ketrick is up to. He's not building condos. He's building a casino."

Claire looked up from her laptop as Liz and Steel walked in. She took one look at Steel's hand. "What happened to you?"

Steel glanced down at his hand. "I cut my hand."

Claire shook her head and grabbed him by the arm and led him into the kitchen. She took his bloody hand and ran cold water over it. "How did you do this?"

"Ketrick," Steel mumbled.

"Liz, look in my backpack. I have a first aid kit."

She dried off Steel's hand and brought him to the kitchen table. "Sit," she commanded.

Steel settled in a chair. Liz handed her the first aid kit, and she pulled out hydrogen peroxide in a small bottle and poured it over the cut. It bubbled but Steel didn't even flinch. She dried it and put antibiotic cream on it.

"Josh said he had a friend," Steel said.

"Yeah, some girl he met. Teenagers!" Steel stood up, and Claire held on to his hand. "Whoa, let me wrap your hand."

Steel looked at her, and his thoughts were obviously far away. "I have to talk to Josh about Summer."

Claire hurriedly wrapped his hand. "What?"

Steel pulled his hand out of her grasp. "Summer is his friend's name. Is he in his bedroom?"

"Yeah. You're welcome," Claire said.

Steel paused and looked back at her. "Sorry. Thank you." He disappeared down the hall.

Josh missed his phone. He wanted to text Ila because he was suddenly missing her. He sat on his bed in the missionary house and longed for something, a tablet, a laptop, anything. He had only brought the one game for his handheld, and he was bored with it.

"What are you doing?"

He turned and saw Summer standing in the door to his room. She closed the door behind her.

"How did you…"

"I missed you. I've been waiting all night and day, and you didn't come back." She sat on the bed next to him and ran her fingers through her hair. The smell of old flowers filled the room, and Josh sneezed.

"Listen, I have a girlfriend in Dallas. I miss her. No offense, Summer. It's just that..."

"And what will happen when that man and your mother get together? Think she'll go back to Dallas? Forget Ila. Forget Dallas. Soon you'll be on your own," Summer said.

Josh blinked in confusion. Where had he heard that before? Someone else had said the same thing. "But he and I are getting along. He's kinda creepy but kinda cool."

"He'll be a terrible stepfather." Summer played with a strand of her hair. "He'll probably send you off to boarding school and make you take out all of your piercings."

"Stepfather? Wait a minute!" Josh touched his lip bead and frowned. "I don't know..."

Summer leaned forward, and he smelled cloves on her breath as she pressed her dry lips against his. "I'll be waiting in the church for you. Later. Think about it. Stay here with me."

Josh closed his eyes and sneezed, and when he opened them, Steel stood in the door. Where had Summer gone?

"We need to talk," Steel said.

Josh looked around the room for Summer. "What about?"

"You said you had made friends with a girl? Was her name Summer?"

"Yeah." Josh sat up. "What about her?"

"You need to stay away from her. She's trouble," Steel said.

Josh watched a muscle twitch in Steel's cheek. "Dude, did you just beat the stew out of someone?" He pointed to Steel's bandaged hand.

"No. Just stay away from Summer. You may be in danger."

Something flared hot and sudden in Josh. "So, are you ordering me as my boss or as my potential stepfather?"

Steel's mouth fell open. "What?"

"Don't deny it. I see the way my mother clings to you. I see how she looks at you. And you've got to be lonely. Right? Well, don't try to take my father's place. Maybe Vivian was right after all."

Steel looked like he had been hit with a bat. He shot across the room and grabbed Josh by the shoulders and lifted him off the bed. "Vivian? Where did you meet Vivian?"

Josh squirmed in the man's painful grasp. "Hey, let me go!"

Steel dropped him onto the bed, and Josh rubbed his shoulders. "I don't know why I said that. I don't know a Vivian." He shook his head trying to clear the confusion. "Why did I say that?"

Steel grabbed him by the chin and roughly pulled his face around so his bright, turquoise eyes burrowed into his. "Don't go near Vivian or Summer. Understand? They're dangerous! They're both working with Ketrick."

Josh jerked his chin out of Steel's grasp. "Dude! So much for me thinking you're cool. You're just crazy." He shoved past him, out the door, and down the hall to the kitchen.

Steel paused in the hallway. How had Josh spoken with Vivian? Someone had planted this crazy idea in Josh's head about him and Claire… "No!" he said. He didn't need love. He looked up and realized he was talking to his reflection in the mirror. His hair was sweaty and filled with twigs. His face was scratched in a dozen places. He leaned over the dresser toward his reflection. *Listen up, Steel,* he thought. *If you fall in love, the enemy will use that person to get to you. Don't do it!*

Steel stepped into the living room. Liz had set up her laptop with a small video projector and had arranged her findings in a multimedia presentation. Claire had printed out a handout with a summary of the findings of her measurements on her portable printer. She set up an easel with a whiteboard in the corner.

Something moved in the corner of Steel's vision. He glanced back down the hall and thought he saw something sinuous and scaly move into the shadows. He rubbed at his tired eyes and flicked on the light in the hallway. It was empty.

"Something wrong?" Claire said.

Steel looked back at her. "Just a little edgy, that's all. I saw a roach. I'm going to go shower and change clothes. Let's plan on going over your findings around five. I need a moment." He walked out the door before they could protest.

[Chapter 17]

STEEL SHOWERED AND redressed his wound. He sat still and quiet for almost three hours, letting his mind sift through the information he had acquired. At 5:00 p.m. he picked up his laptop and walked around the church and up onto the front porch of the missionary house. Something scuttled away from the front door, probably a roach. He opened the door and stepped in. Liz had made sandwiches, and he grabbed one and wolfed it down. He didn't even taste it.

Liz and Claire sat on the couch. Parker sat still and silent in his chair with an old-fashioned briefcase in his lap. Josh was sitting on the other side of the dining room table in the shadows, sullen and quiet. "Care to join us, Josh? You are a part of the team, remember?" Steel said. He picked up a bottle of water.

"Yeah, dude, I remember. I'm fine right here."

Steel fought back a nasty retort and opened the laptop he had brought from his RV. He started up a video chat program. "Cephas, are you there?"

The screen sprang to life, and the woolly-headed image of the old man filled the screen. He smiled and massaged his huge mustache. "I'm here, my friend. Do I see the lovely Dr. Liz Washington across the room?"

Liz raised an eyebrow and chuckled. "Still a charmer, you old coot. It's been a while."

"Yes, dear, it has. Hello, Claire."

Claire smiled. "Nice to see you, Uncle Cephas. It has been a long time."

"Too long. And where is my great-great-nephew?"

Steel turned the laptop to face Josh. "Pouting."

Josh bristled at the remark. "Hey, Uncle Cephas."

"You've grown, young man. You look like your father."

Josh just shrugged and leaned back in his chair and crossed his arms. Steel placed the laptop on the end of the table facing away from Josh.

"So what is this I hear about a giant scorpion?" Cephas asked.

Steel nodded. He recounted the events leading up to their meeting but omitted sharing the details of his encounter with Ketrick with the rest of the group. Cephas frowned. "This is getting quite serious, Jonathan. Let's get on with the meeting."

Liz spoke softly. "My old friend, I think we ought to pray before we get started. Something tells me we're going to need all the help we can get."

Steel started to speak and closed his mouth. The simple act of prayer had never entered his mind. Always he had faced these circumstances with brute force. But he realized he was more tired than at any other time in the last two years. He nodded. "You're right, Liz."

Liz closed her eyes. "Father God, Creator of all the universe, we ask you to watch over us and give us the power to defeat this enemy. Give us the strength to help free Thomas and Emily and their church from this evil. You alone can do this. Amen."

Steel nodded toward Claire. "Claire, let's hear from you first."

Claire turned to her laptop. She brought up a presentation, projected onto the white wall at the far end of the den.

"As Jonathan suspected, the process in the baptistery is an extra-dimensional phenomenon." She pressed a key on the laptop, and a video loop showed on the wall, the energies in the baptistery flowing, swirling, and coalescing hypnotically. "If you try to focus on the energy pool, your mind begins to feel fuzzy, disoriented. We can't possibly sense what is actually before us. Our three-dimensional minds cannot grasp these other dimensions. But"—she brought up another slide—"my computer can reconstruct what we would see if we could see other dimensions." A video loop showed a rotating volume of space filled with multicolored stars. In the center of the image, a swirling whirlpool of black spun, gases and light streaming into it from the edges of the image.

"What is that thing in the middle?" Liz leaned forward as she lowered her glasses over her eyes.

"A singularity," Claire answered. "There is a black hole in the baptistery."

"Wait a minute," Parker protested. "You're losing me. How can a black hole possibly be in my church?"

"Extra-dimensional space," Claire said.

Parker's face collapsed into confusion. "You're losing me."

Claire reached into her backpack and took out a small, plastic item shaped like a champagne bottle. "This is a popper." She held it up and tugged on a white thread. With a loud snap, the contents exploded and confetti shot into the air. "Now, notice that when I pulled the string, the contents of this popper expanded away and slowed down as gravity prevailed. And notice how the contents moved from a very confined space to fill up a much larger space."

She placed the spent popper on the table beside her. "Stephen

Hawking established that when the universe came into existence, our three dimensions of length, width, and height came into being, along with a fourth dimension of time.

"Now, if you think very carefully about my role in pulling the string, you realize I had to exist before and outside of the popper." She picked up the popper. "We are outside the popper. We existed before the popper. We created the popper."

Parker nodded. "I get it. God and His angels exist outside our dimensions because they existed before the universe began."

"Yes!" Claire smiled. "And those dimensions are there, only we can't see them. But God and His angels, as well as the demons, have access to those dimensions as well as our own. But these demons cannot have access to our fourth dimension of time. Otherwise, they would know the future." She pointed to her laptop. "Now, you see why we can't look at what is going on in the baptistery and comprehend it. It lies outside our four dimensions of space-time. Somehow, in a supernatural fashion, the process in the baptistery has tapped into another brane."

"Brain?" Parker asked.

"Sorry, I'm getting into my area of particle physics. Imagine a sheet of paper, and imagine that the surface of that sheet of paper is our universe. It's like our universe exists on a membrane, and the theory is there are other branes out there with laws of physics totally different from ours. The key is that these branes might intersect, and where they intersect, we might be able to access those other dimensions. My theory is that the angels and demons can cross these branes with ease, as can God, since He made them. I believe we have had some confirmation for the ability to reach these other dimensions. Recent research into near-death experiences shows that our consciousness can exist even if our brains are inactive. That's this *brain*." She tapped her head. "In other words, we have a nonlocal consciousness that is somehow attached to a source of energy. I believe this describes our souls, and our souls are attached to the spiritual dimensions of God and His angels."

"Why does the energy pool exist?" Steel interrupted her.

"I believe the pool exists as a source of extra-dimensional energy. I believe the enemy is using the energy field to create the phenomena we see in the sanctuary."

Steel rubbed his chin and studied the rotating image of the energy field. "What can we do to shut it down?"

Claire gestured to the graphs. "If we were to try to interact with the energy field in any way, we might have catastrophic results. A supernatural containment field surrounds the space within. Without the field surrounding it, the black hole would decimate life for an unknown distance from the source." Claire turned back to Steel. "Possibly even the entire planet.

"We're dealing with something we can't control, much less understand." Claire looked toward Parker and Liz. "Now, you see why we must understand the multi-dimensional nature of the universe, the multi-dimensional nature of God, and the limited multi-dimensional nature of the angels and demons." Her gaze turned to the image of the black hole. "Sometimes I wish I could just make that right hand turn into another dimension. Then I could do something about this energy field. If the containment field were to collapse and allow this microscopic black hole into our space, it could end life for an unknown distance."

Josh shook his head and glanced at his mother. "Dude, what I don't understand is if these demons could destroy the planet by releasing the energy field, why don't they just get it over with? Why go to all this trouble with snakes and spiders?"

Cephas cleared his throat, and Steel looked back at his laptop. "Good question. You know the answer. In the Book of

Job, Satan had to ask permission of God before he could hurt Job. The demons are able to do only so much without God stopping them."

"You mean God is letting all this happen?" Josh asked.

"He could stop it any time, Josh," Cephas said. "But God allows evil to enter our lives for a reason. It serves a purpose we can't see just now."

Steel saw empty eyes and a face covered with blood. "Which brings us to the subject of angels and demons. Cephas?"

"According to the Scriptures, Lucifer, the second most powerful being to God, rebelled, and he and one-third of the angels were cast out of heaven. Since then, the forces of darkness have ruled Earth." Cephas leaned into his camera. "Make no mistake, demons exist. Satan is real. As real as the air we breathe. As real as the energy field in the baptistery. Society would have you discount his existence as fictional, the subject of horror novels and movies. But demons are real, seductive, and nasty. They organize human immorality and wickedness. They can cause illnesses and many forms of human suffering. Demons instigate idolatry and false religions. They can be territorial and exercise influence over world governments. But their most vile activity is possessing the bodies of living humans. They do have their limits. They are not omniscient or omnipresent. Although they have access to these extra dimensions Claire spoke of, they can't be two places at once. And they can't see the future. They can possess animals, associate themselves with inanimate objects, and exercise a great deal of control over the individual. And a person can have several demons inside."

"So, is Reverend Parker going to cast out the demons?" Josh asked.

Parker looked up at Steel and swallowed. He was doing a bad job of hiding his nervousness. "I'm not sure I could handle facing these demons when the time comes, but I'm beginning to understand them. And understanding is the first step in overcoming. I believe someone who is right with God and pure of heart in righteous power can command a demon to leave a nonbeliever."

Steel chose his words carefully. "Then we may be in trouble, Parker."

"Wait a minute! All of these problems showed up with Ketrick. He's the villain here, not me!" Parker said.

"You changed something. What was it? Sheriff Sweeney said something about starting a new kind of worship service." Steel sat on the arm of his chair.

"Yeah, well, you'd think I had just invited demons to sing in our choir!" Parker warmed up to the subject. "I felt like God wanted me to move us into a new and more relevant period of this church's sphere of influence. Somehow all of that got lost in the controversy over the possible move to a new location."

"You've got some fundamental challenges to your leadership. Nothing surprising. You're trying to take a different approach to change the way you do church," Steel said. "But the sense I get from this community is the church would never be missed. It's lost its relevance. It's a dying institution about to be replaced by Ketrick's casino. Part of this attack by the enemy could be to stop you from following this new path of leadership. But Thomas, the heart of your church is not in that building up there. The heart of your ministry is within you and within the people of your church. If the church is failing, you can't blame Ketrick. You are the leader."

Parker mulled over the words and crossed his arms. "I'm not to blame."

"What's in the briefcase?"

Parker put his hands over the briefcase. "Nothing."

Steel knelt in front of Parker until his eyes were level with the man's glasses. "You brought a briefcase full of nothing to this meeting? Is that all you have to offer to get your church and your people back? Nothing?"

Conflict warred on Parker's face, and he finally sighed. He popped the latches on the briefcase and opened it. He lifted out a handful of papers. "These are photocopies of something." He handed them to Steel.

Steel stood up and walked over to the laptop. The top sheet showed the cover of a leather-bound book. He couldn't make out the strange lettering. The next few sheets were copies of pages from the book. He held them up for Cephas to see. "What is this?"

"I found this book. It was an ancient text. Emily thought it was a way to find money to pay for our bills."

"Hold it closer, Jonathan," Cephas said as he pulled on his reading glasses.

Liz stood up and came over to read the papers. "It looks like a box."

Parker nodded. "It is was some kind of chest hidden beneath the…"

"The altar of the spiral eye," Liz said. She gasped and sat at the table next to Josh.

"Did you say spiral eye?" Steel asked.

"Let him finish," Liz whispered.

"The text says there is an altar beneath the mound of the red cross. And the book is written by one of the original founders of our church."

Steel handed the sheets of paper to Liz. "Earlier you said a young woman tried to blackmail you. Is her name Summer?"

Parker gasped. "How do you know?"

"Tell me everything."

"I did," Parker said.

Steel bolted up and moved quickly to Parker's chair. He reached down, grabbed the man by the shoulders, and lifted him bodily out of the chair. He shoved his face close to Parker's. "I am getting sick and tired of your lies, Parker. You want my help, you tell me everything. Now!"

Parker started shaking, and tears rolled down his cheeks. "She came for money from the benevolence fund. And then, while we were sitting in my office, she starts telling me she has this child, a toddler. She said he was my son, and she was going to tell my church all about us. But there was no 'us'! She was lying! I confronted her, and she admitted it. So she left. I have always had a policy of making a digital recording of meetings with members for my own protection. I locked it in my safe in case she started something." Parker started shaking. "She did. And then Ketrick came to the meeting. And literally all hell broke loose in the church. She started spreading rumors and my members left and I couldn't get to the office because of the things in the sanctuary and—"

Steel put a hand on Parker's shoulder. "Calm down."

Snot streamed from Parker's nose, and Liz handed him a tissue. He wiped his face and picked up the briefcase from the floor. He hugged it to his chest as if it were a life jacket and settled back into his chair. "She said she would stay in the nursery until I gave her the money. I made it to my office and the recordings were gone. The book was in its place. She said to find the chest and the crosses, and I could have the recordings back."

Liz handed Steel a page. A crude hand-drawn image of two crosses was on the page encrusted with jewels. "Crosses?"

"Covered with jewels and made from gold. Worth a

fortune. It would have been the answer to our prayers," Parker whispered.

"Do you think this is why Ketrick wanted the church?"

"Yes!" Parker said.

"Liz, what do you think of this?" Cephas asked from the laptop screen.

Liz stood up and went back to her laptop. "Honey, I've got the goods." She stood up and tapped on her laptop. She brought up an image of the writings from the sanctuary ceiling. "Let me say that these writings come from a mixture of ancient styles. As you can see, the writings begin here in the center of the sanctuary ceiling and wind outward in a spiral toward the periphery. Time moves from the start of the swirl to the end of the story here on the periphery."

The next image showed a two-dimensional drawing of a man carrying a sack filled with tools. "The first drawing is a glyph dating back to the time of the Incas and Aztecs, I'd say around 1500. Neither of these advanced races had a written language. In fact, the Incas had even less than these pictures. They used a knotted set of strings called a quipu to keep track of transactions."

Liz pointed to the image of the man with her lion stick. "What you see is, in fact, a glyph from an Aztec codex, as it was called." She went to the next picture that showed an image from a textbook of a series of hand-drawn pictures on leather pages joined together like an accordion. "This is the most famous codex, the Florentine Codex written by surviving Aztecs after Cortez wiped out their civilization. The codex contained pictographs and symbols representing numbers and concepts. For instance, see this man with a bird looking out of his feathered headdress? This glyph stands for Huitzilopochtli, the warrior god of the Aztecs."

Liz turned back to her laptop, and her hair was discolored by the images of the codex. "I have spent long hours at the library today looking back at the history of this place. Indians lived here in the early part of the 1500s. The town of Shreveport was an Indian village called Chaguate. Mound dwellers, agricultural Indians who built these great mounds, lived throughout the region, particularly along the Mississippi. In fact, some have called the Mississippi and these cultures the North American Nile."

Liz brought up the next image. It showed a huge, flattened mound of earth as immense as a football field. On the top of the largest mound and several of the adjacent smaller mounds sat thatched huts. Indians carrying sacks of corn and brandishing spears moved through the empty avenues among the mounds. "These civilizations began around A.D. 800. I believe the hill on which the church sits is an undiscovered mound belonging to a group of Indians who lived along Redcross Bayou."

"The mound of the red cross," Parker whispered.

"What happened to the mound dwellers?" Claire asked.

"They suffered and died a horrible death." Josh stood up and crossed to the window. "I helped with the research. The Spanish came through the south in 1540, and by 1600 the mound dwellers had all died out from their diseases. So much for progress."

Liz brought up the next image, and her eyes filled with passion. "The puzzling thing about the drawings on the ceiling is that they contain several different types of communication. They're a mixture of codex drawings, Inca symbols, and Spanish. In fact, in places there is even a little Latin. Why would such a thing exist? Because the author of our codex has a story to tell."

Liz turned away from the wall, and the image of the man

with a sack on his back played across her features. "Someone or something has conspired to bring us all to this place at this time for some purpose. And to understand how these writings and the altar fit together, I will now tell you the story of Jabo Suyu, a man who left his home to journey here to the land of the mound dwellers. I will tell you of this chest and the crosses within. I've learned his story from the codex, and I hope I can do it justice. I'll tell his story in the oral tradition of his time. I have added to the story to give you some frame of reference, but the facts I present are accurate based on the codex." Liz paused. "Jabo Suyu was a good man and deserves our attention and respect." She lifted her lion stick into the light of the projector. Pointing to the picture of the man carrying the sack of tools she began to tell his story.

[Chapter 18]

My name is Jabo Suyu. I was born to an ayllu, or family unit, and learned the trade of stonemason. As an Inca, working with stones was very important. I learned to build walls, bridges, and altars. I am gifted by my God, Viracocha. I could see patterns. I could see the patterns in the rock and stone. I could make the patterns in the walls and bridges. My father, Chopu, said God had smiled on me and I was destined for great works.

Destiny arrived in the form of a man named Felipillo. It was a name given to him by the white men who had come from across the sea. Felipillo found me at my ayllu and learned of my gift. He said I would come with him and learn the language of the white men from across the sea and I would be swift of feet in delivering messages. I did not want to go. I wanted to stay with my father and mother and sisters and work on my stones. But father let me take my tools in a wool sack and told me going was part of Viracocha's plan.

Felipillo introduced me to the white men. Pizarro was their leader. I did not like him. He had a false heart and cared only for gold. I also met Friar Valverde. He told me of his God, who I believe is also Viracocha. But I did not think Valverde listened to his God. He had a false heart. In only days I could hear the pattern of their language just as a quipucamayo can read the numbers stored in the quipu. I also discovered the Christians, as they call themselves, had their own quipu, lines on fabric they call paper. They had huge collections of their writings. I did not tell Felipillo, but I could understand the pattern of their writing. I learned to see the pattern in the words I heard, and I understood the pattern in the written words. Soon I learned to read.

Felipillo told me I was a fast learner and I was a fast runner. I had seen eighteen summers, and God had blessed me with swift feet. I'll tell you now of how I met our great king, Atahualpa. Pizarro had agreed to meet Atahualpa in his royal palace at Caxamarca. I was sent ahead to deliver the message the Christians were on their way. Atahualpa received me with dignity. I was honored to kneel in his presence. As I stood to the side, the advance of one of Pizarro's men frightened me. He sat astride the great llama they call a horse. The sight of this man in his metal jacket and metal helmet astride the huge creature drove my heart into my throat. He rode toward Atahualpa's litter, the horse's feet clattering on our stone road, and he stopped very close to the king—so quickly the horse's spit showered the king's tunic and headdress.

Atahualpa did not flinch. The man was impressed and got down off of his great animal. He said his name was Don Hernando DeSoto. I could see the pattern in his heart. He was a man with a true heart. He had no desire for the gold. DeSoto introduced Pizarro as his leader.

Atahualpa received Pizarro in silence, Felipillo delivering a message in our language, Quechua. And then, the friar Valverde, his brown robe flapping in the breeze, spoke with fervor in his own language. I could understand most of it. He told of the great and only God, Creator of all, who humbled Himself and became a mere man. Jesus Christ was His name, and He dwelt among man until man rejected Him and killed Him on a cross. I could not understand this cross, but I could see the pattern and how a man could be nailed to it. But wait! Jesus Christ did not stay in His tomb! He came back to life and lifted into heaven to join His father. But Jesus and His Father were one along with His Spirit who came to live within us. I could tell Atahualpa could not see this. But I could. I could see the pattern of how one could be three and three could be one. Is not a man son, father, and husband? And yet he is one?

But Atahualpa could not see this pattern. Valverde spoke of a man who was as high and mighty as Jesus and called him the pope. I could not see how this could fit into the pattern. But Valverde had a false heart. Perhaps he did not represent the truth about Jesus Christ. Perhaps he had evil reasons for what he said. Atahualpa was confused by this talk of the pope. He took the quipu of Valverde called the Bible and hurled it on the ground.

Pizarro waved a white scarf in the air, and madness fell upon us. The Christians killed thousands in the streets, their faces filled with the same madness their Jesus must have seen in the faces of His killers. Felipillo took me to safety. Later I learned that DeSoto and Pizarro saved Atahualpa and took him prisoner. That evening they dined together in the palace while my brothers' corpses rotted in the streets. Perhaps these Christians did not worship the one true God I knew. Or perhaps they had betrayed their own Christ after whom they were named.

In the weeks that followed, I was assigned to assist DeSoto as a translator. Felipillo was too busy negotiating with Atahualpa, who had agreed to have our people bring a ransom of gold enough to fill a large room for his release. It was while working with DeSoto that I met Phillip. Phillip was a young man who was a helper to Valverde. He was my age and quite innocent of the bloodshed his Christians had perpetrated on my people. At night, when I was alone with Phillip in the stone houses of Caxamarca, we would speak of God and Jesus and my ideas of Viracocha. I told him of our great king Pachacuti, who abolished worship of Inti, the sun god, when he decided only Viracocha, the creator, deserved our worship.

Phillip, at first, was angry I would suggest our two Gods might be the same. But I told him of our story of the great flood and how Viracocha commanded a man and woman to build a ship and survive the great flood. Phillip told me of his own story of the flood. Might not the same man and woman worshiping the same God have given birth to both of our peoples? I asked him. He could not answer. But I could see the pattern. I wanted more than anything to be able to read his Bible. But I learned it was in another language from the Spanish. It was in an old language called Latin, which only the priests could speak. If God gave the Bible to the people, then why keep it in a dead language? I asked? Phillip could not answer.

One night, weeks after the slaughter, God sent an angel to me in a dream. He told me in the dream that God had a mission for me. I must go north, and there I would find my answers. I would see the pattern of God unfolding. The next day I told Phillip. He smiled because he had just learned that he was to go with DeSoto north to Huamachuco to see if that area was at peace. He convinced DeSoto to bring me along as an interpreter.

While on the way to Huamachuco, Phillip shared a secret with me. Since we had begun to talk about God and the Latin Bible, Phillip had decided to write some of the Bible in Spanish. I know he did this out of friendship to me as I now had learned the pattern of the Spanish words and could read. As we traveled northward, he spent the evenings writing parts of his Bible in a small leather journal for me.

At Huamachuco, DeSoto told me of another white man named Cortez who had come ashore far north through the jungles in a land where the Aztecs lived. I had never heard of these Aztecs. But he wanted me to go north with a small group of men and help with my translation skills. He told me I was smart and a fast learner.

The next morning, Phillip and I, accompanied by five of DeSoto's men, left for the journey northward. After many weeks we came to one of the Christian's settlements with great tents of cloth and many horses. There I boarded one of their ships, and we went to sea. I had never sailed on such a ship on the great ocean and was sick for many days. Weeks passed, and Phillip continued his translation of the Bible.

We arrived on the shore of the great land where the Aztecs lived. Phillip took me over land to their city, Tenochtitlan. I could imagine how grand it must have been before the Spanish conquered the people. Even with many of their temples and buildings destroyed, I could see the pattern of their handiwork. I have never seen such stonework! The great stone pyramids they had built were beyond my comprehension. The meager tools I carried in my stone mason pack seemed far too small to ever compare to these works. But as I studied the seams and the construction of the buildings that remained, I realized these people were ambitious but did not pay much attention to details. Their pyramids would indeed crumble. In only a few summers, the Spanish could bring down their buildings, and the Aztecs' work would be no more. But the houses and walls I had helped build far up in the mountains in Machu Picchu would last for centuries. It is because I saw how the stone would fit the pattern of the land and mountain and the skies. These pyramids were an outrage against the land and sky.

The Christians welcomed Phillip and were amazed at my appearance, at my wool tunic and pants and my wool cap. Here, in the land of the Aztecs, I did not need warm clothing. I was shown their writings, called a codex. They were actually simple to understand, each picture meant to bring to life a memory for the storyteller. Phillip was surprised at how easily I could understand the codex. But he could not see the pattern.

As I studied the codex, I came to pictures of the Aztec religious ceremonies. I had never seen such horror! On the pale leather, pictures showed priests in brown leather thongs and headbands carrying a prisoner up the long, steep steps to the top of their pyramid. There they made him dance and then stretched him out across a stone altar. In the blink of an eye, the priest had cut open the man's chest and removed his beating heart. The man, eyes still open, was pushed off the altar to tumble down the stairs. I had never seen such brutality. In our culture, in times of crises human sacrifices were made to Inti. But since I did not believe in Inti, I had never attended those ceremonies. Here, the killing was wrong. It did not fit the right pattern. The pictures showed the blood flowing down the steps from the man's open chest. I did not feel sad for these people. I learned that four warriors would cut the limbs from the victim's torso and eat the victim's flesh.

I had never heard of such a thing! They were evil. Perhaps it was good that their evil had come to an end.

Cortez soon left to meet a group of his own people at the sea. These people had come to arrest Cortez and take him back to his country. I accompanied the group over the land and watched in horror as Cortez slaughtered his own people. Cortez was an evil man!

Cortez led us back to the city accompanied by many of the lesser tribes oppressed by the Aztecs. Soon he left us behind, since there were so many that we slowed him down.

That night a group of Aztec warriors attacked the camp in our sleep.

Phillip took me into the surrounding hillsides, fleeing from the battle, and we set off on our horses. I had not ridden the horses much, and soon Phillip left me behind. My horse seemed to have a mind of its own, and I could not control it. I fell from the horse and tumbled down a hillside into the forest. When I awoke, a giant eagle looked down at me. A man's face was in its mouth. I could not understand what I was seeing until I realized the eagle beak was a mask. The man spoke to me in a language I could not comprehend and took me to a smaller city called Zultepac.

These were the Eagle Knights, the band of Aztec warriors who opposed the peaceful cooperation of their own people with the Spanish. They argued among themselves for a while as I tended the cut on my head. Then they saw my pack of stone mason tools. I tried to explain to them in signs that the tools were for making stone houses and bridges. And then I found the journal written by Phillip. He had hidden it in my pack.

I think they had planned to kill me as they kept a dozen prisoners in a cave for their own sacrifices. I was placed with the prisoners, who would have nothing to do with me, a stranger to their land. They looked upon my garments with suspicion and fear. In the morning, one of the Spanish prisoners was led forth to a low-lying pyramid and sacrificed, his beating heart ripped from his chest by the largest of the Eagle knights. I hid in the back of the cave and prayed to God for help. Was this where He wanted me to go? Was this part of the pattern? I could not see it if it was.

The man who conducted the sacrifices was the leader of the Eagle Knights. He had me brought before him. He wore a large headdress of green feathers and the opened eagle beak with his face looking out. A black spiral surrounded his right eye. He spoke to me in a language I could not understand, but he made it clear I was to build for them a stone altar for their sacrifices atop the pyramid. I refused, shaking my head. And then they brought Phillip before me! They had made him a prisoner too. He was barely conscious, and there was a bruise on his head. They made it clear they knew we had been together, and if I did not do as they said, they would kill him.

I found strength in that moment and agreed to make the altar only if they would let Phillip go. An Eagle Knight brought Phillip's horse out of the trees and tied Phillip to it.

Phillip never stirred the entire time, and I feared he was dead until I saw his chest move with his breathing. He never woke up as they led him away.

Two days later after two more sacrifices, the warrior returned and handed me a small book along with the journal. It was Phillip's Latin version of the Bible, and a note was written in the front in Phillip's handwriting. It said, "Go with God."

I built them the altar of stones brought to me from the mountains. It took two weeks, as I wanted to make sure the stones fit together well. I think I was trying to put off completion because I knew what it would be used for. During that time I listened to the warriors speaking to each other. I began to hear the pattern in their speech, and by the end of the second week I understood them.

The head warrior called himself Huitzilopochtli. In time I understood this was the name for their god of war, named after the hummingbird. Huitzilopochtli had an evil heart. I could sense the evil within him of such strength it frightened me. He was no ordinary man. Perhaps the god of war did live within him. But I did not believe Huitzilopochtli was a god. There was only one God.

When the last of the white men had been sacrificed on the new altar, Huitzilopochtli decided it was time to move away from their old homeland. The Spanish were becoming more powerful, and in time, I saw the Aztecs falling beneath their heels even as I knew the Inca had. It was part of a pattern. One night, crouched in the darkness of the cave alone, I practiced speaking their language. I looked up, and Huitzilopochtli stood before me.

"How do you speak my language?" he asked me.

"God has given me the gift of seeing the patterns," I told him in my halting words.

"What else has your God told you?" he asked with his arms crossed over his mighty chest.

"I am destined to go north to a faraway land. There I will complete the pattern of my life."

"Then we will follow your pattern. My god has told me to go north to a land he has not yet touched. There we will find many victims to sacrifice. There we will rebuild this great empire the Christians have conquered."

"Who are you?" I asked. "You are not Huitzilopochtli. You are something more."

He smiled at me, his eyes as black as those of a panther. "I have within me the true god Huitzilopochtli, the demon of the spiral eye. He has had many names. Huitzilopochtli is his latest name. And together we will go to the land of the north, and we will take it in his name. You will go with us. And when we find a new home, you will build us a new altar to our god."

I thought for many weeks of dying, but as I journeyed north along the coast of the great sea with Huitzilopochtli and his warriors, I read the journal and the Bible left to me by

Phillip. I had come to understand much of the old language the Scriptures were written in. I learned of the story of the children of God and their great journey out of a place called Egypt. I learned of the great flood and God's judgment. Then I learned of Jesus Christ. I learned of love and forgiveness. I believed God was testing me. Could I find forgiveness in my heart for these most evil of men?

Along the way we found many small villages, more primitive than the Aztecs or the Inca. I watched in sorrow as they all died, crushed under the cruel hand of Huitzilopochtli. If I could understand their language, I could tell them of the one true God and His Son. But we would never stay long enough to learn their language. I could only show compassion and kindness when the warriors were not looking.

Ten summers after we left the land of the Aztecs, and twelve in all after I was taken from my people, we arrived at Huitzilopochtli's new kingdom. We had followed a river up from the ocean and found a great lake in a warm, fertile land. Along a gentle river we found the mound people. My heart hurt for them, for they were no match for the fierce warriors of Huitzilopochtli. He and his men quickly subdued their village and took their women for themselves, saving the men for their sacrifices. I was instructed to make an altar at the top of their earth pyramid where the chief of the village had lived. But I had no stone.

Huitzilopochtli sent his men up the river to the north, and in two months they returned with such stone as I had not seen. It was dark and filled with strength. And yet it was soft enough to be formed. I saw my end in sight. As soon as I built the altar, they would kill me as a sacrifice. Then I could meet my God.

For two months I carved the stone, carefully honing the edges for a perfect fit. But unknown to Huitzilopochtli, I left a chamber inside where I could hide this codex, this record of my life. Someday, someone will find it and learn of the pattern of my life. I also carved a small cross of the dark stone and found some shiny, colored pebbles to place on it. A white stone for a pure heart. A red stone for the blood of Jesus. And a green stone for the shores of heaven I would soon see. I had completed the altar in the waning months of winter as spring promised to warm the land when the Spanish came.

They appeared out of the east, coming from the great lake, led by a man with dark hair and a great beard. Huitzilopochtli's scouts saw them and told us they had gone to a nearby village where salt was made from brine that boiled out of the earth. Huitzilopochtli had reached a truce with the village as well as with the nearby village of Chaguate in exchange for salt. He did not want to draw the attention of the Spanish, and he was angry they had followed him to his new land. The scouts reported the men were tired and sickly and would be easy to ambush.

That night the scouts brought in two prisoners from the Spanish. One of them was an older man, an Indian scout from the east. The other was a bearded man with long, dirty hair. Huitzilopochtli instructed me to speak to them, as I would understand their language. The older Indian spoke some Spanish, which I had not thought of in so long it took me awhile to remember the patterns. He told us they were heading west in hopes of returning to New Spain, the new name for the land of our people. Huitzilopochtli was joyous the Spanish would be leaving his land and would not return. The other man was so sick he could not speak. That night they sacrificed the Indian scout on the new altar.

The other man was placed in the hut I was a prisoner in. He was weak and hungry, and I tried to feed him. When I looked at his face, I discovered it was Phillip! I cleaned his face and hair and made him eat and drink. In two days he was awake and happy to see me. He told of how he had been released by the Aztecs and had sent me the Bible. How he had tried to convince the soldiers to look for me but they would not. Why should they waste time and effort on me? I was but a lowly Inca, one of the people of their newly conquered lands. Phillip had journeyed back to a land called Cuba and had then accompanied DeSoto on his explorations of a land called Florida. I was surprised to hear that DeSoto had almost returned to find me. I could see the pattern of our lives intertwined. I could see that I had reached the end of my pattern, the fulfillment of my destiny. Phillip told me of their great journey across the country, of the great river and the mound builders to the east. He told me of battles and hunger, of death and struggle. He told me of natives who died in their wake from the sicknesses his men carried from their homeland. He had with him a chest of gold he had taken from traders in Florida, and inside the chest were gold bars and many jewels.

It is now the last night of our lives. Tomorrow Huitzilopochtli will offer both of us as the final sacrifice to his god, the demon of the spiral eye. We will die at midnight under the first new moon of the summer on the altar I have built. Tonight, in secrecy, I will place this codex in the altar in hopes someone may find it. The warriors think I need to make one final adjustment to the stones. Tonight the angel who visited me in my dream in my faraway home of the mountains came and told me God was pleased with my life. I was a part of a great pattern that would reach far into the future and touch people for God. I have just prayed with Phillip. I know that Jesus Christ is my God, the fulfillment of Viracocha's promise to reveal Himself to His faithful. I wear the cross of my Jesus, and Phillip wears a gold cross I have made from the gold and the jewels in the chest. We are both tired. We are both going to our death in peace. For we know that the demon of the spiral eye will be defeated. We have seen the sickness bumps on the Eagle Knights. They will not live much longer. To the future readers of this codex I say, find God's pattern and go with God.

[Chapter 19]

LIZ TOOK A swallow of water from her glass. "Everything mentioned in Jabo's story is historically accurate. DeSoto died in southeastern Arkansas, and his men sunk his body in the Mississippi River. They didn't want the Indians to know he'd died as he had represented himself as a god. His men decided to head southwest, thinking they could enter Mexico, or New Spain as it was called, through Texas. They actually passed right through Shreveport and even visited a village on the northern shore of Cross Lake where the Indians made salt from brine. I believe this is where the warriors captured Phillip and the Indian scout. DeSoto started out with six hundred men. By the time the survivors reached safety, only about one hundred fifty men remained." Liz went to the next slide and pointed to a glyph representing a warrior whose right eye was surrounded by a spiral. His head was adorned with the green-feathered headdress of Huitzilopochtli. "This is the leader of the Aztec warriors. Jabo Suyu wrote his name in Spanish here beneath the glyph. He called himself by the name of his god, which I believe is the demon of the spiral eye. But his real name was Ketricoatl."

Steel felt a chill run down his spine. "Ketrick?"

Liz nodded. "That's right. Ketrick is derived from Ketricoatl. I researched Ketrick's genealogy. He is descended from an ancient Indian heritage. I imagine his ancestors may have been the Aztec warriors, survivors of the disease that decimated Ketricoatl and his warriors. This may be another reason why he's so interested in the church."

Liz brought up another image on the screen. A huge, round stone carried the carved image of a woman with severed limbs and head. The stone was identical to the reproduction Steel had seen in Ketrick's den and in his vision of Mexico City. "This is Coyolxauhqui, the sister of Huitzilopochtli. Legend has it that Coatlicue, the mother of these two, became pregnant after giving birth to the moon and four hundred stars. This followed a vow of chastity, and Coyolxauhqui was so angry she decided to kill her mother and the unborn child. But the unborn child sprang forth from his mother's womb and cut the vengeful Coyolxauhqui into pieces, throwing all but her head down the side of a mountain. Thus was born the god Huitzilopochtli and the ritual of human sacrifices of the Aztecs. What is interesting about this stone is that it was uncovered by workers digging ditches for new electrical cable in Mexico City many years ago."

"I've learned some information about Ketrick. He was an exchange student in Mexico when this stone was found. He was present when they unearthed the stone," Steel said. "Ketrick has a reproduction of this stone hanging in his den. His connection probably goes back to the stone." Steel walked across the room and into the projection of Huitzilopochtli. The spiral played across his features as he turned to Liz. "This is the demon I have been looking for."

"What?" Parker sat back at the table. "I thought you came here to help us."

Steel nodded. "I did. But my desire to help others was prompted by my search for the thirteenth demon."

"What is the thirteenth demon?" Parker asked.

"One and the same with the demon of the spiral eye," Steel said. "Right, Cephas?"

"Jonathan," Cephas said, "when you first came to see me, I was unsure of the significance of the thirteenth demon." He moved out of view of his camera for a second and came back with a large manuscript in his hand. It was ancient and contained a hand-drawn wheel with twelve spokes. "I found this in my archives. Notice there are twelve spokes in this wheel with a Roman numeral for each spoke. And here in the corner is the number for thirteen."

"There is a legend," the man's voice grew quiet, "that on the day Jesus named His twelve disciples, Satan called forth from the world around him his own twelve to thwart the work of God's Son."

"Twelve demons?" Steel asked.

"Yes, but there was one demon so heinous, so foul, so uncontrollable that he demanded a role as one of Satan's apostles. When Satan denied his request, it is said this thirteenth demon left and went out into the rest of the world to reign over man with death and destruction."

Steel drew a deep breath. "Then, this demon of the spiral eye is..."

"The most dangerous demon on the face of the planet, Jonathan, because he cannot be controlled by his own master. You and your team must be very, very careful. This demon has been planning death and destruction for millennia. This is just a tiny part of his greater plan. Who knows what he will do once he accomplishes this one small thing with Ketrick. This is part of some bigger plan, and that makes me more frightened than a giant scorpion could."

They were silent for a moment, and then Josh snickered and stood up. "Dude, you're claiming that the most powerful demon on the face of the planet wants to build a casino?"

Steel stared at Josh. "It's not the casinos I am against, Josh. It's Ketrick's intent. He's enlisted the help of organized crime and a corrupt congressman. He's building this casino for the purpose of ruining people's lives, not just to make money. And I believe he'll take this quiet town to hell with him. He's planning on sacrificing the lives of hardworking people to his god, the thirteenth demon."

"That's it, Cephas!" Steel drew a deep breath. "Jabo's story mentioned the first new moon of the summer, and tomorrow at midnight is the summer solstice. On the night of the first new moon of summer, I believe he plans to consecrate the site with some kind of arcane ceremony in tribute to the thirteenth demon."

"What kind of ceremony?" Parker's voice echoed eerily in the silence that had descended on them.

"A sacrifice on the altar of Huitzilopochtli. It must be somewhere under the church," Cephas said.

"What kind of sacrifice?" Josh whispered.

Steel stared at him and then glanced at Liz. She knew.

"A human sacrifice," Liz whispered. "Like the sacrifices of the Aztecs."

Dead quiet filled the room. "Ketrick wants to turn this entire town into a shrine to his god by shedding innocent blood as a sacrifice to the thirteenth demon."

"Dude, call that FBI buddy of yours," Josh said.

"He's already seen an empty church, Josh. This is beyond legal authority," Steel said.

"But this creep is going to sacrifice somebody! Just call five-oh."

"And tell them what? Hey, the man who owns your town is going to perform a human sacrifice in a chamber beneath the church on an altar built by an Inca?"

"That is why I contacted Jonathan," Parker said. "No one takes this seriously."

Josh stood up. "Then, bro, you should leave."

"What do you mean?"

"All you want is vengeance." Josh stepped closer, driving home his point. "Get away from here, and the thing will go after you."

Steel avoided Josh's accusing eyes. "Maybe you're right, Josh. When I first saw the image of the spiral eye in the church, my only thoughts were for revenge. But as I have gotten to know the people in this room and as I have seen the future of Thomas's church, my motives have changed."

"Number thirteen doesn't know that." Josh pointed to the door. "You need to go."

[Chapter 20]

STEEL NEEDED SOME air, and he stepped out onto the front porch. They were in the eye of the storm, and the eye wall would hit any time. He felt Claire at his side. She reached out and touched his arm. "That took a lot for you to admit," she said.

He gazed off into the darkness. "Yes. I've been fighting a battle over my motives since the day I met you."

"And we have a battle ahead of us, don't we?"

"Yes, Claire, we do."

She took his hand and pulled him across the front porch to a swing. Her touch was so foreign and yet so comforting. He gritted his teeth. He could not allow this to happen.

"Sit down. Relax for a moment. Things will change any minute." Claire sat down and patted the empty space beside her.

Steel sighed and settled in beside her. His leg touched hers.

"Now, you are going to tell me about *her*. Now. Before we go any further in this thing. If you don't share this burden with someone, the enemy will use it against us just as it is using the black hole for its energy. Deprive him of that, Jonathan. Tell me. Now."

Steel studied her gentle face and the haunting passion behind her eyes. He had never told anyone everything. He had shared some of it with Cephas. But everything? Could he do this? Could he trust someone again? Could he withstand the inevitable hurt this would bring?

"It's worth the risk," Claire said as if she had been reading his mind. "Tell me."

Steel drew a deep breath. "April took care of me for weeks after I was discovered on the beach with no memory. And then one day she told me I had to leave. She said she couldn't get too involved with her patients. I hated the idea of leaving her behind." Steel blinked and glanced once at Claire. She was still and silent. "She was all I knew. I had no memories. Just the one of the day I became a Christian. I went to work for her and her father taking care of their beach house. By Christmas her defenses were crumbling, and she was beginning to care about me. They came for the Christmas holidays, she and her father. It was perfect. It was wonderful. I knew that Ross was out there and that the one patient of April's, Braxton, had escaped..."

"Who's Braxton?"

Steel sighed. Should he tell her this? To do so was to step onto that slippery slope. She squeezed his hand, and his heart skipped a beat.

Dr. April Pierce escorted Steel down the hallway leading to the high security rooms. Even through the thick walls and doors Steel could hear loud voices and screams of the insane inside the rooms. April paused in front of a door, and the key dangled in her hand.

"Are you sure you want to do this?"

Steel nodded. "Yes. I'm not going to get you in trouble, am I?"

"My father wouldn't have approved. So I didn't tell him."

Steel sighed. "There is something about Braxton that triggers my lost memories. I don't know why, but I want to find out."

April extended the key toward the door and paused. She glanced up at him. "Is this related to all of his religious talk?"

"Maybe." Steel looked into her eyes and swallowed. "Do you believe in God?"

April pulled back the key and smiled. "Of course. I'm a Christian, Jonathan."

"Do you believe in demons?"

April looked up at him suddenly, a confused look on her face. She frowned. "Demons? We all have our own personal demons . . ."

"I'm talking about real demons. Satan's servants. Fallen angels." Steel locked his gaze on hers.

"Well, historically, many patients with schizophrenia and other forms of psychosis were labeled as demons when, in fact, their illnesses were physical. My father and I have had this discussion. He thinks they're purely figurative. I'm open to the possibility they are real." She paused. "What you're really asking me is if I believe in evil."

Steel nodded. "Yes. Pure, destructive evil."

April looked away for a moment in thought. "If you believe in God, you have to believe He is absolute good. And if there is absolute good, then there must be something that is the absence of that good. Evil. So, yes, Jonathan Steel, I believe evil is real. But so is good. You are a good man. You are not an evil man."

Steel looked at the door leading to the room occupied by Rocky Braxton. "How would you know?"

April placed a hand on his chest. "I am an excellent judge of character."

Steel gently pulled her hand away from his chest. "I'm ready to go in now."

April started to say something but instead reached over and unlocked the door. "I'll be right outside."

The room was dark and smelled of body waste. The walls were lined with quilted fabric, and a metal bed sat to his right. In the far corner a lump of white stirred, and Braxton's eyes glowed in the light from the hallway. Steel reached over and felt a flat wall switch for the light and turned it on. The room flooded with white light, and Braxton screamed and squeezed his eyes shut.

"Turn if off!"

Steel ignored him as the door closed behind him. "Too bad, Braxton. I want to talk."

Braxton whimpered, and Steel watched him unfold from the corner. He wore a straitjacket with his arms buckled behind him. His eyes opened slowly, and the hypnotic swirl around his right eye expanded as he allowed his eyelids to open. "You want to talk? To me?" he whispered.

"You know who I am," Steel said.

"Yes. We know who you are."

"Who is 'we'?"

Braxton relaxed and leaned against the wall and slid his legs out in front of him. "Not yet. It's not time, Johnny boy."

Steel felt the anger pulse within him as it built with each heartbeat. His face grew warm. He opened his mouth, and Braxton interrupted him.

"Feel the heat growing? Feel the anger stoking? It feels good, doesn't it? This little charade you've been playing with your girlfriend isn't really you, Johnny boy." Braxton grinned. "The real you is itching to get out. You know, you almost broke my breastbone. I coughed up blood for three days. That was some kick. Ever wonder where you learned how to do that? Ever wonder why you're so strong?"

Steel felt at a loss for words. For a moment, the pent-up anger began to die. "You goaded me into attacking you so I would remember something?"

"Yes," Braxton said. "We don't like you this way. We want you back the other way."

Steel was confused and shook his head. "So, I'm better off as I am now?"

"Not in my opinion," Braxton said. "But in due time the fury will win out. You will become the man you really are. This silly memory of prayer and change and God . . ." He stopped and spit on the floor. "It's just pretend. You just wanted to impress your new girlfriend. But I understand she's let you go; she's sending you off into the big, bad world. The old Johnny wouldn't have tolerated that. He would have slapped her around a bit and set her straight. But you've turned into a little wimpy, doll-eyed Christian."

Steel felt the anger return. "Don't talk about April that way."

Braxton laughed. "Good. I've hit a nerve. Why is she rejecting you? Did she give you some lame excuse about getting too involved with her patient? Wake up, Johnny boy. She would never fall in love with you if she knew what you were really like. Why don't I tell her?"

Steel felt something snap in him, and he found himself across the room, his hands gripped beneath the buckles of the straitjacket. He held Braxton up in the air above him. "Tell me who I am!" he screamed.

Braxton began to laugh hysterically, and tears rolled down his face. The dark spiral around his right eye moved hypnotically. Steel slammed him against the wall over and over, and the quilted fabric tore, letting dust and stuffing fill the air. Braxton never stopped laughing as blood leaked from the back of his head and pooled at Steel's feet.

Steel never felt the hands on his shoulders pulling him away from Braxton. Never saw through the red haze of rage until he was outside with the door slammed before him. As he gasped for breath, his racing heart slowed. April appeared in front of him.

"Are you out of your mind?" she said. "I trusted you, and you attacked him. Again."

Steel gulped for air. "I'm sorry."

April's face was tight with anger. "It's time for you to leave, Jonathan. I've run out of favors."

She turned and disappeared down the hall. Steel stood alone with the two orderlies who had dragged him out of the room and listened to Braxton's insane laugh continue to taunt him. He had found his demon.

Claire touched his face and turned his eyes toward her. "Tell me how she died. Tell me. Josh told you about Arthur. I would have, if you had asked. Let the pain out."

Steel tried to slow his rapid breathing. He was covered in a sheen of sweat. "I don't have normal memories, Claire. You have a lifetime of them. I only have two years' worth. This one is so bad..."

Claire gripped his arm and pressed her mouth close to his left ear. "Relax. Tell me. It will help."

Boulders tumbled, gathering speed, and the barriers he had erected crumbled and fell away down a swiftly tilting slope into the unknown. "It was Christmas Eve at the beach house..."

April grinned and tore off the paper. Inside was a brass box with a heart on the top. She opened the box and withdrew a gold chain with a tiny cross. "Oh, Jonathan, it's lovely. Will you help me put it on?"

Steel reached around her neck and lifted her hair. He inhaled the fragrance of her hair and clasped the chain at the back of her neck. He looked deeply into her eyes. "There, it's lovely. And so are you."

April cleared her throat and thrust a large box into his hands. "Now, open yours."

Steel tore at the paper and opened the box. Inside was a multicolored sweater. He picked it up and shrugged into it.

"It was my first attempt, you understand." April smiled. One sleeve was six inches longer than the other, and the neck was a little lopsided.

Steel rolled up the sleeve. "April, it's perfect. Thank you."

Steel felt her hands slip into his. "Let's try it out. Why don't we go for a walk?"

The ocean was quiet, a sheet of luminescence reflecting a full moon. In the distance, lightning played along the horizon. Ozone tainted the wind off the water. April pulled her sweater around her and shivered. "Why don't you put your arm around me?"

Steel's heartbeat quickened. He settled his arm around her shoulders. She felt small and warm beneath the sweater.

"What happened to your need for clinical detachment?" he managed.

April turned her eyes up toward him. "When will men ever learn to just be quiet and enjoy the moment?"

Steel smiled, and they walked along the water's edge, silent but comfortable in each other's company. Later on they turned back toward the condo, the moon now obscured by rain clouds moving into the area. Within eyesight of the condo Steel stopped and took her by the shoulders. "April, I can't keep quiet. Surely you can't deny there's something between us. Something bigger than us. It's no coincidence God has brought us together."

April reached up to touch his lips with her hand. "Maybe I'm too stubborn, Jonathan. It's taken me this long to realize how much I miss having you around. You're not my patient anymore. You've become my friend. And now, maybe more." Before he could react, she reached up and kissed him. He pulled back in surprise and studied her eyes. She smiled and pulled him down to her. He kissed her and let her fragrance and presence engulf him. He was giddy when he pushed away.

"Merry Christmas," she whispered.

Steel saw something move out of the corner of his eye. He turned and looked up toward the nearby beach house. A figure stood in the shadows shrouded in a long trench coat.

He squinted, and a hand appeared in the shadows beckoning to him. April turned. "What is it?"

"Franklin Ross."

"The FBI agent?" April's words were snatched away by the wind. Steel clutched her hand, reluctant to allow this perfect evening to slip away from him.

"I knew something would happen to ruin this day."

"We won't let him ruin it, Jonathan. Go talk to him, and I'll go back to the condo."

Steel felt that greasy, uneasy feeling that he was slipping away from the world he so desperately wanted into another world of intrigue and evil and despair. "What if he has some bad news about my past? Maybe I'm happy the way things are."

"Nonsense. You've got a whole world waiting for you locked away in your mind. And whatever it is, Jonathan, it won't change who you've become." April shivered and pulled him close for a quick kiss. "Hurry up. Dinner will be waiting." He would always remember her walking away, hair lustrous, her eyes gleaming as she cast one last look at him, her breath faintly steaming in the cool air. The sudden flash of lightning far out over the water illuminated her perfect face.

Franklin Ross sat on a wicker couch just inside the screened porch of the beach house. It was obvious no one was at home, but that didn't seem to bother him. A cigarette illuminated his face as he inhaled. Steel let the screen door slam behind him.

"You've been watching too many X-Files reruns," Steel said. "What're you doing here, Ross? Why are you following me? Shouldn't you be at home with family?"

Ross stood and walked to the screen. His eyes were turned out to the sea. "I saw the two of you walking on the beach from the public pier. I wasn't here to follow you. But when I saw the two of you together, several pieces of a puzzle fell together." He turned, and his dark eyes glittered in the light of his cigarette. "The question, Mr. Steel, is what are you doing?"

"What am I doing? I'm trying to rebuild my life." His breath quickened and his heart raced. He tried to calm down, but he sensed something dangerous looming on the horizon. "Why are you here?"

Ross dropped the cigarette and ground it out against the concrete. "The local officers contacted me about a suspect here in town."

"Who?"

"Braxton. I've been tracking his movements since he escaped." He lit up another cigarette before the smoke from the crushed cigarette had dissipated.

Steel grabbed the back of a wicker chair in a fierce grip. "How long has he been here?"

"A few weeks." Ross squinted in the cigarette smoke, and his eyes were dark pools of suspicion. "Tell me, Steel, how long have the two of you been working together?"

Steel tried to think and recalled the feeling of paranoia, of being watched. The gun club murder! Braxton had probably been following him. Suddenly the impact of Ross's words sunk in. "What? Working together? What're you talking about?"

"I'm talking about an alliance between you and Braxton to destroy the lives of the Pierces. Cooter recognizes you, and you make sure Braxton takes him out before he can warn Dr. Pierce."

"Wait a minute! I love April."

"I bet you do, Steel." Ross raised an eyebrow. "You promised her to him, didn't you? You promised he could have her as revenge for being locked up in that padded cell."

Rage engulfed Steel, and before he knew it, he threw the wicker chair aside as if it were made of matchsticks. He lashed out with his right first and caught Ross on the left cheek. Ross stumbled back and fell over the wicker couch. He bounced up, gun drawn and pointed at Steel. Blood streamed from his mouth.

"What're you going to do, Ross? Shoot me and try to explain to the police why you were here on someone else's property? You're crazy, Ross." He walked toward Ross, and the gun shifted. Ross wiped at his bloody nose.

"Don't come any closer, Steel. I know what you're capable of."

Steel stopped dead in his tracks. "What? What do you know about me?"

Ross laughed and gestured with the gun. "Now you want to cooperate. Well, it's too late, Steel. I'll keep my eyes on you. If you see Braxton, look over your shoulder, because I'll be right there for both of you." Ross put the gun away and walked out through the screen door.

Steel started after him and then stopped as his mind raced with conflicting emotions. Had Ross learned something about his past? Who was he? But the thought of Braxton here in Orange Beach drove everything else out of his mind. He stepped out onto the deck and looked toward the condo. The lights within were blazing, and he caught the strains of music coming from the open doors of the first-level balcony. He did not hear Christmas carols. Instead he heard a scream. Heart thundering, he leaped over the deck railing and sprinted toward the condo.

Steel hurried up the outside stairs into the den and stepped into chaos. The tree was toppled over, and the balls and ornaments were thrown carelessly around the room. The furniture had been overturned. April and Richard were nowhere to be found. He turned off the stereo. Silence descended, eerie and disquieting. No more screams. He reached for a phone and dialed 911.

"This is Jonathan Steel." He gave the address. "I just got back to the house, and something is wrong. No one's here, and it looks like a break-in."

The operator advised him to go outside and wait for a police car, but he hung up. The kitchen and downstairs bedrooms were empty. A large stairway led up to the second and third levels. He bounded up the stairs and burst into the guest bedroom on the second floor.

Richard had been nailed to the wall. His arms were outstretched, and his legs were spread apart, making him look like some bizarre Christmas star. Nails protruded from his wrists and arms, and blood ran down the walls like red tinsel. A nail protruded from the right side of his forehead. His eyes were closed, but his chest still moved. A nail gun from the toolshed lay on the bed.

Steel felt the world shift, spinning out of control, and felt something ill-defined build within him. The past few months of domesticity fell away like the dead skin of a molting snake, and he realized this was what he was meant for. For some reason he did not feel shock or nausea at the sight of Richard nailed to the wall. Instead, a hot center of rage stoked itself in his gut, flowed outward into his arms, his legs, his mind. He yearned to call out for April, but his instincts prevailed, and he paused and examined the hallway for clues.

Bloody footprints led up the stairs to the third floor. Steel leaned against the wall and smeared wetness against his back.

More of Richard's blood. Slowly he inched his way up the stairs, and then he heard the voice.

"Oh, man of steel, where are you?" The voice echoed down the stairs, eerily familiar. It was Braxton! "I came looking for you and found your playmates. I've had so much fun. Too bad you weren't here to protect them."

Steel knew he was trying to taunt him out into the open. He resisted the urge to hurtle up the stairs. The voice came from the third-floor master bedroom, a large room with a huge wraparound balcony overlooking the ocean. He quietly eased back down the stairs and out Richard's bedroom to the balcony on the second floor.

Outside, a fine mist of rain had begun to fall, and he found the railing slippery as he stepped up onto it to reach the railing on the third floor. Slowly he pulled himself up to the third-floor balcony. Through the glass doors he saw a shadow move across the bedroom ceiling toward the inner door. Braxton had moved to the inside stairs. Steel slipped across the balcony and stopped beside the glass door. Glancing in, he saw April tied down to a trunk at the foot of the bed. Her head was slumped, but her chest moved. Scrawled across the walls were bizarre words in a foreign, alien script, written in Richard's blood.

Steel slipped in through the door and hurried over to untie April. She stirred, and her eyes widened in fear.

"He came for you, Jonathan," she whispered hoarsely. "You've got to get out of here. He's demon-possessed." Steel recoiled at the words.

"I know. Somehow we are connected, and this confrontation should not have involved you," Steel said as he untied April. "Quiet. We're getting out of here," Steel said, and Braxton hurtled into the room, moving through the air in an unnatural flip to land on his back. They fell and rolled out onto the balcony into a pounding rain. Steel felt Braxton's arm around his chin, and lightning glinted on metal as he raised a knife. Steel rolled forward, using Braxton's weight against him to flip him over and away from him. Braxton struggled to his feet as blood and rain dripped from his bare chest. He wore a pair of combat fatigue pants and boots—just like in Steel's flashback. The swirling tattoo pulsed around his right eye.

"Look familiar, sonny? Do I remind you of your daddy? They told me all about you and the Captain. Me and my buddy, the thirteenth demon, will kill you and then offer your little girlfriend as a sacrifice to the master."

Braxton plunged the knife toward Steel's heart, and Steel slid beneath it. He struck out with his fist and crushed Braxton's throat even as he diverted the knife's trajectory. Braxton struggled away from him toward the open door into the bedroom, gasping for breath through a crushed windpipe. He stopped and arched his head back. As lightning splattered the balcony with strobe-like shadows, Steel watched the bruised, crushed tissues return to their normal shape with supernatural speed. Braxton laughed and suddenly lurched as April struck him over the head with a fireplace poker. She hurried to Steel and into his arms.

April turned away from him to face the balcony, and suddenly, Braxton was there, blood pouring from a cut in his head. The golden knife arched through lightning and plunged into her chest. Steel screamed, and fury took him. He had never felt anything like it. It was a righteous anger, a holy rage filled with as much supernatural power as Braxton had. He lay April on the floor and reached out to grab Braxton by the throat. Braxton encircled him with his legs and squeezed. The air left Steel's lungs, and his eyes began to fill with pinpoints of light. Without his surge of supernatural power, he would have been crushed. But he had enough strength to lurch across the balcony and backward against the railing. It cracked, and he felt them plummeting through the rain-filled air.

Steel bounced against the second-floor railing, and it shattered and the spindles showered beneath them onto the outside deck. One stubby spindle speared through his sweater, and he came to a halt, hanging from the second-floor balcony. Braxton continued on and crashed through the lower decking to the sand below. As Steel spun on the torn sweater, he saw one of the spindles protruding through Braxton's chest. For a moment he saw something hideous move behind Braxton's open eyes, and then the life left him. The spiral tattoo faded away.

Steel reached above him and grabbed the edge of the balcony and pulled himself up onto the second floor. His sweater tore away in shreds as he ripped away from the broken spindle. He crashed through the glass door into the second-floor bedroom and hurried up the inside stairs. Outside on the balcony April lay on her side, and he pulled the knife from her chest. He tossed it aside and held her to him. Rain splashed on her face and cascaded down onto the deck. She opened her eyes and studied him.

"Don't let them win, Jonathan. Braxton said you were their enemy. That you would stop them if you didn't die . . ." She coughed, and blood stained the corners of her mouth.

"Don't!" Steel wiped at the blood. "Help is coming."

April's eyes filled with tears. "Promise me you'll fight them, Jonathan. Don't let them win. I told my father the demons were real, and he didn't believe me. Promise me."

Steel blinked back tears. "Don't talk like this, April . . ."

She reached up and touched his face. "Just promise me."

"I promise, April. Don't talk. The ambulance is coming."

April smiled, blood on her lips. "I'm sorry I wasted the time we could have had together. Remember, I've always loved you." She died in his arms. He was still holding her, his tears mixing with the rain when Franklin Ross and the local police walked onto the deck.

[Chapter 21]

STEEL STARED OFF into the night. "Her father lived for another six months. I took care of him. He had one week of lucidity, and I had to tell him about his daughter's death. He left everything to me. He made me repeat her promise. He told me to take all of his resources and track down the thirteenth demon. That is what I have done."

Claire sniffed and leaned her head against his shoulder. He wanted to pull away but found the gesture strangely reassuring. "Thank you for telling me. And now I want to tell you something. When my parents died, I saw the other dimensions, Jonathan."

"What?"

"Carbon monoxide poisoning. I was fifteen. There was a hole in the furnace or something like that, and I came home late. I woke up an hour later, and I could hardly think. I found them cold and dead in their beds, and I crawled out of the house and fell down the front steps.

"I saw the white light, the tunnel, everything, Jonathan. I saw my Savior. He was sitting on a rock in the most beautiful garden, and then this man stepped between us. He was tall and handsome like you..."

Claire paused. "Sorry. He was handsome and dressed all in white, and he said he was my guardian angel. I laughed and asked where his wings were."

Claire chuckled and wiped at her nose. "Here I am dying, and I'm wondering about his wings! He said he wanted me to feel comfortable, and so these huge, white wings unfurled behind him! He said his name was Ralph. Ralph? Really? And then he said, 'Raphael, but you can call me Ralph.'

"When I tried to get past him to Jesus, he blocked me with his wings. 'You cannot see these dimensions, Claire, or you will not want to return. But there is much God still has for you to do.'"

She stood up and hugged herself and leaned against a column on the porch. She turned, and her eyes glittered in the faint light coming through the windows. "I saw the other dimensions, Jonathan. I can't even begin to describe them. Colors and smells and tastes and sensations that defy human experience. That is when I vowed that I would find a way to prove they exist." Suddenly she stumbled, and Steel jumped up to catch her and let her slide down back to the swing.

"Are you OK?"

"I'm just tired. Dealing with Josh and..."

"I need to talk to you about Josh."

Steel felt her stiffen at his side. "Will this ruin the moment?"

"Reality always does," Steel said. "He's afraid you're going to leave him."

Claire drew in a breath and leaned forward. Her hands covered her mouth. "I was hoping he hadn't noticed."

Steel felt his heart skip a beat. "He's smarter than you think. It's hard to hide anything from him."

Claire nodded and turned so that she could look into his

eyes. "I've tried so hard to keep it from him. First, he lost his father. And now, he's going to lose his mother."

Steel shook his head. Things were moving too fast. "Listen, Claire, I find you very special." His mouth grew dry. He tried to swallow as he looked into her eyes. "But I'm still reeling from losing April. And relationships formed in the midst of a crisis don't last."

Claire's brow wrinkled, and she studied him intently. Her eyes shifted back and forth between his. Tears formed, and she put a hand to her mouth. "Oh, no! That's not what this is all about."

Steel shook his head in confusion. "What are you saying?"

Claire reached up and took his face in her hands. "My dear Jonathan, I'd never want you to fall in love with a woman who is dying."

Steel drew a sharp breath. "What?"

"I have multiple sclerosis, Jonathan. I developed it when I was pregnant with Josh. I was only nineteen at the time. The doctors said the pregnancy precipitated it and made it worse. I didn't want Josh to know. He would feel it was his fault. So I've hidden it from him. Now it's getting worse. I'm coming out of remission and when I do, it gets really bad. I don't have long to live, Jonathan. That's what I thought Josh had figured out. For you see, I am going to leave him. I'm going to die. And soon."

Steel felt an aching pain. "I'm so sorry, Claire. Josh doesn't deserve this. And you don't deserve to die."

Claire looked into his eyes. "Jonathan, I'm not afraid of dying. I've done it once already! Look, I've known about my disease for a long time. I knew my time on Earth was short. After Arthur died, Josh begged me to remarry. I couldn't bring myself to tell him I wouldn't fall in love with another man and then leave him behind."

Steel looked away. "I feel like I've only lived for two years, Claire. I can't remember most of my life. I'm not ready to die."

He felt her hand on his cheek. "Silly, I don't want to die, either. I said I'm not afraid to die. Imagine you're a caterpillar."

Steel raised an eyebrow. "A caterpillar?"

"Just go with it, Jonathan. Your whole life is spent crawling along a leaf and eating. That's all you do. You have no appreciation of where the leaf is. You have no idea of how far you are from the ground if you were to fall. Your appreciation of the universe is limited. And then one day you feel this horrible sensation of dread. You feel a change coming. You're going to die. You go on eating and crawling, pretending it's not going to happen. It happens. You spin yourself into a cocoon of death and know no more." Claire's eyes were wide with emotion. The night air grew still and close, thick with humidity. Time seemed to slow.

"And then, Jonathan, you awaken. Your cocoon falls away, and you spread out huge, luminous wings. You crawl away from your death shroud and take to the air! You're no longer a caterpillar. You're a butterfly! You fly through trees and fields of flowers. You see the sun and the stars. An entire universe you never could have imagined is yours to appreciate. And suddenly, you spy a caterpillar crawling along its leaf. You watch your former self, and you wonder how you could have ever wanted to stay like that.

"That is death, Jonathan. We're fat, clumsy caterpillars waiting for the day of metamorphosis. We fear the cocoon. But when we emerge on the other side, we'll look back from God's eternal perspective and wonder how we could ever have wanted to stay like this."

"It doesn't make it any easier to accept." Steel looked out into total darkness. "I don't understand why God works the ways He does. I don't understand how He can allow evil to run rampant around us, how He can allow you to die in the prime of your life."

Claire smiled, and her eyes were riveted to his. "God works in the midst of crises. He comes to us in the moments of our deepest change. God will work in all of this, Jonathan. We just can't see it. Just like we can't see the dimensions beyond our human comprehension. I have to know that Josh will be taken care of. I have to know that God will provide for him. As for you, my dear sweet man, guard your heart. It could be your undoing when we face Ketrick. Do you understand?" She reached out and took his face in her two hands.

"This is all Jonathan's fault!" Josh said as he paced around his bedroom. He rubbed his right eye. It was starting to hurt. He saw something out of the corner of his vision, and he jumped. A spider ran across the bed. He backed out into the hall and into the living room. Liz was sitting by Parker, talking to him.

"It will be all right, Thomas. You just need to trust God..."

"The chick who wanted money? Summer? Blonde hair. Dress with sunflowers?" Josh interrupted them.

Parker looked up, and Liz paused. "Josh, we're talking..."

"I need to know, bro." Josh ignored her.

"Yes," Parker said.

Images surfaced in his mind. Vivian. The room with the altar. He looked around. "Where is my mother?"

"On the front porch with Jonathan." Liz stood up.

Josh ran to the front door and threw it open. He glanced toward the porch swing and saw his mother's hands on Jonathan's face. Vivian was right!

"Liar!" The word flew across the porch. Josh stood in the open doorway. "You told me you were just friends. But you lied! Dude, I should have listened to Vivian." Josh ran down the stairs.

"How much more stupid am I going to act before this is over?" Steel said.

Claire placed a hand on his shoulder. "He'll come back. He always does."

Steel watched as Josh ran up toward the church. "I'm afraid that this time he may not come back. I'm going after him." He stood up, but in the near distance from the parsonage he heard the screams. Parker appeared in the open door with his briefcase. It popped open, and papers scattered in the wind.

"Emily?" He ran off into the darkness. Steel looked once after Josh's receding figure and then at Parker.

"Stay here," he told Claire and then went after Parker.

[Chapter 22]

PARKER THREW OPEN his front door and felt Steel slide to a halt behind him. The air poured out of the house, hot and fetid. The foul odor engulfed them, and a wave of clacking, rippling pale brown poured across the floor from the living room. Scorpions, dozens of huge scorpions the size of cats, milled and scooted over each other as they swarmed around Parker's and Steel's feet.

"What the..." Parker gasped. Another scream echoed from deep within the house.

Steel grabbed Parker around the waist and lifted him bodily and threw him over his shoulder. With incredible strength Steel tore through the scorpions, kicking and crushing them as he ran into the house. He jumped up on the couch and put Parker down on the coffee table.

Scorpions swirled on the floor and started making their way up the couch. "Flashlight?" Steel shouted.

Parker pointed across the room. "Closet."

"Stay here." Steel kicked away another scorpion and jumped off the couch to the closet door. A scorpion jumped from the nearby fireplace mantle. Steel hurled the door open, and the thing bounced against it. He fumbled inside, and light gushed from behind the door.

Parker bit his hand at the sight. Scorpions were everywhere, covering the floor. In the back corner of the room was a figure standing still and quiet. "Back there." Parker pointed.

Steel flashed the light across the floor, and the scorpions scurried out of the light. He pointed the cone of light at the corner.

"Like my pets?" Summer smiled back at him.

A scream tore the air from the hallway leading back to the bedrooms. Parker hurdled the couch and landed in the circle of Steel's light. They headed down the hallway. There were no scorpions anywhere to be seen. So why was Emily screaming?

They paused in front of the nursery door. It was shut, and the screams came from inside. Steel twisted the handle and pushed the door open. Something red and spindly launched itself at Parker, and the huge, red spider landed on his face. Parker started to swat at the thing, and Steel swung the flashlight like a bat. The spider flew down the hallway into the darkness. They stepped into the room, and Parker gasped.

Emily stood on the white chest of drawers with a tiny nightlight in her hand. All around the room the huge red spiders spun their webs, covering the floor and the furniture, swinging from the ceiling. Steel pointed the light at Emily, and the spiders moved into the shadows.

"Thomas! Help me."

Parker swallowed and noticed the candle sitting on a nearby shelf. He had to do something, and a formless idea began to gel.

"Wait right here," he told Steel.

He moved down the hall and opened the door to the bathroom. It was pitch-dark inside, but years of using the bathroom in the middle of the night helped to know where everything was. He felt along the wall to his right for the small shelf Emily kept her candles on. Something brushed his hand, and he fought the scream. He touched the cold metal tube of the lighter and grabbed it. He thumbed the control, and the tiny light filled the room.

Parker held his breath. The spiders were also here, but in the tub was something huge and crimson, pulsating with unholy life. It was the mother spider, and from her thorax, new spiders were scrabbling out freshly born. Parker was paralyzed with fear. "God, where are You?" he whispered.

You hold Me in your hand, a voice said. Parker glanced around. Who had said that? He looked at the lighter in his hand. Light. That was the answer. God is light. Evil shrinks from the light. He reached over and threw the medicine cabinet open. He grabbed a can of hair spray and pointed it at the mother spider. The lighter went out!

Parker felt the darkness envelop him like a shroud of death. He felt things touching his neck, felt cold breath blowing against his ears, feelers moving through the hair on his head, and then he heard her voice.

"You belong to me, Thomas. Remember." It was Summer.

"No, I belong to God!" Parker screamed, and the lighter ignited. The mother spider was out of the tub and just inches from his face, its multifaceted eyes glittering with hunger. Parker pressed the tab on the hair spray, and the plume of gas ignited, engulfing the huge spider in a ball of flame. Her screeching filled the air with inhuman sounds.

The huge spider fell back away, and Parker released the spray and headed back to the nursery. Steel met him at the door with Emily in his arms. "What did you do? They're leaving."

Parker looked around him. The spiders scuttled away from them toward the front door. The mother spider rushed passed them, spewing green flames and the smell of burning flesh. The scorpions hurried past them, and Steel led them into the living room.

Summer stood outside the open door holding the ancient book. "This is what I needed, Parker. Mr. Ketrick wants it back. Our deal is off." The door closed with a loud thud as the last scorpion scuttled over the threshold.

Steel lowered Emily to the couch. The house was empty. Parker slowed his breathing and sat beside Emily. She was trembling, and her eyes were focused faraway. Parker glanced up at Steel. "Why did they do this? Because of the book?"

"No." Steel studied the closed door. "It was a diversion to keep me occupied so I wouldn't go after Josh!" Steel bolted out the door.

Liz took Claire by the arm. "Let's go back inside. Wait for Jonathan."

Claire watched Steel disappear toward the parsonage. Josh had already faded into the darkness between the house and the church. "I've got to go after Josh."

Suddenly the weakness hit her, and she fell. Her legs grew useless, and her hands were numb. "No! Not now!"

Liz squatted behind her, and she felt her arms around her. "It's OK, honey. I'm here. I'm here."

Claire let the anguish and sorrow take her. She sobbed, and Liz held her. The feeling began to return to her legs, and Liz helped her stand up. "You come inside and lie down on your bed, Claire. We must trust Jonathan. He will get Josh back."

Claire reluctantly let Liz lead her down the hall. "I'm sick, Liz."

"I know, honey. I've known since I first saw you. Momma

Liz is here. Come lie down." Liz led her into the bedroom, and Claire sat on the bed.

"I have to help Jonathan."

"I know. Give yourself some time. I'll get you some water." Liz disappeared through the door. Claire hyperventilated, trying to flood her muscles with oxygen. Her head grew light, but she managed to stand and stumble to the door. He was waiting for her in the shadows of the hallway.

"Claire?"

It had been years since she had heard his voice. She looked up. Arthur Knight stared back at her. His hair was still unruly with a stubborn streak of gray at the temples. His face was older. He wore black sweats. "Why didn't you tell me?"

Claire grabbed the doorframe. "Arthur? It can't be. You're dead!"

Arthur stepped into the light coming from the bedroom. "Why didn't you tell me you were sick? I thought you were leaving me when you went to California."

Claire shook her head in confusion. Was this her illness? "I was going to a consultant. I told you all of this. You knew. How can you be here?"

"Why did you bring Josh into this danger?" Arthur tilted his head, and his dark brown eyes bored into hers.

"There's no one to take care of him. You're gone, flying off on some foolish hobby of yours, and you left us. You just flew away, Arthur. Why?"

"You were a terrible wife, Claire. And you are a terrible mother. I'm taking Josh from you." He stepped through the door, and Claire stumbled back onto the bed. She sat down and fought the sobs.

"I'm doing the best I can. You can't have him! Where have

you been the last five years if you're alive? Why did you let me raise him alone? Huh?"

Arthur now stood at the foot of the bed, and something moved under the fabric of his chest. He looked down at his shirt, and it bulged and moved. Claire tried to stand and felt the weakness take her legs away from her. She fell back on the bed and tried to crawl away from her husband.

Arthur looked up and smiled, and his shirt split open. Snakes spilled out, writhing and hissing. He opened his mouth, and a huge snake shot forth and his scalp split. Snakes burst forth from his skull, and he collapsed forward on top of her.

Claire screamed as Arthur disintegrated into an avalanche of cold, writhing, hissing scales. She fought the disease that was taking her, throwing the snakes aside. She grabbed a pillow and blocked a striking snake. She looked up at the door. A young girl stood there with perfectly combed yellow hair and a dress of sunflowers.

"Josh is mine, Claire. You failed." She smiled and suddenly exploded into a whirlwind of dust and leaves and dead vines under the blow of Liz's lion stick.

"Go back to hell from whence you came, you vermin!" Liz screamed as she burst into the room. She grabbed snakes by the head and threw them off of Claire. She struck the bigger ones with the lion stick, and they fell away as if poisoned. Liz grabbed Claire's hands and pulled her up off of the bed and shoved her out into the hallway. Snakes fell from the ceiling, and Claire screamed as she brushed them off.

Liz grabbed her around the waist and pushed her out toward the living room and out of the house. Claire collapsed onto the grass, and Liz sat down beside her. They looked back at the missionary house, now a refuse of the devil.

"Did I ever tell you I hate snakes?" Liz said.

[Chapter 23]

JOSH BURST THROUGH the doors of the church and ignored the snakes writhing in the foyer as he hurried into the sanctuary. The huge scorpion squatted over the altar table, and it raised its pedipalpi in the air. Its claws snapped, and it paused to regard Josh with its dark eyes. Josh stopped halfway down the aisle as his heart raced with anger. He felt his face grow warm, and he balled up his fists.

"I knew it!" he screamed. "They lied to me! Vivian was right. How could I have been so stupid?" He paced back and forth, stepping across the dense fibers that covered the floor. Something gently touched his shoulder and turned him toward the baptistery. He looked down at one of the scorpion's claws. It caressed his shoulder, and he looked up into the thing's lifeless eyes. Almost he sensed concern from the thing. The huge tail came slowly down over the scorpion's body and slid between his legs. The scorpion tapped him in the chest, and he sat back on the tail. For a brief second he thought the stinger would pierce through his chest. But instead, the scorpion lifted him into the air and turned toward the baptistery.

He slid down the tail and came to rest on the scorpion's back. Fine hairs grew from the carapace as long as his arm. He grabbed them and twisted them around his arms as the scorpion lifted itself up over the edge of the baptistery and hovered over the energy pool.

"Dude, go ahead. Let's go for it!" he said to the scorpion.

The scorpion plunged its claws into the swirling colors. The head and body followed, and Josh slid into another place. His thoughts became fuzzy as he tried to comprehend the energies flowing around him. The scorpion scurried through the substance of space bursting through nebulae and coiling around suns. Josh felt his body fading away, his entire being contracting to one ball of white, hot energy—his soul. Ahead the black hole beckoned, pulling into itself dying stars and crumbling planets. The scorpion avoided it, but Josh still felt the gravity pull at him, stretching his ball of energy out in strands of flesh and bone. The pull became awesome and painful. He fell, pulling asunder, splintering into a cloud of disconnected atoms drifting down through metal and rock and brick and mortar. His body assumed normal proportions, and he slid into a pool of green luminescence. His feet touched the ground, and his senses returned to normal. He looked around and saw he was in a round chamber. His feet were ankle deep in ash. He stood in the incinerator in the church basement, and his memory of this place returned as the memory of the dimensions outside his own began to fade.

Around him, the ash began to lift and hover upward into the green-tinted air, taking on forms that coalesced into writhing figures. Faces appeared, limbs and appendages took shape, and a group of men surrounded him. Their long black hair hung to their shoulders, and their faces were painted with stripes of color. They wore tunics of cornhusks held together with strips of black cloth adorned with colored stones. The men looked at him with empty eye sockets.

Josh watched them in wonder. "Cool!" he managed through trembling lips.

"You're early." He turned toward the door leading out of the incinerator, where Vivian stood decked out in a long, black dress.

Josh's mouth was dry and his heart raced. "I remember now. You were right about my mother," he said through chattering teeth. "I'm ready."

Vivian stood to the side, and Summer stepped over the threshold. Her smile was radiant, and her eyes were luminous. She came to him, and the men stood and turned their backs to them. She pressed her face close to his, and he smelled the dry mustiness of old flowers and leaves ready for the fire. Her lips came close to his, and he yearned for her embrace. Her hands scratched dry and raspy on his arms, and suddenly she exploded in a gust of dust-filled wind. Leaves and flower petals cascaded around him. The men on the perimeter turned and laughed, slapping each other on the back, pointing and gesturing. Josh glanced around and noticed he stood alone in a pile of dead leaves.

"What's going on?"

Vivian beckoned to him. "You've made the commitment, Josh honey. Now let's get it done. Come with me."

Josh step over the pile of leaves and watched in amazement as the ash men slumped back into piles of gray and white. He stepped out of the incinerator into a round chamber of rough stone. Behind him, the huge iron incinerator dominated the room. In the center, a low stone altar waited.

Vivian slid up onto the altar and crossed her bare legs. An alluring arm drew him to her. "Are you ready to experience life like you've never tasted it? Are you ready to show your mother who is boss?" Her face hovered so close he could see the fine red veins in the whites of her eyes. "Sugar, stop lying to yourself, and give in to the possibility of greatness and power and triumph."

"Yes," he whispered.

Vivian wrapped her legs around his waist and pulled him in to her. She wrapped her arms around his shoulders. He pressed his lips against hers. She tasted sour and spicy all at the same time, and when he pulled away, they were no longer alone. A tall, pale man stood behind Vivian. He was as white as milk and wore a black pair of pants. He ran a hand over his bare scalp, and his red eyes glittered in the weak light. His bare upper torso was covered with dozens of tattoos. Josh blinked as he tried to focus on them. They seemed to move as if trying to escape. The man stepped closer and reached out and grabbed Josh's hand in his icy grip.

"Hello, Josh. My name is Lucas; I've been waiting centuries to meet you."

Josh felt a moment of terror, and then Vivian's hand gently caressed his forehead, pushing back his hair. Her lips tickled his cheek. "Just relax. It'll only take a moment."

Josh tried to resist, but Lucas was pulling his hand toward his chest. There, just below his right collarbone, the tattoo of a scorpion seemed to come to life. Josh watched in amazement as the claws moved and the tail coiled to strike.

"Now, touch your destiny," Lucas whispered as a star-shaped scar flushed with blood on his cheek.

Josh extended a trembling finger, and the tattoo burst from the man's chest fully formed. The scorpion landed on the back of Josh's hand and dug its stinger deep into his flesh. A fire surged into him, coursing down his arm, filling his lungs, and strangling him. Josh struggled to pull away from the hideous pale man and his demonic scorpion, but it was too late.

He had made his choice. He fell away from Vivian's grasp, and fire erupted around him with dark clouds of evil. Images of bloody stumps, severed heads, and beating hearts ripped from living chests swirled around him in a tornado of fiery evil. The woman from the stone appeared segregated into her parts, and she laughed. All was bathed in a cloud of fine crimson blood swirling in a spiral that tightened and entered his mouth. He choked and tried to fight the thing, but Vivian stepped off the altar and held his arms against his side. The spiral became a snake and then a scorpion's tail and then a dark, hideous cloud of black particles that chittered and laughed insanely and entered him.

As Josh felt himself dwindle to nothing, he was pushed far down into the inner recesses of his mind by a new being that filled him to bursting and covered his reason with madness. And as his sight faded, he saw Lucas reach over to kiss Vivian on the lips.

Steel burst through the church doors and found the sanctuary empty. The snakes were gone from the foyer, and the inscriptions were absent from the ceiling. The lights no longer played in the baptistery. He reached out and flipped on the light switch, and ordinary light filled the room.

"Josh!" he cried. He rushed up to the baptistery. The energy field had vanished. Eerie silence filled the sanctuary.

"Hey, dude, looking for me?" He heard the voice behind him. He turned. Josh stood in the aisle with his face beaming. His eyes were filled with fire. The spiral tattoo pulsed around his right eye. "Josh isn't here anymore, Mr. Steel."

"No!" Steel felt a pain in the pit of his stomach he had not felt since he saw Richard Pierce's body nailed to the wall. "You can't have him."

"Oh, but I can. He gave himself to me. We rode together through the fiery energies of the baptistery"—Josh smiled and put a hand up into the air in a delicate gesture—"and orbited that black hole and slipped the surly bonds of earth." He closed his eyes and furrowed his brows, and his voice took on a Shakespearean accent. "We trod the high un-trespassed sanctity of space...put out my hand and touched the face of"—his eyes opened and he hissed—"Satan!"

"So dramatic, sugar." Vivian stood up from beneath the altar, of all places. She was applying lipstick and gazing at her face in a compact mirror. She went over to take Josh's arm. "I didn't know you were a thespian."

"I have graced the stage more than once, milady." Josh bowed and kissed her hand.

Vivian placed a hand on her mouth when she noticed Steel. "We have a guest, Hui darling. Let's invite him, shall we?"

"To the party of the century!" Josh laughed. "Bigger than Mardi Gras. More grand than Holiday in Dixie. Oh, when the saints, go marching in..." He began to sing.

"Enough!" Steel shouted. "I want Josh back. Now!"

"Now, Jonathan honey, Josh and I are going over to Mr. Ketrick's house for a party. I'm going to show him a good time. And you're welcome to come on down!" Vivian took Josh's arm. She gestured toward the choir loft, and a chair flew through the air and caught Steel on the forehead. He fell forward, fighting to keep conscious as Josh and Vivian walked out of the sanctuary.

Claire heard footsteps behind her, and she turned. Steel stumbled across the yard. Liz grabbed him and lowered him to the ground. Blood streamed down from a cut on his forehead.

"Jonathan, what happened to you? Where's Josh?" Claire turned to face him.

"I'm sorry, Claire. I couldn't stop him." His eyes were distant, haunted pools of turquoise.

"Stop who?"

"The thirteenth demon. Josh went with the scorpion into the baptistery and came out with a spiral tattoo around his right eye." Steel's voice trembled.

"Then all of this was a diversion, wasn't it?" Liz said.

"What happened here?" Steel asked.

"Snakes," Claire answered. She drew a deep breath. "I'll go get him." She started to stand and stumbled. She fell to her knees. She groaned in frustration and pounded the ground with her fists. "This isn't fair!"

"You're not going anywhere. Liz will watch over you. Josh is going to Ketrick's. I'll go get him."

Claire looked up into his eyes. "I am his mother! As God is my witness, I will rise and I will walk and I will go with you to get my son back. Do you understand?"

"Honey, never get between a mother and her child," Liz said.

Steel nodded. "Fine. Liz, go check on Thomas and Emily. I'll go get my car."

[Chapter 24]

STEEL CALLED FROM the security gate, and Ketrick invited him up to his house. He pulled up in front of Ketrick's house. Claire climbed out with renewed strength and hurried across the dark walkway. A woman opened the door before she could knock. She wore a black full-length evening gown and was carrying a martini in her hand.

"Oh, Jonathan dear. So good of you to come. And you brought a lovely companion. I'm Vivian Darbonne." She smiled wickedly and held out her hand.

"I don't have time for this. Get out of my way!" Claire shoved Vivian aside and hurried into the house. The sound of partying came from outside. She heard Steel trying to catch up with her, but she ignored him and burst through a back door onto a pool deck.

A group of men and scantily clad women enjoyed the drinks and snacks spread out over three tables. The man who had to be Ketrick was resplendent in a white suit, black shirt, and red tie as he stood at the pool's edge. His ponytail was draped over one shoulder. Claire shoved her way through the crowd and grabbed his arm.

"I want Josh. Now."

Ketrick turned away from the people with whom he was speaking. His gangly neck was loose in its collar. Sweat trickled in a fine line from his thick, black hair. "And who might you be? Vivian dear, where are you? Did you invite these people? Are they here to witness my acquisition of the last available property in Lakeside, the bank?" He sipped at a bloodred drink and sighed. "Tonight has turned into one nonstop party!"

Claire opened her mouth to reply, but Steel lurched to her side and slapped the drink from Ketrick's hand. The red liquid sloshed across his white jacket. The glass shattered on the pool deck. "I want you to release Josh. He's a minor, and I'll contact the police and tell them you kidnapped him."

Ketrick nodded as he shook his stinging hand. His eyes raked over Claire. "Very impressive little tantrum. But you see, Josh doesn't want to come home. He's perfectly happy upstairs in my arcade. And he's no longer sixteen." Ketrick paused, as if in thought. "He's more on the order of thousands of years old. Besides, Sheriff Sweeney had to leave for an unexpected emergency, and I don't know when he'll be back. If you want to file a complaint, Deputy O'Reilly is right over there."

Claire turned and spied O'Reilly standing next to the poolside bar ogling one of the girls in a bikini. She felt like control over the situation was slipping away. She pushed around Steel and planted herself in front of Ketrick. "I want my son, now."

"You must be Dr. Knight. I'm sorry to say your son spoke poorly of you," Ketrick said.

Claire stepped back as if she had been hit in the stomach and gasped for breath. Steel's face reddened as he pulled Claire to the side and struck out. His fist caught Ketrick in the nose. Ketrick tumbled back and fell into the pool.

Claire stumbled backward and fell against a patio table. Food cascaded down around her onto the pool deck. She struggled upward as someone grabbed Steel from behind. Steel whirled, swinging, and his fist connected with the face of a handsome man in a silk shirt. Another man tried to grab him, and Steel pushed him into the pool. Claire struggled to her feet. Deputy O'Reilly pulled his gun from its holster and planted the tip of the barrel behind Steel's right ear.

"One more move and your brain is mayhaw jelly," Deputy O'Reilly spoke through clenched teeth. Ketrick climbed out of the pool, and his tailored suit hung on his skeletal form. Blood streamed from his crooked nose. "Deputy, I want to press charges against Mr. Steel."

Steel opened his mouth to speak, and O'Reilly pressed the gun even harder, Steel's head angling suddenly to the side. O'Reilly reached with his thin fingered hands to his belt and deftly snapped handcuffs on Steel's wrists behind his back. Claire started forward, and Steel's eyes met hers.

"No, Claire. You've got to stay calm. You have to get me out of jail." He winced as O'Reilly shoved him up against a poolside table and planted his face against the metal meshwork. The world tilted in dizzying confusion.

"My keys are in my pocket. Go get Thomas." Steel slurred through his contorted mouth. Claire regained her balance and took the keys from his pocket. O'Reilly jerked Steel's head up, trying to grab him by his short hair.

"All right, Steel. I'm going to put you under the jail." He shoved Steel across the pool deck toward the house. Vivian took her by the arm, and Claire jerked away from the woman's grasp.

"Don't touch me, you witch!"

"Now, honey child, you just need to calm on down," Vivian said. "I was just going to escort you back out to your car. I wouldn't want you to get lost in the house."

"You mean you don't want me to find Josh and take him home with me." Claire mustered every bit of hatred and anger she could into the look she gave Vivian. The woman was evil incarnate. But Vivian failed to meet her gaze, and her eyes were turned upward toward the second floor of the house. Claire gasped as she looked upward. Josh stood in a window. His face was twisted into a vile expression, and the spiral seemed to move around his right eye. He made an obscene gesture and disappeared from view. She felt the tears come in torrents as O'Reilly pushed Steel around her, leaving her to sob in the backyard of a monster. As O'Reilly dragged Steel away, all she could think of was Josh upstairs at the mercy of Ketrick. And somewhere in the small town of Lakeside, Steel would be rotting in jail while Ketrick finished his arcane deeds.

Lakeside had a small city hall with two cells in the back of the cinder-block addition. O'Reilly threw Steel roughly into one of the cells, and he fell against the wall. His cheek raked against the cinder block as he tumbled to the floor. He managed to worm his way up onto the cot and glared at O'Reilly.

"You can take the cuffs off now."

"Yeah, I guess I could, but I got some paper work to finish first." He laughed and disappeared down the hall toward his office. Steel leaned back against the wall and sighed. Unless Claire could find a way to bail him out, he would be in here indefinitely. He replayed the encounter over and over in his mind, mentally flogging himself for his stupidity. He'd fallen right into Ketrick's trap. This is exactly where Ketrick needed him to be. Locked up and out of the way. Cephas had been right. His emotions, his anger, his desire for revenge had cost him dearly. And soon it would cost his friends even more.

An hour later O'Reilly appeared at the door with a twisted smile on his face. Behind him a tall figure in a dark overcoat appeared.

"Ross!" Steel shouted. "You've got to get me out of here."

Ross smiled and nodded toward Deputy O'Reilly. "I'm afraid I have to yield to the local law enforcement until I can get you transferred to FBI custody."

Steel watched the man light a cigarette and blow smoke into the cell. He still wore the crumpled white shirt and red tie. "What are you talking about?"

"Dr. Daniel Brown. The deputy found this in the good doctor's house." He held up a gun in a plastic bag. "It has your fingerprints on it."

Steel felt the world tilt beneath him. "I don't have a gun, Ross. Someone is trying to frame me."

Ross smiled. "That's what they all say. It won't take long to find the body, Steel. And when I do, I will match the bullets with this gun, and I will finally get to put you away for good." He dropped the cigarette on the floor and ground it out with a vicious twist on his face. He whirled and left the room.

Steel collapsed onto his bunk. O'Reilly leaned up against the bars, and his eyes bulged with excitement. "You know, your friends just tried to see you, but it's getting a little too late for visitors. And I told them to forget about bail. The judge who presides over Lakeside's jurisdiction is on a four-day weekend fishing trip at Toledo Bend. Courtesy of Ketrick Enterprises. Looks like you're going to be here until Monday." He cackled as his nervous hands played over his gun butt.

Steel pushed himself up sideways. "At least take off my cuffs?"

O'Reilly's face relaxed, and his jaw worked on chewing gum.

"Back up to me and I'll take them off. But you try something, and I may have to shoot you to keep you from escaping."

Steel slowly backed up to the bars, and he felt O'Reilly's cold hands on his. The cuffs fell off, and Steel turned, rubbing his wrists. "Is Sheriff Sweeney on Ketrick's payroll too?"

O'Reilly grinned as if at some hidden joke. "Sweeney is going to be retiring soon. See, there's a little dark secret in his past that has to do with pornography. And when he finds out Ketrick is going to reveal his dirty little secret, he'll be taking an early retirement. Of course, Sweeney is too dang honest for his own good. We had to use Summer on him like we did on Parker."

"What?"

"Pass around a few pictures via e-mail, and the rumors fly and the church is empty. Parker has to go it alone. Don't you just hate rumors? Yep, Sweeney will have to take an early retirement. And then, after he retires, I'll be the new sheriff of Ketrickville. Sounds nice, don't it? See you in the morning." O'Reilly laughed, and his voice echoed down the hallway as he walked away.

Steel closed his eyes and fought for calm. He walked around the cell. One wall consisted of cinder blocks covered with decades of paint. The back wall was the same. A barred wall separated his cell from the other. He grabbed the bars and shook them. They were solid and unmoving. The ceiling was concrete. No windows. No escape. He backed up and lay back on the cot. He needed a miracle.

Steel brooded in his cell until the next evening. No water. No food. Just time to relive his mistakes. He decided to try and pray. It wasn't working. As darkness was falling outside, he heard Parker and Claire in the hallway arguing with O'Reilly. They appeared, and Claire ran up to the bars.

"We can't find a judge to get you out, Jonathan. I don't know what to do." Her voice trembled with frustration.

Parker leaned against the bars. "I called some of my pastor friends. They've got lawyers looking into this, but it doesn't look good."

Steel nodded. "You've got to go on without me. Thomas, you're in charge. You're the spiritual leader. You've got to do whatever it takes to stop Ketrick and free Josh."

Parker glanced down at his feet. "I don't know, Jonathan."

Steel reached through the bars and grabbed his arm. "You can do this, Thomas."

Parker looked up. "I will do my best."

O'Reilly appeared behind them. "Time's up, folks. Mr. Steel has a long weekend to spend alone."

Claire stumbled against the bars, and Parker reached out to take her by the arm. Her hand lingered on the bars as they walked away. O'Reilly slammed the door at the end of the hall.

[Chapter 25]

CLAIRE SAT QUIET and still on the couch. "Liz, we only have an hour until midnight. I don't know what else to do."

"Honey, we've tried everything. Now, here is what you are going to do. You are going to go to Jonathan's RV and lock yourself in..."

"What? And what are you going to do?" Claire stood up and felt dizzy.

"I am going to go get Thomas and Emily, and we are going to stand up to Ketrick if he shows up." Liz took her lion stick and rammed it on the floor. "We will stand together against Ketrick, and we'll get Josh back."

"With me in the RV?" Claire put a hand on her hip.

Liz sighed. "Claire, Ketrick will use Josh against you. In fact, I have an idea. You go to the RV and contact that FBI fellow. Sweeney is gone and O'Reilly is with the enemy, but Ross is an outsider. Maybe he can help us."

Claire nodded. "Not a bad idea. I have Jonathan's keys to the RV. Will you drive me over there?"

A few minutes later Claire stood in the middle of the RV and looked around. "OK, he's bound to have some way to contact Ross." She sat down at the computer consoles, and lights flashed at her through the windshield. She stood up and felt her legs go weak. Outside, Liz was pulling away in her rental. "Liz! Don't you do this to me!"

She slumped back in the chair too weak to go out the door. Tears ran down her cheeks, and she slapped her hand down on the table in frustration and hit the keyboard.

"Claire? I have been trying to call since last night."

Claire glanced over. A window had opened on the desktop with the image of Dr. Cephas Lawrence. "Cephas! I hit the keyboard..."

"Where is Jonathan?"

"In jail!" She wiped tears from her eyes and quickly told Cephas what had happened since their meeting the night before. "We didn't even think of calling you for help."

"What can I do from New York City, my dear? I know a judge in Dallas, but that would do Jonathan no good at all. I warned him to be careful, but he is a very stubborn man." Cephas massaged his huge gray mustache. "Now, what can we do? We are running out of time. Ketrick will make his move any moment. Do you know how to get to the altar room?"

"No. Josh said he went through the baptistery with the scorpion, so it must be somewhere beneath the church," Claire said.

"Then you must free Jonathan. No matter how hard it is. Or how illegal. The true legal representative of Lakeside has left, and these false authorities have no real moral power."

"What about Ross?"

"I would think that man is very happy Jonathan is rotting in jail. I would not count on him for help. But that doesn't mean you can't take matters into your own hands." Cephas pointed a gnarled finger at the screen.

"But I can hardly walk, I'm so weak."

"Who said anything about walking?" Cephas raised an eyebrow with a twinkle in his eye.

Parker stood in the dark on the sidewalk outside the church, uncertain where to begin. The car was packed, and he had decided it was best to run. Again. In spite of Jonathan's plea. "I'm just not ready." He looked up to the sky. When he had finished packing, he discovered Emily was gone. She had left a note that she was going to go to the church nursery to find the chest.

Parker glanced at his watch. "We have less than an hour before Ketrick carries out whatever he is going to do, Emily. Why did you do this now?" Above him, rolling clouds skittered across a new moon, its bloodred crescent reminding him of the sleepy eye of the devil awakening to a new night of terror.

Parker walked carefully across the dark, shadowed ground and made his way down the side of the base of the stairs toward the basement of the church. A dark opening yawned into a hallway leading beneath the stairs. He ran his hand along the rough brick wall and grasped for balance. A rough wooden door on his left opened into the basement.

Parker reached in and threw the light switch. The room flooded with light from bare, hanging bulbs. A short set of stairs ran down into a long hallway that stretched into the distance. The hallway led right beneath the aisle in the sanctuary above. Doorways led off the hallway into rooms. The floor was bare concrete and the walls were of old wood, painted so many times they looked grainy and pebbly. It had been months since Parker had visited the nursery in the basement. It reminded him too much of the child he did not have.

At the end of the hall, light moved back and forth across

the floor from within a room, swaying in a dizzying pattern. He reached the edge of the doorway and peeked inside. A bare bulb hung on a wire from the ceiling, swaying back and forth. A rocking chair creaked in the corner, surrounded by baby beds and toys.

"Emily?"

She stood up and smiled at him. "Look, Thomas, a little boy." She held the black-haired toddler on her hip.

"Put him down!" Parker barked.

"But he's scared."

The little boy reached a hand toward Thomas. "Boobah!" he said.

"Emily, why are you here?"

"I came looking for the chest. There has to be a secret passage from the nursery to the altar room. I just know it. And then I heard this little boy crying." She smiled at the little boy, and he put a hand on her face. "He's adorable."

"He should be."

Parker whirled. Vivian Darbonne stood in the doorway to the nursery. She was dressed in a tight, leather jumpsuit. "He could be yours."

"Mine?" Emily asked.

Summer stepped into view and moved around Vivian into the room. She pushed toys away with her feet. "He's our baby, isn't he, Thomas?"

"No!" Parker glanced at Emily. "She framed me. She said she would tell them it was my baby. But I had the recordings from my office proving she was lying. Emily, you have to believe me."

Emily blinked and looked at him. Then she looked at the child. "Oh, I believe you, Thomas."

"It's time we joined Mr. Ketrick," Vivian said.

"I'm not going anywhere." Parker moved over by Emily.

"We're leaving town. I'm giving in. Ketrick can have the church. I just want my family back."

Emily put the toddler on the floor, and the little boy walked over and picked up a toy truck. She looked at Parker. "It's not that simple, Thomas. I was hoping to find the chest, and then maybe I could trade it to Mr. Ketrick for letting me out of our deal."

"What deal?"

Vivian laughed and jerked the toy out of the boy's hand. The boy began to cry. "Enough, Emily. There is no going back on your bargain. I find it interesting that you both have kept secrets from each other. Good choices. But time is running out." She mouthed a word that sounded so vile and so inhuman that it grated on Parker's ears and made no sense in this universe. With that one strange word, the baby stopped crying and ran over to Emily with unnatural speed. She stepped back.

"Boobahhhh!" The toddler opened his mouth, and huge, black dung beetles poured out onto the floor. Parker pulled Emily to him. The boy's skin crawled with bumps and lumps, and he exploded into a shower of black, chitinous evil. Beetles swarmed around Parker's and Emily's feet, streaming up their legs and encircling them in a tight, unbreakable bond.

"Thomas, do something!" Emily screamed. The beetles were swarming up their abdomens, and Parker was paralyzed.

"Vivian, as God is my witness..."

"I think not, Reverend Parker. You abandoned what little protection you had when you made the choice to lie to your wife. I just love it!"

Parker felt the beetles' cold, tapping legs move across the base of his neck, and behind Vivian and Summer, Liz appeared in the doorway.

"Thomas, are you in here? I saw you go into the church..."

Parker opened his mouth, and before he could speak, beetles streamed into him and covered his screams with darkness.

Liz watched the last beetles cover Emily and Thomas, and she hefted the lion stick into the air and brought it down on Vivian's head. Vivian spun around with inhuman speed and caught the lion stick. She jerked it out of Liz's hands and motioned to Summer.

"Take care of this."

Summer's hands became scabrous and rough with scales and tiny rootlets, and before Liz could move, they shot out in tendrils and fine vines and wrapped around her arms. Summer's arms bifurcated into dark green vines, and they wove their way around Liz's torso.

"What do we have here?" Vivian studied the lion stick. "I do believe you have no idea what you're got, Miss Liz. But it needs to be far away from this church before midnight." Vivian released the stick, and it soared over Liz's head and out into the hallway. "I'll toss it in the trash upstairs."

Liz started to speak, and Summer suddenly pulled her close to her face. Her eyes grew dark green, and her face became fibrous and leathery. Liz struggled against the creature.

"Summer and the baby are my two demons, Liz. They serve me, not Ketrick. They do my bidding. And it is time for you to go to sleep."

Summer's face exploded into a huge obscene sunflower, and a mouth formed in the center of the acrid yellow petals and closed on her face. Liz knew no more.

[Chapter 26]

STEEL SIMMERED IN silence, sullen and desperate. "OK, so I messed up, God. I know Claire brought her son into this, but I made him a part of the team, and I need to save him. It's my fault, so we need a little help." He closed his eyes and then opened one eye and glanced at the ceiling. "Please." He sat in silence and waited to hear from God.

But instead of a still, small voice, Steel heard a growing thunderous noise. The door to the office opened, and O'Reilly stepped in, his eyes wide with panic.

"She's crazy, man."

The wall behind him exploded in a huge cloud of dust and broken cinder blocks, and a pair of headlights burst through the darkness. The wall collapsed onto O'Reilly. Steel jumped up and stared through the windshield of his RV at Claire.

O'Reilly's body was shoved up against the bars. Claire smiled and waved at him. "Sorry about the damage. I didn't think you would mind," she said through the broken windshield.

Steel laughed. For the first time since April, he actually *laughed*. He reached through the bars and grabbed O'Reilly's arm and pulled him closer. He retrieved the keys and unlocked the cell door. It took several shoves to push the broken debris away, and he stepped over O'Reilly's motionless body toward the RV.

The front end was wedged into the wall of the jail, and Steel could not get to the RV door. "Are you OK?"

"Yeah. This was Cephas's idea. Go on to the church and get Josh. I'll be fine. I promise." She reached out of sight and tossed Steel his cell phone. "Call me when you get to the church, and I'll find Liz, Thomas, and Emily."

Steel nodded and ran across the broken rubble and out into the middle of Main Street. A few cars had stopped, but near midnight, the town was essentially deserted. He looked up the sloping street toward the church at the end of Main Street. Its steeple pointed hopefully to heaven, and the lights in its windows, though flickering, promised hope and a future. Steel would make sure it happened that way.

Josh looked around the dark, dank room. Mold and mildew covered the rough stone walls, and a meager torch in a rusty bracket cast light into the chamber. He stood up and paced around the walls and could find no doors or windows. There was no ceiling, only a darkness more profound than the deepest night.

"Hello! Hey, dude, I want out of here."

The light from the torch flickered and grew dim until only a faint glow illuminated the base of the torch. In the darkness above him, an eye appeared, huge and lidless, and a spiral of blood pulsed around it.

"Too bad, Josh. You made the choice. I'm in charge now." The voice thundered in the room.

"Where am I?" Josh screamed. "I want my mother. I want Jonathan."

"I want my mommy!" The voice mocked him. "You are lost in your own jumbled imagination, Josh. And before you can find your way out, I'll be done with you."

The eye disappeared, and the torch grew brighter. Josh slumped onto the hard, wet dirt floor and pounded it with his fists.

Steel found the open trap door under the altar table and the stone stairway leading down into total darkness. He felt his way down the winding stone stairs until he stepped into a larger opening. A sound came from his right.

"Hello?" He spoke into the darkness.

"Jonathan?" Liz called from nearby. "We're here."

"We're chained to a wall," Parker said.

"Vivian took us prisoner," Liz said.

Steel reached out and tried to feel his way to the nearest voice. He touched flesh, and his hands strayed over a face. Young. Short hair. A lip bead.

"Surprise!" a raspy voice said. Steel tried to back away, but he felt hands grip his arms in a rock-hard pinch. "You're not going anywhere, man of steel."

Steel tried to back away, and the light on his cell phone cast pale blue luminance over Josh's face as it rang. The spiral pulsed and moved with unholy power.

"Let me answer that." He grabbed the phone out of Steel's hand. "Hello. Mother? Oh, so good to speak to you. Yeah, Hui and I are getting along famously. And I have your friends here. We're going to have a party. You're invited to join us, but don't plan on leaving. This party is to die for!" He glanced once at the phone and then squeezed it with supernatural power. It shattered into a hundred pieces of metal and glass, and the room plunged once again into darkness.

"I will stop you," Steel said. He felt his anger build, felt the fury ignite him, and was about to lash out with his fist when light to his left danced against ancient brick walls. Josh turned him around with superhuman speed so that he was facing the light coming down the stairway. He looked around. Stone walls led up to an ancient wooden ceiling. They were in a sub-basement of the church. The wooden rafters appeared to be over a century old, and the bricks of the walls seemed handmade.

Jonathan saw Emily, dimly illuminated by the flickering light approaching down the stairway, bound by ropes on a stone altar. Her hands and feet were tied to stone notches at the bottom of the great stone altar. Its interlocking blocks formed an intricate pattern. It was the altar of the spiral eye. On the far wall, an old iron incinerator squatted like some beast in the shadows.

"The altar from the codex," Liz said.

"Precisely!" A voice boomed from the stairwell. Ketrick stood at the foot of the stairs. His face was painted in streaks of bright color. His head was adorned in a huge green, feathered headdress. His long, black hair hung loosely upon his shoulders. He wore a breastplate adorned with bright, colorful stones over his bare chest. A golden cloth encircled his waist, leaving his legs bare. He held a flickering torch in his hand. "It is the altar of the spiral eye, the altar of Huitzilopochtli. Upon this altar I shall offer my continued allegiance to the thirteenth demon."

Josh released one of Steel's arms and grabbed his chin so he could look in his eyes. "Dude, Josh invited the big man in to stay. Willingly. He's inside somewhere. Would you like to see him?"

"Yes," Steel said through clenched teeth.

Josh smiled, and suddenly his face twisted into a mask of fear. "Jonathan, help me. I didn't mean for it to go this far. I…" And then Josh was gone, replaced by the fearsome mask of a demon. "Well, they all change their mind once we settle in. But it's too late, baby, now it's too late."

Josh got one quick glimpse of Steel, and for a few seconds, he was back to normal and in control. But before he could finish his thought, he was back in the stone chamber.

"OK, dude, remain calm. You've gotten out of worse…no, maybe you haven't. Think." Josh studied the stone walls again. "Wait! I know this place! It's a chamber on level twelve of my video game! There has to be a way out of here. So my opponent is the thirteenth demon. Yeah, Huizilowhatever." He looked at the dark ceiling. "Why did the light dim when he appeared? Maybe he can't stand the light!"

Josh stood up and approached the torch and put out a hand. It gave out no heat. Gingerly he reached forward with a finger and touched one of the flames. Sight and sound exploded around him. He saw himself sitting in a pew in his church watching a baptism. He was strumming his bass guitar, really down with the praise song he was singing. He was sitting on his mother's lap, and she held an open Bible before him while reading him the story of Goliath.

Josh jerked his hand away. "OK, so the light is connected to all the good things in my life. Good things that are tied to, uh, God! That's it! God is light!" he said, looking around the musty chamber. "God, are You there? Can You help me?"

The light flickered, and something brushed his cheek. He whirled, and a butterfly fluttered through the air. It landed on the metal bracket of the torch.

"That's my answer? A butterfly?" Josh said. The butterfly's wing fluttered up and down, and the flames of the torch flickered with it. "The torch? That's the answer? So, how can I use the torch to open a doorway?" He frowned. "I'm talking to a butterfly!" He sat in the middle of the floor. "Dude, were you sent by God? So what does He want me to do? I haven't done anything wrong. It's the thirteenth demon that is the bad dude here."

Josh sighed and looked around at the empty room. Could he be the problem? "Look, I'm a good kid. I haven't done drugs. I don't steal. I keep those commandments, bro. So why do I have to do anything else? Huh? I'm good enough to get into heaven."

The butterfly left the bracket and fluttered across the room and landed on his ear. Josh brushed at his ear and felt his ear hoops. He pulled his hand back, and the butterfly sat on his thumb, slowly opening and closing his wings. "The piercings? Come on! Give me a break. I did this for Ila! That doesn't make me a bad kid. And yeah, I was rebellious to my mom. But hey, I'm a teenager. And…"

Josh watched the butterfly's wings slow to a standstill. "I can't be good enough on my own, can I? Dude, I need help. God, can You help me?" He looked up at the ceiling.

A huge scraping noise came from behind him, and he turned. The wall separated as huge stones slid aside, telescoping into each other to reveal a door. "Awesome!" He jumped up, and the butterfly flew off toward the door.

"Ketrick, let's get on with it. It's getting close to midnight, and it has been far too long since blood last ran on this altar," Josh said.

Ketrick pressed a button on the side of the incinerator. In

the depths of the dark chamber, fire exploded, and the incinerator came to life. Its orange and red face grinned at them through the slits in the door. Ketrick opened the door to the huge incinerator, and the heat instantly engulfed the room.

"What are you going to do, Ketrick?" Steel strained against Josh's grasp.

"Well, for starters, my new 'nephew,' Josh, is going to practice heart surgery. Let me see. We have five potential sacrifices. You'll enjoy it, won't you, Josh?"

"Yes, Uncle Bobby," Josh said. "I need the practice. It's been a long time since I dismembered anyone."

"I have longed to see you in action since the day I looked upon your handiwork in that pit in Mexico City," Ketrick said. "You see, Steel, I have spent a lifetime in service to the thirteenth demon. And now, the thirteenth demon will give me my heart's desire."

"Ketrick, how do you expect to cover up five murders?"

"Oh, my poor Mr. Steel," Ketrick said. "There will be a terrible fire in the church basement. The entire church will burn to the ground, and the five of you will be lost, trapped in the inferno while investigating your silly rumors of demon possession."

"Why Emily?" Steel asked.

"She is the important ingredient in tonight's ceremony." Ketrick gestured to Emily with his free hand. "I must insure my heir arrives in this world unharmed. You see, Emily bears my unborn child. And like the child that sprang forth from its mother's womb to bring destruction to the world, this child shall be the house of the thirteenth demon. Dr. Brown has worked his genomic magic, and the child that grows within Emily is derived from my altered DNA and will have powers that defy explanation."

Parker lunged against the chains. "I don't believe you!"

"Vivian, would you come in?" He glanced toward the stairway.

Vivian appeared from the stairway. She sauntered across the room and leaned against Josh. "Hey, sweetheart."

"Hi, girlfriend," Josh chuckled.

"Tell them what happened to Dr. Brown," Ketrick said.

"Emily approached Dr. Brown to help her find a donor for a baby." Vivian smiled at Parker. "He told her he had an anonymous money donor who would pay for the procedure, but one day, that person would show up and try to buy the church. She was supposed to urge you to sell the church! Dr. Brown performed in vitro fertilization while she was heavily sedated and told her the child would look like Reverend Parker. But the embryo was from Ketrick! His son."

"Dr. Brown promised me it would be from someone who looked like you, Thomas," Emily cried. Her desperate eyes turned toward them. "We couldn't have our own baby. It was our only chance. I didn't know any of this. Thomas, you've got to believe me."

"It doesn't matter what your husband believes, Emily. The child is my son," Ketrick interrupted her. "Only he will be like no son that has walked this planet since that accursed Messiah of yours. With Huizilopochtli's help, my son will grow up to be the ruler of all of humanity. Such power! Such abilities! Pyramids will rise across this land! Blood will flow once again, and beating hearts will be eaten alive! And your God will taste defeat!"

"No!" Parker screamed. "Ketrick, ask your demon friend here what good it does to offer these sacrifices. Go ahead. Ask him. Emily is a child of God. She belongs to Jesus Christ, or he would already possess her. All he is doing is manipulating you into murdering innocent lives. It is your own soul you are condemning, Ketrick."

"Stop your preaching!" Ketrick screamed as he brought his hand up clutching the knife from his desk. The golden blade glittered in the firelight. "My god demands a sacrifice. I will perform the surgery and remove the unborn child. Vivian will take him to a private clinic, where they will insure the baby is healthy. And then, Josh and his friend, the thirteenth demon, will remove your wife's beating heart and hurl it into the fire." He grinned, and his perfect white teeth gleamed. His eyes were brilliant with reflected torchlight. "It will be a glorious, symbolic gesture to the thirteenth demon. The end of your reign over this sacred ground and the beginning of my reign over the lives of the people of this town."

"And what about Josh?" Steel asked.

The dark, dank hallways smelled of rotten, putrid things. Josh passed a pile of garbage with flies. He stepped over raw sewage. He gagged and moved on down the stone hallways toward fresh air. "What is all this trash?"

The butterfly paused and landed on the edge of a pool of rancid water. Josh looked down, and his own reflection stared back. He was startled at what he saw. "Hey, I forgot I dyed my hair black. I'm really blond." He touched the lip bead. "This trash is me, isn't it? It's all the bad things I've done. Dude, I really stink inside, don't I?"

The butterfly lifted and continued down the hallway. It paused in front of an open doorway and disappeared from view. Josh stepped through the doorway and gasped.

The rough hewn stone pyramid towered above him with four sides straight out of an Aztec nightmare. The sky was turbulent with red- and orange-tinted clouds. Thunder rolled across the jungle around the pyramid, and lightning flashed. At the top of the pyramid the eye from the ceiling stared down at him, red, lidless, and surrounded by a spiral of flame.

"Great! This is the one level I can't beat in my video game. But I never had your help before." He nodded at the butterfly and started up the steps toward the eye.

Josh was exhausted by the time he reached the platform at the top of the pyramid. An altar sat before him, dark and perfect in proportion. On the far side a man stood with long, black hair and a loincloth of cornhusks. The spiral pulsed around his right eye.

"You are stronger than I anticipated, Josh. But I only have to hold you off for a few more moments. Then I will claim your soul and send your friends to their deaths." He smiled, and scorpions ran out of his mouth, across his cheek, and down to his chest. A dozen of them paused, quivered, and then became trapped tattoos on his chest.

"I'm game if you are, Hui," Josh said.

The man pulled out a golden knife and lunged for Josh. Josh ducked and ran around the other side of the altar. Hui laughed and motioned to the altar. A flame emerged out of the center of the altar. "I will cut out your heart while it is still bleeding and eat it in front of you as you die, and then I will burn the rest of your body in these flames." He laughed, and red spiders poured from his mouth and onto his chest.

"Dude, you need to see an entomologist," Josh said.

Hui paused. "What?"

"An insect doctor." And Josh reached into the flames and

grabbed a handful of fire and launched it toward Hui's face. Hui gasped in shock and fell back away from the altar.

"Don't like the light, do you?" Josh gathered up another ball of flame. "Then you should never have played with fire." Josh shot the ball of flame at Hui's head. He ducked, and the flame fell down the pyramid.

"I'm growing tired of this," Hui said. "It is time for you to die."

"And when I do, what happens to you?" Josh asked.

"I will be free, and your soul goes to hell."

"If that's what it takes to save my mother and my friends, then that's the price I'm willing to pay. Hey, butterfly. Why not land on his face?" Josh said to the butterfly.

The butterfly soared down from the sky and landed on Hui's nose. He shrieked in pain and horror, and the insects burst forth from his chest and scampered away. Josh ran around the altar, grabbed the golden knife, and plunged it into Hui's chest.

"Dude, get out of my head!" Josh screamed.

Hui lashed out, and Josh fell backward. He thudded onto the first step, and as he tumbled down the stairway, he saw Hui disintegrate into a thousand scorpions.

[Chapter 27]

CLAIRE STUMBLED THROUGH the door into the church sanctuary. It had taken far too long to climb out of the wreckage of the RV. And then it had taken far too long to walk up the street to the church. But adrenaline had given her the energy she needed.

"I am here, Jonathan. Nothing is going to stand between me and my son." She looked around. The plants had returned. Along the edge of the sanctuary snakes moved along the base of the stained-glass windows. The energy pool glowed in the baptistery.

"Oh, no! You are not going to stop me now!" She climbed over huge vines and roots and leaned against the altar table. "Where are you? How do I find you?"

She felt the snakes closing in on her. A spider ran across her hand, and she brushed it away. What to do? How had Jonathan found the room? There must be some kind of door hidden somewhere. She pulled out her cell phone and dialed Steel's number.

"Jonathan?"

The voice that came over the speaker made her jerk up in shock. She looked down at the screen. "You are not my son.

You have taken my son prisoner, and I will come and find you and send you to hell!" She threw the phone across the room, and it disappeared into the baptistery. She gasped and ducked, waiting for the inevitable release of energy, but nothing happened.

A snake crawled over her shoe, and she kicked it away. She stood up again, and more snakes covered the altar table. Jonathan said Josh had ridden the scorpion through the energy pool. He had needed supernatural help, but he had passed through extra dimensions to reach the altar room.

Claire felt renewed strength as she made up her mind. "Josh, I am coming." She shoved snakes aside and brushed spiders from her shoulders and strode through the choir loft until she climbed up onto a stool and looked down into the depths of the energy pool.

"Ralph, or Raphael, whatever your name, you said you were my guardian angel. So, Lord, let him now guard me as I go through the extra dimensions to rescue my son." She took a deep breath and stepped into infinity.

She was somewhere? Nowhere? Darkness and a tight ball of light. She had seen this before, and there below her was her body spinning through space, stretching in the gravitational pull of the black hole. She felt her soul soar across magnetic fields and through gaseous nebulae into the very heart of a red star, boiling and teeming with energy and the life of the universe given by the Creator. Then, darkness and a light came fast and furious, and she floated toward it.

"Ralph!" she called. "I need you! Ralph!"

The dimensions shattered and shimmered around her like a kaleidoscope. Space and time rippled, and she *saw* the branes! She saw the ultimate reality as she was pulled with superhuman speed through all of her memories and her entire life to a rock in a garden filled with gardenias. She reached down and inhaled the blossom. It was heavenly and sparkled with light. A butterfly landed on her hand.

"Raphael, I told you." A voice came from the butterfly. "Were you looking for me?"

"A butterfly?"

"I like your butterfly story. Just remember. Humans can't become angels. However, as a butterfly, I was sure you would recognize me."

"I need your help. I must save my friends."

"Claire, I am but a servant of God. I am a messenger. I can do nothing that God does not allow." The butterfly fluttered its wings, and suddenly, the manlike creature she had met before stood before her. He wore a bright, white tunic, and his dark, blue eyes were filled with such power, such wisdom. "Oh, yes. You like wings," Raphael said, and his wings unfurled behind him, a perfect match for the colorful pattern of the butterfly. He reached out and put a hand on Claire's shoulder.

"Claire, even if God allowed me to help you, there is a problem. If you return now to your world, I can put you back with your body. But if you stay here to help your friends, you will not be able to return."

"I know," Claire said. "I guess I have always known. My time on Earth is limited. I have to make my life count for something, and I love my son enough to do this. I will become like the butterfly."

"I can let you taste what you will be like when you are transformed. For God has given me permission to help you."

"You think I care what happens to this body?" Josh glared at Steel. "When I'm done with it, I'll kill the shell and harvest the soul. It is our way."

Behind Josh, Vivian stepped back and reached into the pocket of her black jumpsuit. She pulled out a syringe, uncapped it, and held it up like a knife. What was she doing?

"Wait!" Josh shouted, but he was looking at Steel, not Vivian. His brow furrowed, and he started muttering to himself. His grasp on Steel relaxed, and Steel stepped away just as Josh screamed, arched his back, and looked at Steel. "No!" he shouted. He looked over at Ketrick. "I have to leave this body, and I will have yours."

Josh collapsed, and his head bounced against the edge of the altar. Ketrick's eyes widened in fear as he shouted, "No, you cannot have me!" He reeled back, and his lifted knife severed one of the gas lines entering the incinerator. Steel heard the hissing sound. He had to get them out of here now!

Josh slumped to the floor. His chest barely moved, and his face was pale and slack until suddenly, his eyes widened and his mouth gaped open wide enough to almost unhinge his jaws. Something hideous and foul streamed out of his mouth, all dark particles of dirt and stone and dust and clumps of clotted blood that whirled in an obscene spiral of putrid energy. The stench was overpowering, and the spiral filled the rafters with dark smoky material that mixed with the escaping gases of the severed hose. The clumps of smoke and mist hardened and condensed into dark brown chitin and glistening eyes and clacking claws. A huge scorpion clung to the roof. Vivian dropped her syringe and ran up the stone stairway and out of the chamber.

Parker's heart burned with bitter despair. He pulled against the chains even as Ketrick raised the ugly knife above his wife's body. He watched her eyes widen with fear. Claire appeared before him, and her face was blurry and insubstantial.

"Thomas, you'll soon be free to rescue Emily. Remember, your heart must be righteous as you face the demon. And in the aftermath, you must remember to forgive and to love unconditionally." He studied her deep, green eyes even as he felt the chains fall from his arms. Claire faded from view, and Parker realized he had just witnessed the miraculous, supernatural power of God. The sudden recognition of God's infinite power drove itself home into his heart and soul and filled him with resolve.

Parker burst across the room, freed from his shackles. "Listen to me, you spawn of hell!" Parker's voice built in volume and echoed across the chamber, strong and vibrant. He crouched near the altar, glaring up at the scorpion on the ceiling. "I am a man called by God to preach the gospel of peace. You have no power over us. We are bought with a price, and that price is the blood of Jesus Christ."

"I don't have to listen to you, pitiful human." The thing spoke in a raspy voice. It released its hold and fell toward the floor. Parker ducked, and the scorpion twisted and landed between Parker and the altar. It was over twelve feet in length, and its tail easily scraped the ceiling. The tail coiled above the body, and the stinger dripped venom. "You are a broken and fear-filled mortal weakened by greed and doubt. I've killed millions just like you over the past millennia. Ultimately, you are a failure. A mere man who has lost his church. Who has lost his congregation. And now, who has lost his wife."

Parker should have fallen back in whimpering, abject fear. But the power that burned within his heart grew hotter. He had seen Claire in her transformed state. She had shown him the power of God. Why had he ever feared? Why had he ever doubted? He stood up and threw out his chest and balled up his fists. He tossed his glasses away and glared at the scorpion. "I'm not perfect, demon, but I'm forgiven. And you can't stand against the power of the Holy Spirit. It is time for you to go, to leave this place!"

"No!" The tail lashed forward over the demon's head, and the stinger glittered with poison. Parker dodged the tail. Ketrick had backed away from the altar, and he had to free Emily. He started to untie the ropes holding Emily. One of the demon's claws dipped down and grabbed him at the waist, lifting him into the air. Parker felt the cold, slimy touch of the carapace and felt the constricting power of the claws closing upon his waist.

Steel stumbled back as the scorpion spun around and grabbed Parker with one of its huge claws. "Put him down!"

The scorpion turned in his direction and paused. Steel jumped up onto the huge claw and pulled at Parker. The scorpion was too strong. A shadow passed over him, and he ducked as the tail whistled by his head. The stinger thudded into the stone floor beneath him.

Steel dropped to the floor and grabbed the chain that had bound Parker to the wall and jerked it from the ancient stone. Just as he turned, the tail came at him again. He rolled to the side and jumped over the thing's tail as it lifted into the air.

He threw the chain around the base of the stinger, catching the other end in his hand. Leaning back he pulled with all his might, and the tail tilted to the side. The scorpion whirled, trying to dislodge Steel, and it took its attention away from Parker. Parker slid loose from the creature's claw and fell back onto the chamber floor.

"Steel, command him to hell. You can do it," Parker screamed.

Steel stood up on the tail as it whipped around the chamber and jumped toward the scorpion's head. The momentum brought the tail with him. He landed just behind the scorpion's eyes, and he pulled with all his might. The stinger plunged into the open carapace behind the eyes and into the scorpion's nervous center. Steel opened his mouth to speak, and the world shimmered around him.

Claire hovered in front of him. Her face was radiant.

"Hello, Jonathan. I don't have much time. The more time you spend outside our four dimensions, the less you'll remember of it. Our minds can't comprehend the other dimensions, you see. But my dear sweet Jonathan, it is so beautiful! I understand so much now. I can see the big picture, and I know why all of this is happening. I can see Jabo Suyu's pattern. It will bring good. You have to remember that. All things work together for good for those who love God. I'm going to free Liz. You must get them out of here quickly, you understand?"

Steel tried to speak but stopped when, behind Claire, he caught the impression of movement, of pearly light, of motion of wings; in the distance he saw April smiling. Claire touched his face, bringing him back to her. "My guardian angel helped me."

"How?" Steel glanced around the room. In slow motion he watched Claire's body appear through the very fabric of the roof and fall to the floor. "No, not the energy pool!"

He felt a warm caress on his cheek, and he turned back to Claire. "I knew the price, Jonathan. Only I could do this. You know that. For me, there will be no return, Jonathan. Do you understand? You must promise me you'll see that Josh is taken care of. Get him to Cephas. Will you promise me, Jonathan?"

Steel tried to focus on her face, but the pain gripped him. He blinked and whispered, "Yes. I promise. But I don't want this to happen. It isn't fair."

"Though He slay me, still I will trust Him, Jonathan. Now, forget about the thirteenth demon."

"What?"

"Listen to me. It is your obsession, and it has ruled your life. Let it go. You will have a chance to fight it another day. For now, you must save Josh. He is dying, but if you get him to breathe again, he should be fine."

"How can you know?"

"Other dimensions, remember? I know a lot now, Jonathan. I see your past, and you must remember you are a good man. There isn't much time. You must choose. Now. Josh, or the thirteenth demon." She brushed his lips with hers and was gone.

Time moved around him again, and Steel felt the thirteenth demon beneath him. He glanced over at Josh's crumpled form and slid off the scorpion.

Parker shouted, "Steel, what are you doing?"

"Saving Josh. It's up to you." Steel hurried across the room to Josh's slumped form. His face was deathly white. He wouldn't let Josh go like April. Not again. He put his head against Josh's chest, and he heard the slow thumping of his heart. "Come on, Josh. Breathe! Move!"

He started chest compressions, and then ripped open Josh's mouth and pressed his mouth against Josh's. He breathed into the boy's lungs. Josh's chest inflated, and Steel pressed on his chest again.

"Come on, Josh. Don't do this to me!" He screamed and hit Josh with a mighty blow on the chest. Josh jerked and gasped, sucking in air. His eyes flew open, and he looked around. His gaze focused on Steel. He reached up with a weak hand and touched his mouth.

"Dude, you put your mouth on mine! Gross!"

Parker watched Steel slide off the giant scorpion, and the thing turned to face him while it tried to disengage the stinger from the carapace behind its eyes. "It all comes down to this, doesn't it? Every sermon I have preached. Every Bible verse I have read. Every prayer raised to God, and I almost lost it all because of my fear and my greed." He glared at Ketrick holding the knife on the other side of the altar. "I don't care what life stirs within Emily. You will not kill her."

Ketrick raised his knife. "Wrong again. Time to choose, reverend. Send the demon to hell or save your wife."

Parker glanced once at the scorpion and hurled himself forward over his wife's body in protection, but he never felt the knife fall.

Claire smiled as she took the chains from Liz's arms. Liz reached out and touched her cheek. "Honey, thank you." Her eyes glittered with tears. "I understand the price you'll have to pay."

"Thank you for becoming my friend. You must help Josh. And Jonathan."

Claire turned and watched Steel blow life into Josh. She watched as Ketrick lifted the knife for the final blow over Thomas and Emily.

"Raphael! Send me back! Now! If for only a moment. Please."

The butterfly floated before her. "You will only have seconds."

Claire nodded, and suddenly she was falling through darkness and endless pain and confinement and bitter disappointment at leaving the extra dimensions behind. She gasped for breath as she sat up on the floor of the altar room.

She looked up at the scorpion and Parker's body draped in protection over Emily. Now, she had to make the choice. Her body no longer felt weakened by the disease. She felt powerful and alive, her muscles responding to her every command. With uncanny grace, she launched herself toward Ketrick. Her outstretched arms met his arms in midair, and the knife halted before it could touch Thomas or Emily. The momentum of her jump carried them backward into the roaring fire of the incinerator, where the flames blossomed out through the open door to explode in the gathering gas cloud near the ceiling of the basement. They continued on into the fire as her hands gripped Ketrick's arms with unnatural strength.

Claire watched his face fill with horror as they landed on the red-hot ashes of the incinerator. She watched his hair burn away in a smoky cloud of grease, and she saw his mouth open in a scream of pain that was lost in the roar of the fire. She watched his eyes grow in horror as he drew his last, fiery shuddering breath. And she watched as his soul left his body on its final trip to hell. Only then did she release his arms, having fulfilled her task of seeing that he met his fitting punishment. He lay crumpled in the flames, blackened flesh, arms, and legs contracted in the same posture as the mutilated woman in the Aztec carving. Ketrick had fulfilled his final destiny, arriving where he had begun, a victim of the destructive power of the thirteenth demon.

As Claire stood up, she realized she did not feel the wrath of the flames. And she glanced down to see her own body blackened and crisped by the fire. Her cocoon. She looked out through the open door and saw Jonathan and Josh staring forlornly into the fire, longing for her to return. She wished they could understand. She wished they could see from her perspective. She was no longer the caterpillar. She was the butterfly. And she smiled as she realized she was not alone. She reached out her hand to His.

Josh tried to sit up and instantly felt dizzy. As his vision cleared, he watched in horror as his mother hurtled over Parker and into Ketrick. Even as his breath surged back into his lungs and his mouth opened to scream, he saw the two of them tumble into the incinerator. Fire poured from the door and ignited the hissing gas pipe above the door. A silent explosion bathed the old timber rafters above him with flame.

"Mommy!" he screamed hoarsely as he clawed his way up Steel toward the open door. Fire gushed out into the room. He felt Steel's hands clasp around his arms, holding him against his chest. Josh struggled, but he was far too weak from the blow to his head. He felt Steel's breath on his ear.

"Josh, it's too late. We can't save her."

Josh felt tears fill his eyes and struggled until he felt Steel relax beside him. They froze in amazement as they both saw

Claire standing in the midst of the flames. Her hair was lustrous, her body robed in a shining white wrap that sparkled with colors the human eye had never seen. Claire smiled, her eyes filled with such happiness, such understanding it made Josh's heart ache. She reached out, and they saw a man standing beside her. It was not Ketrick. The man reached out a hand to take Claire's, and Josh saw the wound at the wrist. Steel pulled him tighter, and he felt the weakness overtake him, the darkness beckoning him as he spiraled into unconsciousness, the sight of his smiling mother the last image in his mind.

Steel hugged Josh to his chest even as he watched Claire disappear forever. Josh lapsed once again into unconsciousness, but this time, his chest still moved. The fire exploded above them, and the scorpion swirled in pain and agony as burning rafters fell upon it. They were the rafters of a church, of a building anointed by the power of God, planks laid by the shedding of tears and the sweat and blood of generations of Christians. The scorpion screamed and whirled to face Jonathan.

"I'll see you again." It exploded into a black spiral cloud of cinders and energy and streamed up the stairway toward the church above. Liz was suddenly beside him, and he pushed Josh into her arms. She carried the unconscious Josh toward the stairway. Steel helped Parker untie Emily, and they started after Liz up the stone stairway. Steel felt something crunch beneath his foot. He reached down and picked up the broken syringe Vivian had been carrying.

An explosion rocked the basement, and Steel tumbled into the ashes and embers as the roof collapsed above the altar. Burning timbers folded down over the opening into the stairway, and his exit was blocked. Nursery beds and rocking chairs poured through the hole in the roof from the basement. And then, from high above in the main sanctuary, the pulpit and altar table fell headlong, completely blocking the only exit from the room.

Steel stumbled up from the floor and glanced back at the altar. Something glittered from among the broken rocks. It was the golden chest from the book, and it sat against a tube of stone, hewn out of rock with a cap mortared into place. He scooped up the chest and tucked the stone tube under his arm. As he straightened, more burning timbers fell from above, and a huge pew thundered down from the sanctuary. He grabbed the edge of the pew still propped against the hole in the sanctuary floor and began to climb.

He pulled himself up into the sanctuary, now filled with fire and smoke. Flames were already gushing through other holes in the floor and ate away at the pews. The stained-glass windows burst from the heat. Smoke and flames licked at him, and he hurried down the corridor of fire that had once been the aisle and fell through the front doors. Already the others were at the driveway, where he saw his car cranked and waiting.

Steel jumped on the wide stone banister and slid down the slick stone to the sidewalk and tumbled across the gravel and up against his SUV. He shoved the chest and the stone cylinder in the back of the SUV as Liz was putting Josh in the backseat next to Parker. Emily was in the front seat, and her face was contorted in pain. Steel hurried around and piled into the driver's seat and threw the car in gear. For an instant he saw Liz's face in the rearview mirror, illuminated by the growing fire, and then he thought of nothing else but the road.

Parker reached up over the front seat and grabbed Emily's hand. "Honey, just hang on. We'll be there in a minute."

Steel barely heard them, his heart heavy with the loss, his

mind back in the basement where already the images were fading, where already the memory of Claire in the other dimensions was becoming distant. *The more time you spend outside our four dimensions, the less you'll remember of it,* Claire had said. He knew the others would soon forget the details of what had transpired in the basement, remembering just the general horror and loss of it all. In addition to the events of this night, he prayed that God would help him remember Claire's last words and the promise he had made.

[Chapter 28]

STEEL SMELLED LIKE a fireplace, and his reddish-blond hair was dotted with soot. His face was smeared with sweat and ash. He looked at himself in the mirror above the examining room sink and saw the incredible fatigue and loss in his turquoise eyes. He looked at the open wound in his hand and dozens of blisters on the back of both of his arms.

"Mr. Steel?"

"Yes." He turned to see the doctor standing in the doorway.

"Josh Knight is recovering from the blow to his head. He'll have a headache for a day or two, and I would like to keep him in ICU overnight. I imagine he'll be fine by Sunday morning. I don't think there will be any residual damage."

"What about the syringe?"

"I had it tested. Some kind of neurotoxin. Very deadly. But there is no trace of it in Josh's system," the doctor said.

"Good. Listen, Josh's mother is, uh, dead." Steel slumped against the counter. "Can I stay with him?"

"You can't stay in ICU. I'm sorry. Why don't you go home and rest?"

"What about Mrs. Parker?"

The doctor pointed toward the ceiling. "Upstairs in labor and delivery. Would you like some directions?"

Steel pushed past him. "I know the way."

Emily's tear-streaked face beamed from the pillow as she held her newborn daughter. "See," she smiled up at Parker. "I told you she was our baby. She has your eyes."

Parker felt tears form as he looked at the tiny life in his wife's arms. "Ketrick almost took her away from us." His mind went back to the events in the basement. "I don't remember much of what happened, but I know that demon is gone for now, and we are back together."

"And you were willing to die to save me, Thomas." Emily's face clouded. "I knew nothing about what Ketrick was up to, Thomas. You have to believe me. I just wanted us to have a baby. You understand, don't you?"

Parker felt his heart breaking, and he leaned over and kissed her on the forehead. "Let's talk about this in the morning. Right now, let's just enjoy our new child." He looked up as the door opened, and he saw Steel peek in. Parker joined him in the hall.

"How are Emily and the baby?" Steel asked.

Parker took in his appearance, his singed hair, his bleeding hand, his soot-coated clothing. "Emily is fine. We have a new daughter. It's our baby, Jonathan. Not Ketrick's. Ketrick said he was to have had a son. I don't know what happened."

"Perhaps it was a miracle, Thomas."

Parker's face was flushed with excitement. "What about Josh?"

"Josh is holding his own and will be in ICU." He felt a hand on his back and turned to see Liz standing beside him.

"And Liz is right here." She smiled. Her hair was dotted with ashes. "Jonathan, the police are waiting for you at the church. One of them brought me here."

"We left you at the church. I'm so sorry."

"Don't be, hon. You had to take care of Josh and Emily. Someone had to stay and tell the fire department what happened."

"What about the church?" Parker asked.

"Only the annex is still standing. They didn't get there in time to save any of the rest of the building." She paused, and her eyes turned to Steel. "They haven't found any bodies, yet."

"They won't," Steel said. "Between the gas and the old timbers in the basement, the whole church was nothing but a bonfire waiting to happen."

"Go and rest." Steel felt Liz's hand on his arm. "I'll stay here with Thomas and Emily, and I'll check on Josh."

Sheriff Sweeney was waiting for Steel at what was left of the church. Seems he had gotten back from his conference in Monroe.

"I was hoping you'd show up, Steel." Sweeney wore a blue, one-piece jumpsuit instead of his uniform. "Dr. Washington told us what happened. I don't know what got into O'Reilly."

"Ketrick," Steel whispered.

"Yeah. Can't say I'm sorry to see him out of the picture. I had someone move the RV back over behind the annex. Didn't drive so well. Had to get it out of the jail so I could find O'Reilly. He won't be arresting anybody anytime real soon." He handed Steel his keys and held up a clear evidence bag. Inside, the golden knife glittered, shiny and impervious to the fire. "We found this here knife down in the basement area. You recognize it?"

Steel stared, amazed it had survived a fiery inferno that had even melted the old incinerator. He was more convinced than ever the knife had supernatural qualities. "Yes. And so does Special Agent Ross. It belonged to Robert Ketrick. Check out his house. You'll find a picture of Rocky Braxton. He was his 'nephew.' The knife belonged to him, and tonight, Ketrick tried to kill Emily Parker with it. Claire Knight saved her life and died in the process. She saved us all." He turned to walk away and paused. "Oh, and Sheriff Sweeney, you need to check out your house. O'Reilly and Ketrick planned to frame you and force you to resign. They tried to frame me too."

"Yeah, that gun Ross was crowing about is missing. I'd say you're off the hook," Sweeney said.

Steel found the RV parked roughly in the same spot. He was amazed they had gotten it to run after hitting the jail. He hurried inside the darkened, hot interior to retrieve something and saw Liz's lion stick on the couch. He guessed she left it there. He returned to the church's smoldering ruins. Yellow police tape surrounded the apex of the mound where once Indians had lived out a peaceful life and two Christians had been slaughtered on the altar of the thirteenth demon.

In his hand, Steel held the small, brass box in which he had given April her cross necklace on that fateful Christmas Eve. He knelt to scoop some ashes into the box. Later he would have a proper memorial for Claire.

Steel heard a sound behind him and turned. Two figures moved across the ground as if they did not touch it. Their footsteps failed to stir the ashes. She wore the same black jumpsuit. Lucas walked beside her.

"Good evening, Mr. Steel." Vivian stopped before him. "Visiting the dead?"

Steel closed the lid to the brass box. "I wondered what happened to you. You managed to escape unscathed."

"I want to thank you for taking the thirteenth demon out of the way." Vivian smiled.

"Out of the way? He's not in hell where you and he both belong."

"You understand so little, don't you? These here demons take decades, sometimes centuries to pull off their plans. You mess them up real good, and they just have to start all over. You failed to send Hui to hell, but it'll take time for him to regroup. The important thing is that he is out of my way, and I can claim his territory. You see, with him out of the way, I can take my aim at the Council of Darkness."

"Council?"

"Oops. I let that one slip, didn't I?"

"I don't think you do anything by accident."

"You're right, sugar. Who do you think sent Summer with the book to entice the Parkers? Or Parker that e-mail about your website? Who do you think made sure you would need a physicist? I knew the old man would call his niece. He is quite predictable."

"You planned this all?"

"Of course. I needed Parker and his bride to stay around and not run. Summer and her baby saw to that. I played on Thomas's fear and Emily's greed. I wasn't sure what would happen to Hui with you around. He could have been sent packing to hell. Or he could have gotten away. I had that syringe to kill Josh so Hui would have to leave his body. You can't send a demon to hell while the vessel is willing to let it reside. Remember that little tidbit, Jonathan dear." She adjusted her hair and smiled. "All that mattered was that Ketrick was eliminated. Not only do I get to move up Satan's corporate ladder, but poor Robert left his entire company to little ole me," Vivian said. "Oh, by the way, when Dr. Brown started to implant his embryo, he found out Emily was already pregnant. If Miss Claire hadn't have stopped Ketrick, he would have been in for quite a surprise!"

"Don't speak her name!" Steel growled. He looked down at the box in his hands and tried to recall the fading images of Claire in her other dimensions. He pushed the thought away and glanced back at Lucas. "So, the Council of Darkness? There are more of you?"

"Of course," Lucas smiled. "And in time, we will prevail."

"Not if someone tries to stop you," Steel said.

"Stop us? Why, we're here to thank you," Lucas said. "You've performed flawlessly. You fulfilled a plan that began years ago. So now you can move on with your life and leave the business of good and evil to the experts."

Vivian glanced up at the sky, and her eyes came to rest on the horizon. "Yes, the crescent moon has made its journey this night. So many souls have been harvested."

"Ketrick is defeated. His plans for the casino failed. There's nothing else you can do here in Lakeside," Steel said as he stepped toward them. Lucas suddenly stepped back, caught unaware by the movement. Steel smiled. "You lost, Vivian. The church will rebuild. Thomas Parker will preach again."

"Well, maybe one little ole thing." Vivian leaned forward and placed a black-tipped finger on his chin. "Soon, we'll visit the boy again. Remember what your own Bible says about a man whose house is empty?"

Steel shook his head. "What are you talking about?"

"When an unclean spirit goes out of a man, he goes through dry places, seeking rest; and finding none, he says, 'I will return to my house from which I came.' And when he comes, he finds it swept and put in order." Vivian stepped closer to him, and her breath blew cold on his face. "Then he goes and takes with him seven other spirits more wicked than himself, and they enter and dwell there; and the last state of that man is worse than the first." She blinked slowly and cocked her head. "You've lost, Jonathan Steel. Everything you've ever cared about is either dead or belongs to us."

Steel glared at her and turned his gaze on Lucas. "Are you afraid of me?"

For a fleeting second Lucas was motionless, his eyes riveted on Steel. He averted his eyes. "Don't worry yourself with supernatural politics, Steel. You came out of this encounter relatively unscathed. You won't be so lucky next time. Just stay out of our way."

"You told me you were just a pawn." Steel glared at Vivian.

"Jonathan, you're the pawn, and I'm the queen." Vivian leaned forward suddenly and pecked him on the cheek with a quick kiss. She giggled and waved her hand in his face. "See you later, alligator." She turned and walked across the ashy ruins of the church. Her high-pitched laughter echoed in the dying night. Lucas remained behind, hovering above the ashes.

"Ashes to ashes, dust to dust. Forget about the Council of Darkness, Steel." He vanished into thin air.

[Chapter 29]

STEEL MOVED TO the missionary house where he could at least be cool and slept almost through the next day. The next afternoon he started up the hill toward the church and saw Ross's car parked at the ruins. Steel paused in the yard of the missionary house. The feeling of loss was so overwhelming. He groaned in pain and suddenly recalled the last time he had felt this loss.

Had it been six months already? Steel stood alone by the flower-covered casket. The sun was hidden by a gunmetal gray cloud that leaked rain over the cemetery. A few local physicians had come to bid their farewell to Dr. Richard Pierce. After April's death, he had cared for Richard at the condo. He had awakened from a vegetative state only once for a few days and then faded away, but Steel had not left his side. Two days ago, a year to the day when Jonathan Steel woke up on a beach in Alabama, Richard had gone on to join his wife and daughter in heaven.

Steel studied the tombstone with April's name on it. He tried to find sorrow. But it was gone. He tried to find understanding, but he had none. All he was left with was a cold, smoldering fury that kept him going from day to day. Cigarette smoke drifted through the rain, and he turned to see Franklin Ross leaning against a tree with an umbrella above his head.

"You're soaking wet, Steel. You might rust," Ross said as he exhaled a cloud of smoke.

"You defile the ground you walk on, Ross. What do you want?"

"To pay my last respects to a great man. And his daughter."

Steel only stared at him, unmoved by the man's verbal taunts. "I don't have time for you."

"Oh, but you will." Ross dropped the cigarette butt and ground it into the wet soil. "I understand you took care of Dr. Pierce for the last six months. Never left his side."

"That's true."

"I heard you were given power of attorney."

"Yes."

"Did he leave you everything in his will?"

Steel stepped closer to Ross and underneath the umbrella. Ross backed up against the tree trunk. "Out of the last six months, Richard had one lucid week. I had to tell him how his daughter died. I had to tell him about the demon who killed him. He made his will, and he was very clear to me. I was to take everything he owned and track down the thing that killed his daughter."

Ross laughed. "Thing? It was Rocky Braxton."

"Do you remember the tattoo?"

Ross blinked in thought. "The spiral around Braxton's eye? Yes, what of it?"

"It was gone after he died. How does a tattoo fade after someone dies?"

Ross shrugged. "Beats me. You're saying it was a demon?"

"The mark of the demon. The demon of the spiral eye."

Ross' smile faded. "You're serious, aren't you?"

"Disappointed?"

"What do you mean?"

"Did you expect me to take the money and head off to the Vegas? To find some wine, women, and song? I loved one woman. She's dead. I don't care to do that again. I'm taking the money, and I'm going to find that demon."

Ross rolled his eyes. "And how do you do that? Register as a demonbuster?"

Steel looked down. "I already have a private investigator's license."

Ross opened his mouth and closed it again in confusion. "You're out of your mind! How do you know when 'demons' are involved? Get out your demonmeter? Call on ghostbusters?

All you're going to find are people who need help with their little tawdry affairs and unfaithful lovers."

Steel stood very still for a moment as he digested Ross's words. There was some truth in what he said. "I'll find people who need help. People in need who are surrounded by evil. Where there's smoke, there's fire. Where there's evil, there are demons."

Ross reached inside his coat and pulled out an envelope. "No matter where you go, Steel, I'll be looking over your shoulder. Do you know what is in this envelope?"

"A Dear John letter?" Steel said.

"It's a warrant. I can now listen in on your telephone conversations. I can tap into your e-mail. I can even search your possessions and your house at any moment's notice."

Steel looked at the envelope and noted with curiosity he didn't feel any anger toward the man. "Ross, I'll have to give you credit. You got one thing right. They are dead because of me." He turned and walked away in the pounding rain, leaving Ross silent beneath his umbrella. He had a demon to find.

Steel walked up the hill and paused beside Ross. He had his sunglasses off as he watched the wind stir the ashes in the hot noon sun.

"I was about to come and find you. I went to Ketrick's house. Found this." He held up a silver disc. "Digital recordings. In fact, I found a bunch of these. Ketrick had security cameras all over his house. He recorded everything. You should see the horrors we found in his basement." Ross met Steel's gaze. "Ketrick was a monster. He took in stray young men and perverted them, turning them into killers. Braxton was just one of Ketrick's many 'nephews.' Ketrick never killed anyone. He just enjoyed it from a distance."

"What about the Pierces?"

"Nothing to tie Ketrick to them. I think Braxton came after them because of you." Ross glanced off toward the church ruins. "We have enough evidence here to go after Ketrick's associates. Seems Ketrick was bribing a state representative to approve a license for a riverboat on Redcross Bayou. I'm turning this all over to the Justice Department."

"What about Vivian Darbonne?"

"Can't place her at the scene in the church. All we have is your word she was a part of this." Ross squinted. "She also filed papers claiming she and Ketrick got married yesterday right before he died. She gets all of his assets." Ross shook his head. "I thought *you* were clever. Oh, by the way, this is for you." He held out a manila envelope.

"What's this?"

"We found it in Ketrick's papers. I had it checked out. It's legal and binding."

Ross put his sunglasses back on and walked over to his car and climbed in behind the driver's seat. "I'll be seeing you around, Steel." He drove off down the hill into the distance.

Steel stood there, shaking. The papers in the envelope tumbled out onto the street. Steel knelt down on the same spot where he had first seen Thomas Parker and gathered them up. As he examined them, for the first time in days he smiled.

[Chapter 30]

PARKER'S DAUGHTER SNUGGLED against Emily's chest as they sat together on the couch in their living room. The baby cried, and Emily placed a bottle in her mouth. She quieted, and the sound of her suckling filled Parker with a sense of deep satisfaction.

"Thomas, I am so sorry for all the grief I caused. I only wanted us to have a baby. When Dr. Brown offered to help me get pregnant, I agreed. But then I got scared, and I suspected it might not be my baby. I was going to ask Dr. Brown for that morning-after pill. But I couldn't do away with this new life inside of me, no matter whose baby it was. You have to believe me." She started to cry.

Parker stared off into the distance as he listened to his daughter cooing. He heard the soft beat of his wife's heart and her labored breathing as she gently sobbed beside him. What was he going to do? "You said that I see good in everybody." He turned to her. "I see the good in you. I may have lost my church, but I will not lose my family. I want us to go on from here and hope that God will heal us."

Emily wiped at her wet cheeks and smiled. "Thomas, I love you so much. I don't ever want to hurt you again." She fell against him. Between them, the baby wriggled, and Parker held Emily as she cried.

There was a knock at the front door. Parker opened the front door and was glad there were no insects scurrying around his feet.

"Am I interrupting something?" Steel was actually smiling. He stepped in and closed the door and took a backpack off his shoulder.

"What are you doing here?" Parker asked.

"Well, I've got some encouraging news. I found out that when Dr. Brown got ready to perform the procedure so Emily would bear Ketrick's son, he discovered Emily was already pregnant. He never told Ketrick."

Parker felt a chill run down his spine. "So it's certain Claire is our daughter?"

Steel's eyes widened. "You named her Claire? I love it." He dabbed at his eye. Parker smiled. Probably got something in it.

Steel reached into the backpack and removed a golden chain with a tiny gold cross. "I bought this for April. I kept it so I wouldn't forget her. But that reminder became a thirst for revenge. I'm done with that quest. I want Claire to have it as a gift."

Emily reached out and took the tiny cross. "Thank you. That means a lot to us. Jonathan, I'm sorry for the way I treated you. I want to thank you for helping us. You really are a helper in the time of crisis. And I hope you go on helping people."

"I will. I made a promise, and I always keep my promises."

Emily laughed, and it sounded good to Parker. "Well, besides the necklace, what other surprises do you have in your magic backpack?"

"I'm here to make sure Thomas is ready to preach this morning."

"Preach?" Parker laughed. "Jonathan, in case you haven't noticed, I don't have a church anymore. It burned down."

"Well, I wouldn't count on that." Steel reached into the backpack and pulled out a sheaf of papers. "You might want to look at this."

"What is this?"

"A legally binding document substantiated by a local attorney and delivered to me by an authorized representative of the federal government. It was to have been Ketrick's last, desperate move. You'll find a deed for property on the highway signed over to the pastor of Lakeside Community Church, along with $500,000 to build a new worship center. Ketrick thought it would be a nice tax-deductible donation."

Parker's mouth fell open. "What?"

"I imagine if the business meeting hadn't turned into a slug fest, Ketrick would've pulled these documents on you at the meeting. It would've been hard for anyone to pass up this deal." He tapped the papers. "Sign the deed, and the new property and the money belong to the church."

Parker thumbed through the papers and held up his hands in exasperation. "But what about the current church property?"

"Technically it will belong to Ketrick Enterprises. It will be tied up for years in court, but I have a feeling in the meantime the state of Louisiana will declare it a historical site, and nobody will build anything on it."

"What poetic justice," Emily said.

Parker looked at the papers and then looked into Emily's eyes. "Do you think I can make God's dream for this church come true? After all, my dream can't come true with just a building. The church is people, not property."

"You're absolutely right." Steel stood up and stepped to the doorway and threw it open. Sheriff Sweeney stood on the doorstep in a three-piece suit.

"Morning, Reverend. I know this is a bit of an intrusion, but Mr. Steel wanted me to deliver this news to you in person."

"What news?"

"About last night's business meeting. I got together the members of Lakeside Community Church in the elementary school auditorium, and we voted unanimously to move to the new property. It was Mr. Steel's idea. We're all outside if you want to see us."

Parker took Emily's hand, and they stepped out onto their front porch. The congregation of his church filled his entire front yard. Emotion engulfed him, and he felt tears in his eyes. Emily squeezed his hand.

"Reverend Parker, as chairman of the deacon board, I'd like to offer our sincerest apology for not supporting you throughout this ordeal," Sweeney said. "We'd like to make amends this morning, and we've all brought food for breakfast before you preach."

"You brought us breakfast? And you want me to preach?" Parker asked.

"Mr. Steel said you had a sermon ready for this morning."

"But where will we have church?"

"Right here under the trees." Sweeney smiled.

Parker felt Emily melt into his side, and he put an arm around her waist for support. Things were happening too fast. Just moments before his world had crumbled, his calling to his church over with. Now it had all been handed back to him. He wiped at tears.

"I want to apologize to all of you for not being the kind of leader this church needed. Throughout this ordeal, God has given me the strength to overcome fear." He glanced at Emily, and she smiled. "But from this day forward, we will strive to overcome the forces of evil in this community and in the world around us. We will learn to love unconditionally and to forgive each other. Yes, today we will have church!"

The crowd erupted in applause, and Emily motioned the women into the house with their baskets of breakfast food. Parker shook his head in amazement. God was full of surprises. And if it had not been for Jonathan Steel, none of this would have been possible. He craned his neck, searching the crowd for Steel, and saw his figure halfway up the hill toward the ruins of the church. He hoped someday he would see him again.

Liz leaned against her car as Steel came up the hill. She smiled at him, gripping the lion stick. "Jonathan, honey, thank you for finding my lion stick. I thought Vivian had turned it into splinters."

"You're welcome, Liz."

Liz reached out and adjusted his shirt and brushed away some dust. "Well, I have a lot of work to do trying to prove my theory about that mound. The story of Jabo Suyu will bring the anthropology field to its knees. The idea that an Inca could come to the Americas and that he believed in God will be amazing."

Steel tilted his head in thought. Something had been bouncing around in the back of his mind since the last visit to the sanctuary of the church. "I don't understand why the demons would put the codex on the ceiling for us to read. It seems they were defeating their own purpose."

"I don't think the demons put it there," Liz said. "I think God did. He sent an angel down to make sure we would learn of Jabo's life. That's why the vines could not cover it. The demons were trying to hide it." Liz looked at Steel closely. "I'm sorry the thirteenth demon escaped. I don't remember much of what happened in the basement after Claire appeared to me. I should have known she, of all people, would have gotten some help from her precious extra dimensions."

"I'm sure I haven't seen the last of him." Steel took the backpack off his shoulder and pulled out the stone cylinder. "You might find this helpful."

"What is it?" She studied the cylinder.

"I found it under the altar, along with this." He reached inside to remove the golden box. Liz's eyes grew wide, and she thrust the lion stick into his hands and took the box. She released the golden clasp. Inside were the two crosses of Jabo Suyu.

Steel lifted up the golden cross encrusted with stones. "Like April's cross, they are reminders of the sacrifices of the past. And I imagine the cylinder contains the codex."

Liz's eyes widened. "They were under the altar?"

"Yes. Right where the book said they would be. The gold one probably belonged to Phillip, the stone one to Jabo. I'd say they'd go a long way to proving your theory."

Liz hugged the box to her chest. She clutched the stone cylinder and its precious gift of the past. She turned slowly, her gaze taking in the mound and the burned church. "God completed the pattern of Jabo's life. He has given us the proof of his faith." Liz looked toward the parsonage. People milled in the front yard of Emily and Thomas' house. Their voices drifted up the hill, singing an old hymn in perfect harmony. "Listen, Jonathan. They're singing 'Tell Me the Story of Jesus.' They're telling the story to end all stories. They will carry Jabo's legacy into the future."

"The big picture. Jabo's pattern," Steel said. "Claire told me she understood it. I wish I could."

Liz looked up at him. "Sometimes we can't see the forest for the trees. We can't see God's purpose in the midst of our trials. But God uses ordinary people for His extraordinary purposes, Jonathan. Just like He used you. And me. Just think. This entire mound will one day be a historical site. Archeologists and paleontologists from around the world will come to hear Jabo Suyu's story. And his story will tell them about Christ."

She turned to face him, tears glittering in her eyes. "Thank you for letting me join your team. My life has been changed forever. If I were any younger, I'd court you."

"'Court' me? Just how old are you?"

Liz smiled, and she tucked the stone cylinder into the backseat of her car along with the gold box. She climbed into the driver's seat and smiled. "Almost as old as God, honey." Her eyes twinkled as she drove away. Steel waved at her and realized the lion stick was still in his right hand.

Josh sat at the dining room table in the missionary house. He played with the gold bead protruding through his lip. The hospital had cut off his hair to look for head damage. The short, bristly reddish-blond hair made him look so different from when his hair was long and black. At the hospital they had removed most of his piercings, except the lip bead. He had a large bruise above his left eyebrow. Steel leaned the lion stick in the corner and sat at the table. Silent. Waiting. He didn't know where to begin. He had not spoken to Josh since he left the hospital.

"She hated these things," Josh whispered. "I knew she hated them. I did this for Ila, but I knew it would tick Mom off." He twirled the bead. Suddenly he twisted the ends off and hurled the lip bead across the room. It ricocheted off the wall and clattered onto the floor. “I hate her! I hate her for trying to save me! Why couldn’t it have been me?”

“It almost was,” Steel said.

Josh finally turned to look at him, and blood trickled down his chin from the lip bead hole. “Dude, what’re you going to do with me?”

Steel studied Josh’s eyes, filled with a mixture of rebellion and loss. “Uncle Cephas.”

“Uncle Cephas? Bro, he must be what? Sixty?”

Steel fought off a smile. “You’ll like Cephas’s New York City loft. He has a lot of creepy stuff.”

“I’m done with creepy stuff.”

“I promised your mother I’d see you were taken care of.” Steel sighed.

“I don’t want you to put yourself out just to keep from breaking a promise,” Josh said.

Steel drew a deep breath and let it out slowly. “I wish I could have died in your mother’s place. You need her more than you need me. But it didn’t happen that way. She gave her life because she loved you.”

Josh drew a shuddering breath. “It hurts.”

Steel saw April’s dying face in his memory. Now, that memory would be joined by the image of Claire standing in the flames of the incinerator. “I know. And it will keep on hurting every day. But in time, the hurt will lessen and maybe become bearable.”

Josh stared into the distance. “You hurt too, don’t you?”

“Yes.”

Josh blinked back tears, but it did no good. They ran down his face and mixed with the blood from his lip. “When that thing was inside of me, I felt so powerful, so mighty, but it just used me. If I hadn't have let it in, my mother might still be alive."

Steel saw the guilt rising like a beast from the sea of regret, saw it eat away at Josh. They both had a lot of regrets over the past few days. "I need to tell you something, Josh. Your mother told me she had an incurable disease. She was already dying before she made that sacrifice."

"I know," Josh whispered. "I figured it out about a year ago. At first I thought I was to blame. Then I got mad that she was going to leave me like Dad did. I tried to make her life a living hell."

"That's something you'll have to learn to live with, Josh."

"I feel so empty."

"You were never a Christian, were you?"

"I walked the aisle. I joined the church. But I guess I never made it real. I lied to myself. And my mom." He pulled into himself, his face pinched, his eyes closed, and Steel once again saw the little boy who had lost his father at the age of eleven. Now he had lost his mother, and he had no one left in this world to care about him. For a second, the fleeting memory of the alleyway and his friend Kevin surfaced. He swallowed. Could he help Josh like Kevin had helped him so many years before?

"I need to get rid of my trash," Josh whispered. Then his shoulders heaved as his face dissolved in wracking sobs, and he put his head down onto the table. Steel sat quietly, watching the boy's shoulders heave with his sobbing. In that alleyway someone had cared enough about him to come to him in his hour of greatest need. That someone had helped him take his trash out. Maybe it was time to return the gesture. Steel let the crying subside, and then he gently put a hand on Josh's back.

"It's time to forgive and forget and find a reason for living."

Josh looked up but did not shove his hand away. "I'm tired of being empty. I want the power of Christ in my life. Will you help me?"

"I promise."

Coming in 2012...

The Twelfth Demon,
Mark of the Wolf Dragon

[Chapter 1]

Dallas, Texas

THE ASSASSIN PRESSED her face into the stock of her rifle and rubbed her cheek across the hatch marks carved into the stock. Twenty-seven. Soon to be twenty-eight. Each one represented a life poorly lived and a death richly deserved. She squatted on the maintenance catwalk and sighted through her scope across the huge expanse of the shopping mall. The lawyer sat at a table on the balcony outside his favorite Chinese restaurant overlooking the ice skating rink. Her employer's reason for the man's death was of no interest to her. It was just a job. But she always sought for justification and had found it. She didn't kill indiscriminately. After all, she wasn't a monster.

Someone moved at the edge of her vision. She shifted the scope ever so slightly. A teenage boy sat next to her target. He had short, red hair, and his gaze was directed at her. He motioned to someone sitting across the table behind a support beam and then pointed directly at her. She felt a chill. He couldn't possibly see her! *Pull the trigger,* she thought. *Take care of the target and ignore the boy.*

The lawyer lifted a teacup. A shadow fell across the table, and someone leaned forward into view. Bright, turquoise eyes glittered in his lean face. Ice ran in her veins, and she gasped in shock. He was supposed to be dead! She squeezed the trigger prematurely, and the rifle slipped out of her grasp toward the ice skating rink below.

In a panic she ran down the length of the catwalk toward the roof. She burst through the maintenance door, and rain swirled across the roof of the shopping mall. She sprinted down a jogging track until she reached an angle in the roofline. She hopped up onto the metal support between the glass panels of the roof.

She had failed! Of all the people to surface out of limbo, why him? He had nothing to do with her target. Or did he? She cursed her employer for not warning her and deftly maneuvered across the wet metal support.

She heard the doorway bang open behind and knew it was the man. She pulled the brim of her cap down to hide her face and slid her hand into the overall pocket for her knife. Irony of all ironies, it was the same knife she had used on him years before. She spun and watched the man awkwardly run toward her. She slowed her breathing, concentrated, and released the knife even as she completed her turn.

The man stopped, and his hand lashed out with inhuman speed and caught the knife. She gasped in amazement, and he stopped, his eyes fixed on hers. For a moment that seemed to stretch into eternity, the rain slowed, and the air grew thick and quiet. They looked at each other over the intervening years, and she saw his hideously beautiful eyes and his square jaw, smelled his masculine fragrance, felt the stubble of his cheek on her hand, tasted the saltiness of his lips, and then she was back in the present. Their stare broke, and he stumbled sideways and fell onto the glass panel. With a sudden explosion of cold air it collapsed, and the man's free hand lashed out to snare the edge of the support beam.

She walked gingerly along the beam and squatted down. A flash of memory, and she was looking down at her pet lamb. She smelled the blood, felt the shock of loss. She shook her head and pushed away the memory. This man was not an innocent lamb. He looked up at her, and rain pooled in his haunting eyes. She grabbed his hand just as it was about to slip and pulled him up onto the beam. The man turned over onto his back and gasped for breath. She took the knife out of his hand.

"You're supposed to be dead." She leaned close to his face. "I should finish you."

"Raven?" he mumbled.

There was a shout from the distance, and she glanced up. Three security men were coming out of the door onto the rooftop. She cursed and slid the knife back into her pocket. She hurried along the beam and down onto the roof. She hopped over the retaining wall where the rope waited and rappelled down to her waiting car. She slid in and sped off toward the now uncertain future. Her gun was gone. Her target was still alive. She glanced once into the rearview mirror and saw the man standing at the edge of the shopping mall roof. Now that he had returned, her life would never be the same.